Right of Possession

Naomi Young-Rodas

TSL Publications

First published in Great Britain in 2021
By TSL Publications, Rickmansworth

Copyright © 2021 Naomi Young-Rodas

ISBN / 978-1-914245-22-0

The right of Naomi Young-Rodas to be identified as the author of this work has been asserted by the author in accordance with the UK Copyright, Designs and Patents Act 1988.

All characters and events in this publication, other than those clearly in the public domain, are fictitious and any resemblance to actual persons, living or dead, is purely coincidental.

All rights reserved. No part of this publication may be reproduced, stored in a retrieval system or transmitted, in any form or by any means without the prior written permission of the publisher, nor be otherwise circulated in any form of binding or cover other than that in which it is published and without a similar condition being imposed on the subsequent buyer.

Cover image by Unsplash

Chapter break : https://pixabay.com/vectors/ornate-decoration-banner-greeting-3068591/

*There is no property in a corpse.
If the Coroner has jurisdiction, he or she has
the right to possession of the body.
Coroners Act 1980 – Section 24*

Thwack. His right hand against my left cheek. I stared at him in utter disbelief. Time stood still, and then I could hear him apologising. All these words that didn't make any sense, and the slap rang in my ears and hung between us like a curtain separating love and reality. But it was a net curtain, the kind you could see and touch through because I couldn't separate my love for Michael from what he'd done.

We'd had a good marriage, at the beginning. Michael had been everything I'd hoped for in a husband. Strong, well defined muscles, a toned body. Not classically good looking, not what you could really call handsome, but when he turned his head and the light caught his profile; sometimes it took my breath away. He had very intense eyes. I should say 'has', he's not the one who's dead, but you always talk about ex-lovers in the past tense, don't you? There was something dark and slightly scary about his eyes, which should have clued me in, I suppose, but they were gorgeous too. I never could resist dark brown eyes.

He was ambitious, and he needed me to be the perfect wife, and I was, for a time. So I suppose you could say it was my fault for ceasing to be what he wanted me to be; for thinking I could just be me. But battered women always think it's their fault. It is not. I know that now all these years later. But the things I've had to endure to come to that knowledge. I hope this record might help you realise sooner.

It was just a slap that first time. *Just* a slap, ha listen to me! Across the face. It was the shock that got to me more than anything. He never hit me on the face again. He didn't want any marks to be seen. Everything had to remain perfect on the outside. Oh, did I mention how clever he was? That was another thing I liked about him. We had fantastic conversations about films, books, politics. He had such interesting opinions on things. It was later I realised only his opinions mattered; he didn't want to hear mine. But I digress, I'm waffling a bit, sorry, it's a foible of mine, it all just comes tumbling out.

So, the slap. It wasn't hard, in retrospect, but hard enough. It smarted. It stung. And what stung the most was the fact that he'd done it. He was so apologetic afterwards, so sorry. I was convinced he'd never do it again. We made love, oh how we made love! He was always good at that. I couldn't understand that – how the man who hurt me could make such beautiful love. He was gentle, almost caring, though he still liked to be in control. But I liked that. He never went too far with it, not in the beginning, anyway. I liked the thought of just lying there and him taking me. So, you see, I gave him licence, in a way.

I can't remember what caused it – the slap. What we were arguing about. What I'd said, or done, or not done. But it doesn't matter. Whatever it was, it was just an excuse. He would have hit me sooner or later whatever I did. I know that now.

I didn't tell anyone that first time. But what am I saying? I didn't tell anyone, ever, well not for a long time, and then only Anna, but I'm getting ahead of myself. It's not the sort of thing you talk about, is it? 'What did you do last night?' 'Oh my husband slapped me about a bit. How about you?'

My cheek was still red the next day, but not bruised. Fortunately it happened on a Friday, so by the time I went to work on Monday there was nothing to show. He'd been good to me all weekend. I'd almost convinced myself it hadn't happened, that I'd dreamt it. The worst bit was the moment of silence just afterwards when we stared at each other in disbelief. Then the spell broke and he started with the apologies. In retrospect it was overkill. And he wanted to touch me! Soothe me like a child, kiss it better. I wouldn't say I cowered like a mistreated animal, cowering wasn't my style, but it felt like that. I flinched inwardly. I told him I was going to have a bath and walked away. Wisely he left me alone to soak. I stayed there a long time in a daze, steaming, condensation running down the mirror and sweat trickling down the back of my neck. It was unbearably hot. I like my baths hot and that night the heat was more necessary than ever. Did I think about leaving him then? No, of course not. I loved him. This was just a one-off, a misunderstanding, it wouldn't happen again.

I got out of the bath with great carelessness, dripping everywhere. I left the wet towel on the floor, hoping he'd feel obliged to pick it up. Then I wiped the mirror with my hand, something I never do because of the smear it leaves, and looked at my face. I was good looking for my age, mid-thirties at the time. We hadn't married young. Bright green eyes that dulled to brown when I was sad, which I rather considered my forté, a slight hint of red in my blonde hair, a few flecks of grey above the ears, not enough to worry about, just enough on close inspection to show that I wasn't a twenty-something; laughter lines around the eyes that I perhaps wished weren't quite so obvious; an ordinary sort of nose, nice enough lips, and a hand print on my left cheek.

I cleansed. I toned. I moisturised. Usually I'm a quick wipe over with the cleanser type of woman. I care, but I've got more important things to do with my time, but that night I watched my face, I admired it, I observed it for any symptoms of slipping, any clue that it might give way and slide into tears. I was not going to afford him that luxury. I watched it for a long time. So long that he knocked on the door asking if I was all right. I ignored him. Then I applied Witch Hazel to the red welts and went out. I was in my bathrobe and slippers, feeling as comfortable in my skin as I could. I let him fix me a drink and tell me how sorry he was and I believed him. How could I not? He had a pathetic lost boy look in his eyes like when he'd told me about his brother, and I believed he hadn't meant to, that he really was repentant and that he wouldn't do it again. He just kept saying how sorry he was, how he was stressed at work, but it was wrong to take it out on me. 'I love you so much,' he said.

I wonder what he did all that time. Did he have a drink? Probably. Call a friend? Doubtful. Did he watch television? Read a book? Did he think about what he'd done? Difficult to say. I found it very hard to get inside his mind. Over the next few years the beatings became so frequent, so vicious, that it took all my energy just to hold myself together. I didn't have time to wonder about what Michael was thinking. I came to believe that he enjoyed it.

That he got off on the power of seeing me in pain, though more and more I tried to pretend it didn't hurt me. You get used to these things just as you can acclimatise to anything.

The violence came to feel as though he planned it. He was calculating. He knew just where to hit to inflict pain with minimal visible results. I imagined him reading martial arts books to find out the pain spots, like the opposite of erogenous zones. But that's probably far-fetched. Apart from that first slap, it never felt like he just lost his rag, like he couldn't control his temper. I think he took pleasure in it. And he was hardly ever drunk, so we couldn't blame the drink. The blame was all mine. It was usually preceded by some argument, by some choreographed shouting match that he could blame it on. It gradually grew to be less, 'I'm sorry, I didn't mean it' to 'look what you made me do, you bitch.'

Anyway (sorry, I'm rambling again), on that first occasion, after the bath and the apologies, we watched something on the telly that I don't recall at all. I only remember making sure that I didn't brush up against him on the sofa, making sure my robe was tied tightly. Later, in bed, we lay without touching. I was very aware of him being naked while I was wearing my frumpiest pyjamas buttoned up as high as they would go. He was smart enough, or remorseful enough not to try to touch me. I slept with my back towards him, feeling his presence. I say slept. I lay awake for hours until I was sure he was asleep and then I finally relaxed.

The pattern would remain the same from then on except increasingly after a while in bed he would say, 'how long are you going to punish me?' in a petulant manner and I came to know that it was best to submit to him. To just give in and let him have me or it would be bad for me. And I hate to say that after the initial resistance I often enjoyed it. I hated myself for that because it wasn't about making me feel better, comforting me; it was about him and what he wanted. It was about my self preservation too, I came to know that eventually. I submitted to spare myself more pain. He always came very quickly after he'd beaten me and collapsed in an exhausted heap, and then I could sleep.

The next morning, he brought me breakfast in bed with a flower on the tray with the newspaper. We read the paper and gradually the tension eased and we made love. I'd forgotten how wonderful that was until just now. All I'd remembered were the bad times, the pain, and wanting to get away from him. We stayed in bed all day, like newlyweds. I suppose we were still newlyweds, come to think of it. Eventually we got up, he ordered pizza and we watched videos. I got to watch everything I wanted. He pandered to my every whim and I forgave him. It's not like he would ever do it again. I don't think we had another day quite like it, not even on our honeymoon. I make it sound beautiful, don't I? Must be the distance between us. Absence makes the heart grow fonder and all that. Only it doesn't, I still hate him.

We met at a party. Lynn's I think it was, her thirtieth presumably. I've never really been much of a party person. I'd done the chit chat with all the people I actually liked, been stuck with boring balding guy from finance, and was hovering near the nibbles wondering whether I could make my escape yet without seeming too rude when Michael appeared out of nowhere. I know it sounds corny but I really can't remember where he sprang from, I just remember talking to him.

'Hi, I'm Michael.' He extended a hand.

'Isabel, pleased to meet you,' I replied politely, feeling rather sorry that I'd got myself stuck with another half hour of drivel before I could get away. So you can see he didn't bowl me over immediately.

'How do you know Lynn?' I asked, thinking the sooner I got some small talk out of the way, the sooner I could make an excuse to leave.

'I don't really, I'm a friend of her boyfriend, Pete,' he added, as though I didn't know who Lynn was going out with. We'd had enough discussions about him down the pub. I almost said, 'the loser' as that was how we spoke about him and I'd almost had enough Pimm's for that, but politeness won out. 'I think he was worried the girl boy ratio would be off.'

'And we wouldn't want that, would we? Aren't we a little old to be called boys and girls?'

'Yes,' he looked at his shoes, and then up at me again. 'I seem to have annoyed you. Shall we start again? Would you like a drink?'

I looked around to see if I could see anyone I knew, anyone I'd rather talk to than this jerk, but as luck would have it all my friends were either hiding in the kitchen or had managed to tunnel their way out. 'That would be nice, thank you.' At least more alcohol might dull the awkwardness. I nibbled on crisps until he came back.

'There you go. That's a lovely dress.'

'Flattery will get you nowhere.'

'Oh come on, give me a break. I don't know that many people here and you're the prettiest person I've spoken to.'

'Well what took you so long to find me?' I was starting to enjoy teasing him. I didn't realise until it was out of my mouth that probably sounded like a come on.

'Pete started on a rugby story, and didn't draw breath for at least two hours. I always think it's too rude to leave mid sentence,' he said switching to a mock public school boy voice.

I laughed. 'We could just leave, you know. I was planning my escape when you cornered me.'

'Cornered you? Did I? I think that's a little harsh.'

'Well, I am rather hemmed in between the shed and the table of snacks.'

'Hmm, I suppose you have a point. So what was your plan?'

'Nothing too technical. Just a smooth sort of slink out without anyone noticing. I have a theory that if one moves very slowly, in short bursts, most party goers won't notice you've moved until you're well out of the building.'

'Or garden.'

'Yes, or garden, in this particular case; although we would have to cross the kitchen and living room to make it to the front door and freedom. Kitchens can be very tricky, people tend to loiter there and invariably there will be someone you know who comes out with that classic, "not leaving already, are you?"'

'I could cause a distraction.'

'Would you? I'd be unbearably grateful,' I said fluttering my eyelids and putting on an equally posh voice. Makes me cringe to think back to it now, but it was amusing at the time. Mr Pimm has a lot to answer for, a hell of a lot. 'OK, walk with me,' I said, 'nice and slowly.'

We gradually made our way down the length of the garden and into the kitchen. As I feared, my path was barred, by Lynn of all people. 'Isabel, darling, how are you enjoying the party?' Clearly too much birthday good cheer and gin there.

'Um oh lovely, but I've got to...'

'Oh shit. Oh God, I'm sorry Lynn, how clumsy of me.' I looked back to see Michael trying to mop up the fruit punch he'd knocked from Lynn's hand, fortunately onto the floor and not onto the brand new £120 dress she'd bought for the occasion. He shot me a glance and I made for the front door.

Once outside, it wasn't long before he joined me. 'I don't think I've made myself very popular there, hopefully she won't remember tomorrow.'

'Yeah, I don't think she'll remember much tomorrow.'

'So, where to?'

'I would say the pub, but I think I've had enough.'

'How abstemious of you!'

'That's a very big word for this time on a Saturday night. Are you more sober than I thought you were?'

'No I'm a researcher for the Oxford English Dictionary, such words come easily to me.'

'Are you really?'

He smirked. 'No of course not!'

I smiled at him. He was turning out to be quite funny, maybe he wasn't such a jerk.

'So how were you planning to get home?'

'Oi, I'm not that sort of a woman, I haven't known you anywhere near long enough to invite you back to mine.'

'I wasn't suggesting that, though I'm glad the thought crossed your mind long enough for you to discard it!' He smiled again. 'I just meant if it's on your way, we could walk through the park. It's still early and it's a lovely evening.'

'Oh. Well, yes, we could.' I felt stupid, but you know what men are like, especially men who've had a few drinks, and done you a favour, they think you owe them something. The pattern was set then, correcting me came to be one of his favourite occupations. But back then I only saw that he was funny and reasonably good looking, and it was a beautiful evening, and I was happy and tipsy and had my whole life ahead of me, and why shouldn't I walk through the park with him?

'So what do you really do for a living?' I asked.

'Merchant banker.' I looked at him to see if he was having me on again. 'No, seriously, I'm a merchant banker.' How appropriate I thought many times after that, but I think I've already mentioned the beauty of hindsight. 'And you?'

'I'm an insurance account manager.'

He looked somewhat nonplussed. 'Really? Sounds erm, interesting.'

'Liar! You think I sell insurance, which I don't, but let's not talk about work. Read any good books lately?'

'*Post Mortem*.'

'By Cornwell? I loved that.'

'You're into crime books?'

'Yeah love them, why not?'

'Dunno, I just always think women read more, um...'

'Girly kinds of books?'

'Well yeah.'

'Oh you're not a sexist are you? I was almost starting to like you. I'm going to have to get rid of you now.'

'Not literally I hope.'

'You never know, you can pick up some good tips from crime books.'

We walked in silence for a while. I kind of hoped he would take my hand, but he didn't, I suppose I wasn't making it very easy for him. But I had fond memories of that walk for a long time.

At the other side of the park I said I'd better get a cab.

'Right, yeah sure.' He hailed one for me and opened the door. 'Can I see you again?'

'If you must.' I smiled. 'Have you got a pen, I'll give you my number.'

'No. But it's OK, just tell me it, I'll remember.'

'Are you sure?'

'Yeah, I'm good with numbers. Come on tell me.'

I could see the driver looking at me in his rear view mirror, so I rattled off my number. 'Bye.'

He did remember the number and called me the next day. I sometimes think he remembered everything about me – everything I said and did. He certainly remembered how much money I spent on what he called 'fripperies' – added them to his spreadsheet and kept account. But at the time it was thrilling to be called the next day. I loved the attention and I loved that he had remembered the number.

I didn't go home from the party on cloud nine or anything. I wasn't in love. It had been pleasant, but I remember thinking that if he didn't call I wouldn't have been that upset. I wish now he never had called me.

Michael was very attentive from the start, very keen, though not what I'd really call romantic. He called me the day after Lynn's party and we went for a coffee. I usually hung out with Anna on Sundays if she didn't have to work. Anna was my best friend from when we were children. Apart from university we always kept in touch and now that we were both in London we saw each other often. So I had to fob her off at the last minute.

'Oh I suppose you met someone at that party, didn't you?'

'No.' I didn't want to divulge anything just yet. Anna had a propensity to malign all my potential boyfriends and put me off them. I know she meant well, but sometimes it got tedious. Just because she had no love life, didn't mean I shouldn't. I didn't want her killing this off before I had chance to see if it was going anywhere. I hadn't been out with anyone for quite a while at the time, and if nothing else a bit of sex wouldn't come amiss! 'Last minute family thing. Some Louise crisis; mum's issued a three line whip to Sunday lunch.'

My younger sister Louise could usually be relied on to provide some kind of minor crisis, so this was a totally credible fib.

'Oh well, if you must.' Anna feigned disappointment, but I knew perfectly well that she would have no problem entertaining herself without me and was probably relishing the Isabel-free time. 'I suppose I'll just have to go out with Molly.'

I met Michael at some non-descript café and after kissing me on both cheeks which surprised me (this was before continental style kissing had really taken off) he moved quickly to acquire coffees and bring them back to our pavement-side table.

'So...tell me all about yourself.'

'Wow, well, don't hold back there!' It seemed an unusual opening gambit, but what does one say on a first date with someone you've only just met and don't know?

He looked sheepish. 'Sorry. But I want to know all about you. What you do, what you like, brothers and sisters, you know.'

'Yes, OK.' I liked that he seemed so interested. So often men only want to talk about themselves, but in a boring way, telling you about their work in minute detail, or explaining how they took a car engine apart just for fun. 'Well, um, standard sort of middle-class family, parents, one younger sister. Oh I could tell you stories about her!'

'Could you? Go on then.'

'Er, maybe later.' I remember his hair flopping over his eyes as he squinted into the sun, and he seemed young and a bit vulnerable, which was kind of endearing. I got a funny feeling in my stomach for a second. 'What about you? Have you got brothers and sisters?'

'Er no.' He hesitated a bit and looked off into the distance. 'I had a brother but he died.'

'Oh no, I'm so sorry,' I said, touching his hand. 'Was it, um...how...'

'Oh no, it wasn't recent. When we were kids. Suppose I was about six, I'd started school. He was four. We were mucking about near this river on holiday and he fell in. I shouted and shouted, but by the time mum got there…'

'That's terrible.'

He shrugged, as though it was no big deal, but obviously it was. Over our next few dates he told me more and more about the drowning and how bad he felt. How he always thought his father blamed him. His father sounded like quite a tyrant from the way Michael described him. Not violent, but very strict, always telling him off. It made me feel like I'd had such a charmed life when he told me stuff like that.

'Well that puts the whole Louise thing in perspective.'

'Louise?'

'My little sister. She's ten years younger than me and mum thinks the light shines out of her…She's always getting into scrapes of some kind, you know runs out of rent money, unsuitable boyfriends, doesn't know what she wants to do, and that's all all right, but I'm expected to be all sensible and do everything right.' I don't know why I said all that, I felt like I was about five years old telling tales out of school. Louise could be a pain, it was true, but really I thought she was great and didn't mind that she seemed to get away with murder as far as our parents were concerned. I'd grown out of all of that. But Michael seemed to understand somehow.

'So we're both the eldest child. It's tricky isn't it? Nobody seems to get how responsible you're supposed to be, they just think you're jealous of the younger one.'

'That's it exactly!'

I hate to say the time flew by because it's such a cliché, but honestly I don't know where the afternoon went. I had to stop drinking coffee in the end or I'd get too wound up. I've never had a first date like it. I got to know so much about him and he never mentioned work once.

'Gosh, look at the time. It's nearly six.'

'So it is. Why don't we go to dinner? Do you want to go to dinner?'

'Um, no, I don't think so. This has been great, honestly, but I've got some stuff to do.'

'Oh OK. Well in the week then?'

'Yeah.'

It was weird, when I got home, I kind of missed him. I felt like

I already knew him and I'd spent so long with him it was strange he wasn't there. We met on the Wednesday for dinner, and by then he'd already called me twice. I was gagging to tell Anna about him, but I resisted. I didn't want the excitement dampened by her laconic wit. I wanted to see where it was all going before Anna brought me back to reality with one of her, 'if it's too good to be true, it can't be true' remarks.

'What the hell's this?' Michael held up a shoe box.

'It's a shoe box.'

'You know what I mean.'

Unfortunately I did know what he meant. Recently Michael had got all weird about me spending money. As soon as we got married he insisted on a joint account, which seemed like a perfectly good idea at the time. Why should I worry about the house bills when I had a banker for a husband who was willing to take care of all that? He loved spreadsheets and numbers. I didn't. So I was happy for us both to pay in, but I never expected that would give him the right to question whether I bought shoes when I wanted them, or anything else.

'I needed some new shoes, all right. It's not a crime.'

'Needed?'

'Yes, needed for work.' I stood up then, annoyed, and rooted around in the wardrobe, pulling out my old court shoes and pointing to the scuffed toes and worn down heels.

'You could get those repaired.'

'I don't see you getting your old shoes repaired.'

'I don't have time.'

'Well, neither do I and they're not fashionable. I need to look half-way decent to meet clients.'

'Oh yes, these so-called clients you meet. And what do you really get up to with these clients, eh?'

'We talk about insurance Michael, it's not exactly sexy. For goodness' sake, what's your problem? It's just a pair of shoes, they weren't even that expensive!'

'I'm sorry. I'm sorry, you're right, I overreacted. I had a shit day at work. John is banging on about targets again and…I don't like you having to worry about money or anything. I'll give you money for clothes if you need stuff.'

'I know you would, but I like shopping. You know it's a girl thing, it's what we do. Anyway, I made the money, I can spend it.'

I don't think he liked that, you could tell by the look on his face.

'I'd rather just take care of you. You don't have to work, you know.'

'I know, but I want to.'

He put his arms around me then and snuggled into my shoulder so I could barely hear him when he said, 'I love you so much Iz.'

Our arguments never lasted long. Sooner or later he always told me how much he loved me and that ended it. And I loved him too. He really only wanted to take care of me, and be the man. I'm no woman's libber. I'm not like Anna, all self-sufficient with no need for men. I liked being taken care of. But actually Michael was a big softy. He needed me and he wasn't afraid to show it, at least when we were alone, when it was just the two of us, and I loved that about him too.

By the third date, when I eventually invited Michael inside my flat, I think I was in love. I had been in love before, at least once, probably only once if I'm entirely honest. Jason, when I was seventeen. That was love at first sight, well lust at first sight. I first saw him in a swimming pool, so I pretty much saw the whole package right away. I thought he was gorgeous – dark brown eyes, dark hair, good muscle tone, smooth chest, just my type. He was shorter out of water, but then I was tall for my age. He turned out to be a bastard, but the good-looking ones always are. So I should have been onto a good thing with Michael given that he wasn't really super gorgeous, though of course I thought he was very handsome.

Anyway, back to date three. We'd been to dinner, Chinese I think, I can't remember. Funny that's usually the sort of detail I do remember – I love food. He paid, as he had on the previous two occasions. He didn't become penny pinching and demand that we paid for everything jointly until after we were married. We'd walked home, and since it was still early I invited him in for 'coffee'. We did actually drink coffee too and had some discussion on crime noir, and he told me more about his father, which ended up with me cuddling him in a rather sisterly way, or so I thought.

Up to this point the only physical contact had been a fairly chaste kiss at the end of each evening and some hand holding, and I was beginning to wonder if there was something wrong with him. The thought that he might be gay had even crossed my mind, the way he talked so much about personal stuff, but yet he was so manly too. Now, I don't want you getting the wrong idea about me. I'm not 'fast', but we all know that the age of chivalry is dead and your average man makes a move on the first date, or, if he really likes you, the second and we'd had such intimate conversations already it felt like we knew each other really well. I'm not one for casual sex, and I'd not had that many boyfriends, possibly because I'm not loose enough, or maybe I'm just too picky. (See where that got me! At least I can see the hint of a funny side to it all now.) But I have had a few flings where it got hot and steamy pretty quickly, and in comparison Michael was exuding about as much passion as a bowl of porridge. But even so, I felt so close to him, I wanted it to be physical. He was interesting, and so understanding, it felt like he was inside my head sometimes. We just fit. Anyway, the cuddling led to a slightly lacklustre kiss during which I'd almost regretted having invited him in, followed by probably the best sex of my life right there on the sofa. The sofa never quite recovered, and I never entirely got the coffee stain out of the rug either, which just goes to show how little you can tell from initial impressions, nor for that matter how much you can tell from the quality of the sex, because he was definitely the best sex ever and ended up being the most horrible man I have ever known.

It was after the third date that I finally told Anna about Michael. I told Anna everything sooner or later.

'What are you looking so smug about?' she said.

I raised an eyebrow, trying to be nonchalant, though I was gagging to tell her. I hadn't said anything when I'd first met him, but now we'd done the deed, 'the nasty' as Louise, my sister, liked to call it.

'Oh. Who is it this time?'

'His name's Michael. We met at Lynn's party.'

'So you did meet someone at that party, you little liar. And you saw him the next day, didn't you? That's why you stood me up! There was no Louise crisis.' She looked mock shocked. 'A slow mover then,' she said, sardonically. 'And you've been keeping secrets from me, haven't you, Isabel?' She poked me playfully in the ribs. We were sitting in Clissold Park, Anna's ridiculous folding bike propped against a tree.

'So, anyway...' I drew breath for dramatic emphasis, 'we chatted at the party, and I gave him my number, and then we went out for dinner, and he's called me loads, you wouldn't believe some of the things we've talked about, and then last night...'

'Last night you shagged him.'

'Yes, last night I shagged him, as you so delicately put it.' I was a bit pissed off that she'd stolen my thunder, but I ought to have been used to it, she'd been pre-empting my stories since we were about seven, like she has some sixth sense or something.

'Don't say it. You're going to say, but it wasn't just sex Anna.'

'Are you telepathic or something? You've got cappuccino froth on your lip.'

She put her face further into the cup and came out with froth all over her nose. Then, smiling, she licked it off (she could touch her nose with her tongue, something of which she was very proud).

'It was the best sex ever.'

'Really? I thought Joe was the best sex ever? Didn't you bring any pastries, Iz? I'm starving.'

'You're always starving. Yes, Joe was pretty good, but now I've had better.'

'What was so great about it?'

'I don't know. He didn't seem that exciting up 'til then. I was starting to wonder if he might be gay.'

'Oh, the famous Izzy Gaydar in action!'

'Oh shut up!' I said. 'But then…well he was just very passionate. I felt so close to him. It's like I've known him for so long.'

'What all of about a week? You sound like a feature in Cosmo!'

'Since when do you read Cosmo?'

'I like to try and learn what makes straight woman tick; you're such an alien species!'

I hit her arm. She was always coming out with this kind of nonsense.

'Passionate. Right,' she said, 'can you be any more specific?'

'Not really,' I said coyly.

'Were you drunk?'

'No, not particularly.'

'Going to see him again?'

'Definitely.'

'Suppose I'll have to vet him then?'

'Oh no Anna, you never like any of my boyfriends.'

'I'm only looking out for your best interests.'

'You just don't like men, you little man-hating dyke!'

'Some of my best friends are men. I just don't happen to need them like you do.'

'I'm going for a full English. Coming?'

As it turned out, I didn't see Anna again for ages. Michael and I quickly dropped into that new love thing where we only wanted to be together. It must have been weeks before I realised how little I'd seen her. Just the odd phone call or week day lunch. Strange that she didn't say anything either. Maybe she was remembering her thing with Siobhan, she'd pretty much abandoned me for a while when they were all hot and heavy. She knew I wouldn't ignore her for long. Boyfriends came and went but Anna was constant. But Michael didn't know that and he wasn't very pleased when he realised.

I can't remember the second time. The second time he hit me that is. After a while they all tended to blur into one. He perfected his technique; I'll give him that. Practice certainly did make perfect. Maybe he should have given up banking and taken up tae kwon do or kickboxing. Maybe if he'd had a suitable outlet for his anger he wouldn't have used me as a punch bag. And what was he so angry about anyway? I never worked that one out. He had a good job, plenty of money, a pretty nice life, I'd say. OK, so he'd had a strict upbringing, but so had lots of people. His parents seemed nice enough whenever I met them (which wasn't often it has to be said) despite what he said about his father and his being mostly estranged from them. His father always seemed rather gruff and military-like on the rare occasions we met. It wouldn't surprise me if he'd ruled Michael with a rod of iron.

Michael didn't like his family, so it's odd that he seemed to want to start his own as soon as possible. Before we were even married he used to say how great it would be to have kids. I wasn't bothered either way, but I went along with his enthusiasm. I suppose if I'm totally honest, I didn't really want any, and later on I was glad I never got pregnant. Glad any children were spared the violence, or the witnessing of it. But why am I talking about him? This is my story. Well it's all tied together isn't it? And for a while, for a long time, trying to work out the reason he did it obsessed me. I thought if I knew why, I could avoid it. I could change what I did so he wouldn't have to hit me.

We hardly ever saw his family and he didn't like to see mine. He liked it best when it was just me and him on our own together. Families were overrated, he said. We didn't need them if we had each other. He said things were never the same after his brother died. His father took his grief out on Michael and blamed him for everything. I could see why he wasn't keen to see them. I tended to go and meet Louise for lunch without him. More so in the beginning before the noose tightened. It felt odd having to sneak around to see my own family, but if it kept the peace…

Did he feel guilty about his brother because he was supposed to be looking after him and he'd failed? But he was only six; no one could expect a six year old to keep his little brother safe. Not alone, not without help. Michael never liked to fail at anything. Never did fail at anything at least as far as anyone knew. His marriage was a disaster, but no one knew that. People thought we were the ideal couple. He was very good at pretending. No one ever knew what was going on and I certainly didn't tell them. That became part of the problem later; when I did start talking about it, no one believed me. People shouldn't be so gullible – there's no such thing as perfect, if there aren't a few perceptible cracks, chances are there's a gaping San Andreas Fault underneath.

It must have been after the second time that I asked him why he did it. The first time I was too shocked and upset and later on as it continued, I got more and more scared of him. Scared that he really would injure me, or that he would kill me. He threatened that later on, and I believed him. Later I started altering my behaviour to second guess him, to pre-empt situations that might rile him. I wonder how bad it would have been if I hadn't? If my efforts made any difference?

'Why do you do it?'

'Do what?'

'Hit me,' I mumbled, not wanting to say the words out loud.

'I don't know. We were arguing, weren't we?'

'Were we?'

'Of course we bl…of course we were.' He lowered his voice from the shout that had started, already backing down – the prelude to his apologies. He always had a reason – he loved me so much, that's why he got jealous; he just wanted to protect me, that's why he didn't like me going out. 'Most men don't hit their wives when they argue.'

'Well, I'm not most men.'

No, you're certainly not, I thought. This was getting nowhere. 'Why don't you tell me what's bothering you? You must be upset about something. All I did was suggest we go and see my mum and dad on Saturday.'

'I play squash on Saturdays.'

'Yes, I know that Michael, but I was talking about the afternoon. Anyway it's hardly enough to get violent about is it; potentially having to change what time you play squash?' I was starting to get exasperated with him. What was the point? Except from a self-preservation point of view – if I could understand why he did it, maybe I could make him stop. Maybe I could get him some help and that would help me. How naïve I was. If only I'd known then that I had no hope of ever changing him; that things could and would only get worse. I gently rubbed my arm where he'd grabbed it. I could feel the dull ache of a bruise forming.

He shrugged. 'I had a hard day at work I guess. I overreacted. I'm sorry. But you know I don't like family stuff.'

'Why not? Is my family really that bad?'

'No.' He smiled. 'A bit weird, but not so bad. It's just, you know... I don't like my own family much. I like it to be just you and me. You know it's best when it's just us.'

'If you like it to be just us, why do you keep trying to mess it up?'

'I don't know.' He moved over and sat next to me on the sofa. He stroked my hand. 'I don't know Iz. I'm sorry. You're everything to me, you really are.'

I felt sorry for him, I knew he meant it. I wanted to help him. I wanted us to be together just as much as he did. 'Maybe you should see someone.'

'You mean like a shrink? No, I'm not doing that. I'm not sick; I'm not some monster who needs fixing.' He voice was starting to get angry again.

'I'm not saying you are. I just mean an anger management course or something. Loads of men do that sort of thing. It can help with work too, it doesn't have to be all touchy feely,' I said, trying to appease him, trying to make it sound like a manly thing to do.

'Yeah, maybe. I'll look into it. I'm really sorry Izzy, I won't do it again.'

'You said that last time Michael. I'm not going to take it you know. I'm not going to be your punch bag. I'll leave.'

'OK, OK, I promise it's the last time.'

Just like broken New Year's Resolutions, nothing changed. Michael never did look into anger management, and any time he mistreated me I forgave him, because he was still my Michael and most of the time things were great. What I said must have registered on some level and things were better for a long time. He didn't want me to leave. I know now that he couldn't manage without me, that he needed me, far more than I ever needed him.

I wouldn't call Michael a romantic by any stretch of the imagination, but he certainly made an effort in the early days. He was so attentive. He listened to any suggestion I made of things we could do, especially if it involved us being alone together. We had what you'd probably call an old fashioned courtship. We had a lot of dates. And I mean *a lot* of dates. We saw each other nearly every day, almost from the start and if we didn't he would call me. Anna used to joke that we were worse than lesbians, though I didn't really get what she meant. And while most dates ended up with us staying either at mine, or more usually at his, we didn't officially move in together until after we were married. Though we were married within a year so that's not saying much. Maybe if we hadn't got married so quickly I would have been able to get away more easily, but I doubt it. It was when I started trying to get away that things got really bad. It might have been easier legally to dump him than divorce him, but from Michael's point of view it would have been the same. But I was talking about the good times, wasn't I?

One of my favourites, I'm often reminded of it here, being near the lake, was the picnic in Hyde Park. We used to quite often meet in parks, I don't know why, and one time I'd said how I'd like to go rowing.

'Wouldn't it be lovely if there was a lake here, with boats?'

'Would it?'

'Yes, it's romantic. You rowing me around in the sun. A picnic hamper, and champagne. Sort of *Brideshead Revisited*.'

'That was punting in Oxford wasn't it?'

'Yes, but it's all the same kind of thing. Ooh, yes, you could take me to Oxford if you want. It's not far. Or Cambridge.'

'Rowing,' he said, in a pensive way, as though he couldn't really fathom what would be romantic about it, but that it was something he could arrange.

A few days later he called me and said, 'I've got a surprise for you. Meet me at Speakers Corner, Hyde Park, 11 a.m. Sunday.'

'OK, what are we doing?'

'Well it wouldn't be a surprise if I told you, would it?'

'No, right. I just meant what should I bring, what should I wear?'

'Bloody women!' he quipped. 'Wear whatever. No, actually, wear something summery and girly and shoes you can walk in.'

It was a glorious sunny day, although I think it was only May. Or was it June? It doesn't matter. Strange how the few good memories I have of Michael always seem to be bathed in sunlight. A trick of the mind, or was it really like that? Anyway, that day I'm sure it was. Michael was waiting for me, looking rather nervous, I have to say. He was wearing jeans and a polo shirt and carrying a large rucksack, which wasn't like him. I watched him for a moment before he saw me, thinking how squeaky clean and public school-boyish he looked, though he hadn't in fact been to a public school.

'Hello. You look nice.' He gave me a peck on the cheek. He never liked showing too much affection in public, only when we were at home.

'And you look…sporty. What's with the rucksack?'

'Classified information, I'm afraid. Shall we wander?'

'Oh, yes, OK.'

I seem to remember feeling a bit nervous myself, or excited. Part of me was enjoying the expectation of some kind of treat or surprise, and part of me was slightly uncomfortable at not knowing where we were going and what we were going to do. It hadn't dawned on me what he might have planned. Perhaps that's just me projecting what I know now onto my memories. Probably at the time I was just happy to be with my new boyfriend on a sunny day out in Hyde Park.

So, we walked. Not hand in hand, needless to say. There were loads of runners, walkers and cyclists all doing their Sunday thing. Young couples with toddlers, teenagers playing with Frisbees, older people with dogs.

'I'm surprised Anna isn't here, whizzing around on her bike!'

'Anna?'

'Yes, you know, my best friend Anna. I must have told you about her.'

'Oh yes, the doctor?'

'Pathologist, yeah. She's the intelligent one. Come to think of it, she's probably reading some medical journal rather than being out having fun. She's a total workaholic.'

'And she rides a bike a lot?'

'Oh God, yes! She bought this nerdy folding bike and she takes it everywhere.'

'I must meet her, she sounds like a character.'

'You must. Love me, love Anna,' I joked.

'Really?' He looked worried.

I laid my hand on his arm. 'Not literally, no. But she is my best friend, from when we were kids. It would be awful if you two didn't get along.'

'So, here we are.' I must have looked a bit blank or something. 'You wanted boats.'

'Oh wow. Oh Michael how lovely. You sweetheart!' I loved that he'd remembered my comment about rowing. That was *so* Michael, going out of his way to please me and make me happy.

He looked very gallant as he rowed me out on the Serpentine. He got the hang of it quickly though I doubt he'd rowed before. It never occurred to me that he was scared of water because of what happened with his brother. I only realised later that he didn't like swimming, or beach holidays, or any of those water related things that I adore, so taking me out in a boat was a huge sacrifice on his part and I loved him even more for it. No wonder he looked slightly on edge until we reached land again.

Sunlight glinted off the water, and we dodged children in pedalos, and other boats. It was pretty busy; you know how the English are – first hint of a nice day they swarm to the parks and beaches. So it wasn't quite the romantic experience I'd pictured, but the fact that he'd done it was superb, and I think he liked showing off his sporty macho side. He wasn't a jock, but he was a man's man. He ran sometimes, and played squash, and was generally up for any sporting endeavour that came his way, though he wasn't really a team player.

We weren't on the water long; he must have hired it just for an hour. Afterwards, we threw ourselves down on the grass and he opened up the rucksack. '*Voila*, the picnic,' he pronounced as he starting unpacking Tupperware. I want to say that there was chilled champagne and dainty sandwiches and fruit. There wasn't. There was warm white wine, cheese rolls, pork pies and Mr Kipling's cakes. But it's the thought that counts, and Michael had put so much thought and effort into that day.

I never understood how Anna and I became friends. She was always such a geek! While I was at ballet, she was creating stinks with her chemistry set. When we formed our spy club, it was really Anna who did all the spying, collecting fingerprints, setting booby traps for people (the hair stuck with spit across a closed door), while I was just her pretty assistant. I wonder sometimes why she bothered with me. I suppose it would have been less fun without someone to order around, someone to observe how brilliant she was, and every great detective needs a slightly dumb but appealing side-kick. Perhaps she needed an audience, but Anna was always a happy loner.

We were, are, complete opposites. Anna's on the short side, dark hair, dark eyes, sort of Mediterranean looking, with funky glasses (about the only thing about her dress sense that was). I'm tall, green eyes, fair hair. She's a total workaholic, really lives for nothing else, spends her spare time reading the latest journals in her field, I've even heard she eats her lunch in the morgue! Yuck, with that smell of decomposition, and all those nasty implements around, I don't know how she can, and she's got a nice office she could sit in. She wouldn't even have to go out for lunch like normal people, but she could at least sit in her office. I'm a good influence on her in that respect, I get her out of that awful place now and then. But I digress. She hardly ever has lovers. I can't imagine her ever living with anyone.

I must confess I only really work for money. I've never had a passion. I haven't even made a career out of not having a career! Didn't do the super housewife, voluntary worker, or the yummy mummy perfect mother to three or four immaculately raised children, though to be fair that wasn't entirely my fault. Maybe I never found the right person, or maybe it's me, maybe I've got no soul! Although things are a little different now. Maybe I'm finally finding a passion…passions, after all this time. Anna would be pleased.

And we were opposite in another way too. Anna liked women. She never fancied me, as far as I know, and I never really thought about her being a lezzer. Anna was just Anna. I'm not a fag hag. Nothing against it, I just don't happen to have many gay friends and if I'm honest, I can find camp gay men somewhat annoying, but I never really saw that side of Anna's life. We mainly met for lunch, or at each other's houses, just the two of us. She never took me to gay bars, and like I say she rarely had lovers. When she did, she didn't like to talk about them, none of them ever seemed important enough to her to talk about them, or maybe she just liked to keep her private life private, even from me. It was always my boyfriends and disastrous liaisons we discussed and laughed about. If only I had been more like her maybe I wouldn't have ended up in this mess.

Before Michael got too clingy, I went to a couple of small parties at her house, and I suppose the guests were mainly female couples, but I didn't really think about it. I wish I'd asked her more about it all now; it might have come in handy. I wish I'd asked her about a lot of things.

Anyway, we were always there for each other, uncritical, whatever happened, I'm in your corner kind of friends. I had a sense that she never really liked Michael, but she didn't come out and blatantly say so until I'd told her about the beatings. In fact she was the 'best man' at our wedding. That's pretty sad, isn't it, when the bridegroom can't find a friend or relative he likes enough to be best man? I wondered why he didn't ask Rob, his squash buddy, but Michael said it was me who wanted the big wedding so I could have the person giving the 'humorous past' speech. Now, I think about it, perhaps he felt that such a task should have been taken by his brother, but since he couldn't do it, it was better not to have a male best man at all. Or I could be cynical and say that Michael thought of himself as the 'best' man in everything and so couldn't give the role to anyone else!

Of course Michael didn't like Anna. He didn't like any of my friends, though he never let them see that. He only maligned them in private to me, implying that my poor collection of friends reflected badly on me, and him. He never complained directly about her being a lesbian, I'll give him that, though he certainly had things to say about the growing number of lesbians in Stoke Newington. No, I think he resented the fact that I was closer to Anna than I was to him. Whatever he did he couldn't get rid of her, in the end she got rid of him in a way.

She wasn't, isn't, a political lesbian, she always said who she slept with was nobody else's business. She was just Anna, the pathologist. That's what defined her, her work, her papers, her triumphs in the lab, playing with microscopes and scalpels just like she had from age six. Sounds like she never grew up, but she was more grown up than I'll ever be. But she did manage to get lesbians into the best man speech. Something about how Michael must be a reasonably good man because she'd tried to convert me and hadn't been able to, and if she couldn't do it, nobody could (roars of laughter). How wrong she was on both counts – Michael being a good man, and me converting. It didn't dawn on me until years later that she really had wanted to convert me and not just to the general cause, but to her very specific expression of it.

I don't know how I talked Michael into it, because he wasn't remotely interested in art, but one Saturday afternoon I managed to get him to the Hayward to see the Toulouse Lautrec exhibition. When we were first together Michael wanted to do everything with me, even if it wasn't really his cup of tea. We couldn't get enough of each other and to my chagrin I barely saw Anna in those heady first weeks. I love the Impressionists, and while Lautrec is a bit 'post', I liked what he did, the people he chose to paint, the fact that he was a misfit. Strange, because I always thought of myself as very ordinary, a going along with the flow, not sticking out from the norm, kind of person. I was a bit of a 'material girl', I liked the good life, and I liked stuff. I gave to Live Aid and Comic Relief, but everyone did that. The 90s were just my decade, decadent and money grabbing. But now, I am a complete outsider, living on the fringes, and being well…I don't know what you'd call it – beatnik? I like that, very Kerouac! If people here only knew my story…

Anyway, I suppose the Impressionists are not that exciting in art terms, everyone likes them, and most people can name one, but I've never been that into modern art, I like the classics, and I'm not going to apologise for it. When I think about art I can't believe I stayed with Michael so long. He just wasn't interested. Oh he tried in the beginning, but it was too far removed from his interests. I wouldn't say art was my life, but I had done my degree in Art History and as far as I was serious about anything it was art. I think Michael was mainly interested in money. At first he loved doing everything I liked, but he got to be so controlling. Eventually it was all about money – having money, getting money, and showing he had money, but in a very understated way. He wasn't showy. He kept tight rein on our finances and invested well. Michael liked routine. He liked squash on Saturday, *The Times* on Sunday (*The Financial Times* during the week), and me at home making his dinner.

So, he must have been still trying to impress me, it was certainly quite early on in things, because it was the first time he met Anna. Afterwards we walked along the Southbank.

'You didn't really enjoy that, did you?'

'I wouldn't say that,' he paused. 'It was OK, he…no, not really.' He gave in. I was already beginning to see that he always said what he thought and meant. He was always very understanding and loved it when I divulged 'secrets' about my past, but he didn't beat around the bush to save anyone's feelings.

'What's not to like?'

'I wouldn't say I disliked it, but you're not interested in cars, are you? You wouldn't want to look at a car exhibition.'

'No, but I would if it made you happy.'

'You would?'

'Yes, that's what couples do, they compromise to make the other person happy, so they can do things together.'

'But wouldn't you rather just go round the gallery on your own?'

'Yes, I think I would after this conversation. But it's fun to do things together. Hopefully it would be something you both enjoyed, but if not, what's wrong with a bit of give and take?'

He shook his head. 'I don't see the point, if you're not both enjoying it.'

'Oh, you're such a man!'

'Um, well yes.' He looped his arm through mine then, though he didn't usually do that kind of thing in public. 'You're a silly old stick sometimes.' I looked at him, not quite getting what he meant. 'You know I want to be wherever you are.' I smiled. 'They're not great paintings though, are they?' He teased. He always had to have the last word. We walked along in silence for a bit, then suddenly Michael turned and sort of looked behind him.

'Did you see that woman?'

'No, what woman?'

'The one who just went past us in a red leather jacket.' I turned round too and saw the back of a woman in a red coat walking away. 'She looked just like you.'

'Really?'

'Yeah, the spit, it was spooky.'

I turned round again. 'Don't be silly, Michael, she's got much longer hair for a start.'

'You didn't see her face. Seriously, she really looked like you.'

'OK, if you say so. Oh look, there's Anna.'

Anna was speeding towards us on her Moulton, paying scant regard to the evening strollers. She skidded to a halt in front of us, like a teenage boy on a skateboard.

'Well hello. So is this the new squeeze?'

'Anna, don't attempt street slang it, doesn't suit you! Yes. Anna, Michael. Michael, Anna.'

Anna removed one of her fingerless cycling gloves and gave Michael a firm handshake. I wanted to ask her why she wore them, but we'd had 'fashion' conversations before – they just didn't work. She could just about manage smart and businesslike for work, but beyond that she was a hopeless case, and twenty plus years of our friendship had made no dent on her appalling fashion sense.

'Pleased to meet you,' said Michael, ever the gentleman in public.

'I'm glad we bumped into you,' I said. 'Not only have I been trying to get you two to meet, but we're having a male/female dilemma that you can help us with.'

'Well I'm going to need refreshment if we're getting all philosophical.'

We sat outside at a nearby pub, and Michael went in for drinks, after looking slightly shocked at Anna's order of a pint of bitter.

'God, I haven't seen you for ages. I hope it's not all because of him. He's not exactly the world's most handsome man, is he?'

'You can't judge a book by its cover, anyway what are you doing over here? Not like you to be out and about.'

'I do go out sometimes, you know. I was at the lesbian and gay film festival, if you must know.'

'Nice. What did you see?'

'Oh, some arty lesbian flick you won't have heard of!'

'Hmm. Go with someone?'

'No.'

'Meet anyone?'

She raised an eyebrow. But just then Michael came back and I never got an answer as Anna fell on the accompanying crisps as though she hadn't eaten all day.

'So what's this male/female dilemma then?' she said, licking salt off her fingers.

'Well, I think it's nice to do things together as a couple and it's OK to compromise sometimes and go to something you're not crazy about to make the other person happy – case in point, the Toulouse Lautrec we just went to, which Michael hated.'

'I didn't hate it! It's just not my thing, and I don't see the point of trailing round pretending to enjoy it, when you probably would have enjoyed it more if you'd gone on your own.'

'I think you should just split up now,' said Anna. 'The sexes are never going to see eye to eye on this issue. Men don't like doing stuff to please women if there's nothing in it for them.'

'You're saying men will only be nice to you if they think they'll get you into bed?'

'Not just bed. Other stuff too, like getting their meals cooked and their laundry done, and some men like companionship, and showing off a pretty woman – makes them look good.'

'You make men sound quite objectionable!'

Anna shrugged. 'They're OK, for certain things. Anyway women do it too.'

'Do what?'

'Use men.'

I thought about that for a bit. I didn't want to get into too deep a conversation; I just wanted a nice day out! I suppose there were things I wanted from Michael. Hadn't I wanted to parade around the gallery with a well-dressed man at my side, rather than be taken for a sad loser with no boyfriend or friends to go out with? But I genuinely wanted to be with him too. We were spending so much time together, I almost couldn't imagine what it would be like to go somewhere without him.

Anna had already finished her pint. 'Can I get anyone a drink?' she said standing up.

'I'll get them,' said Michael.

'No, it's all right, you don't have to buy all the drinks. I'm a liberated woman,' she said heading inside to the bar.

'She's a bit, um…'

'What?'

'I dunno…unusual.'

'You mean she doesn't act like most women.'

'Well, she's not exactly feminine, is she? The bike. And that T-shirt!'

'I know her fashion-sense is atrocious. Maybe it's a lesbian thing.'

'What?'

'Oh, hadn't I said?'

'No, you hadn't,' he said, in his annoyed voice.

'Look out, she's coming back.'

'Thanks,' he said, as she put a pint of lager next to the one he'd only half finished. He picked up his old pint and almost drained it in one, clearly not wanting to be shown up by a woman. 'So, that's an unusual bike, you've got there.'

'Yes, it's a Moulton, got it second-hand in 88.'

'Don't get her started on the bike, Michael, or she'll never shut up.'

'What would you rather discuss, shoes?' she said, putting a trainer shod foot up on the table.

I groaned. 'You've got a male brain, haven't you? Maybe I should just leave you two alone to talk about sport and car parts.'

'No, I'm not really into cars or sport. We could discuss bike accessories, or maybe yesterday's post mortem.'

'Really, you do post mortems?' said Michael, suddenly showing some interest.

'Yeah, it's really cool,' said Anna. 'First you make a big cut...'

'Oh gross, I give up!'

Later, back at Michael's, he seemed in a bit of a huff. 'What's the matter?' I asked.

'You showed me up.'

'What do you mean?'

'You embarrassed me with your friend Anna, saying I didn't want to go to the exhibition with you. What will she think of me? It's not right. You know I adore you. I'd go to anything you want.'

'Oh come here, you ridiculous boy! I was just teasing. I didn't mean anything by it. I love that you want to be with me. I love you.'

'Do you?'

'Of course I do.'

Later, in bed, I said, 'it doesn't really bother you that Anna's a lesbian, does it?'

'No. It was just a bit of a surprise, that's all. You two have never, you know...'

'No, of course not, we're friends.' I didn't know how he could think such a thing. It had never crossed my mind that Anna might fancy me.

'OK, OK, I was just asking. She looks at you in a funny way.'

'No she doesn't. She looks at everyone like that.'

'OK.'

'You're not going to be weird about her, are you? 'Cos she is my best friend, and she means the world to me.'

'Ooh, means the world to me,' he said in a teasing, childish voice, 'see you're just adding fuel to the fire Iz.'

'Oh, shut up!' We both laughed. But while they seemed to get on initially, Anna and Michael never became friends, and he soon became more and more jealous of her.

Although Michael had promised not to hit me again, inevitably he did, but I was still in the days of denial. I wasn't prepared to accept that my new marriage was a mess, or that the man I loved, and who had never raised a hand to me while we'd been going out, could change so radically. I spent many hours in reflection, trying to work out what had changed, why he did it, was it something I did that provoked it? But I never really came to any conclusions.

It must have been not long afterwards that I was having lunch with my sister Louise. I don't know if I winced or something reaching across the table, but she asked me if I was all right.

'Of course I'm all right.'

'Well you don't seem very,' she paused searching for the right word, 'happy.'

'I'm just tired that's all.'

'Oh newlyweds,' she said rolling her eyes, 'I see.'

I'm embarrassed to say I think I blushed.

'Well…'

'Are you sure he's the right bloke?' I looked mildly surprised. 'Only, don't get upset for me saying this, but I don't really like him much.'

'Well it's a bit late to say so now I'm married!'

'I couldn't very well say before, could I?' Her voice was starting to enter its exasperated range. She has a very pliable voice that expresses a vast range of emotions (she would have been a great boon to the theatre). 'Mum had gone into hyper-drive with the wedding and all the invites and everything; can you imagine what she'd have been like if you'd called it off?'

'You don't think I should have called it off, do you?'

'I don't know. It was all a bit quick though. Do you?'

'What a question to ask, of course I don't. I'm very happy,' I said a bit too defensively. 'You could have said something before we got married.'

'What, in the whole six months before you rushed down the aisle with him?! Anyway, you've always had crappy boyfriends, how was I to know he was going to be any worse?'

'In what way is he worse? At least he's got a proper job and he doesn't smell.' I thought back briefly to Rodney. The name for a start should have given me pause, never mind the smelly feet.

'I don't know. I can't quite put my finger on it. He's a bit smarmy.'

'Well, maybe you shouldn't try too hard to put your finger on it. How's your love life going?'

'You could always get a quickie divorce,' she said trying to deflect attention back to me. 'I hear they're quite easy to get these days.' She laughed. I let her get away with that, because sometimes you have to allow youth a bit of licence and she is a lot younger than me and generally doesn't know what she's talking about. 'I know a bloke who'd shag you if you need proof of adultery or anything.'

'Thanks for the offer, Louise, but I don't think that'll be necessary.' I put on my most superior older sister voice. 'And anyway Michael would kill me if he thought I'd slept with someone else.'

I never said a truer word in my life.

Louise had never really liked any of my boyfriends, she was right there. But unlike Anna, who, with hindsight, I think was a bit jealous, Louise just liked any excuse to poke fun. She took great delight in teasing me about them, not that her taste in men was great. She went out with lots of lithe, tanned boys whose hair went almost white from being outdoors too much, but who never seemed to have proper jobs. Louise was a bit the same, a kind of loafer with no real ambitions. She wore a lot of beads and went through a stage of thinking everything was far-out, though I don't think she ever actually did any drugs. She was more stable and sensible than she made out, but was very emotional and liked to 'talk through things' that were troubling her. I always thought she would have done well as a character in a Jane Austen novel, doing little but getting very excited about insignificant things and waiting for a man to whisk her away. Currently she is a yoga instructor and happily between men. I wouldn't be the least surprised if she's tried women too. She always thought it was cool that Anna was gay. I've no doubt that one day she'll grow up, get married, have lots of children and be very good with them, although she'll never be grown up in the staid boring way I am. I can't let go in the way she does, but I'm giving her a run for her money now.

That evening, in the bath, I thought a lot about that conversation. We hadn't been married long, a matter of months, so I should have been happy, but was I? Michael hadn't hit me often then, probably only three or four times. I know that sounds like a lot in the first months of marriage, and it is, but it's nothing compared to what came later.

I've always loved water. We used to swim a lot as children. Dad taught us. He thought it was very important we knew how to swim in case of accidents. Swimming was one of the best things I did with him, and completely second nature to me. I think I love baths so much because they were my only real escape from Michael. I know I was still in the same house, he could have been standing right outside the door for all I know, and he didn't like me to lock the door, but he never came in while I was in the bath. Hot water is so soothing not only to the mind but to the body. Many times I added salt for its healing properties, but that's another story.

I lay there for a long time wondering if I was happy. I think that answered my question really – if I had to think about it, obviously I wasn't, because if you are happy you just know it. You don't consciously think to yourself, I'm happy. It's like that first time you have sex with someone new, even if it wasn't that good, you go around all the next day with that stupid grin on your face, the clothes hanger grin, you just can't help it. Well you can't be that sort of happy all the time, but a lot of people, I'm assuming, are generally happy most of the time. In the last years of our marriage, I found it hard to remember a time when I had been happy. I was of course, before I met Michael – reasonable childhood, no major angst at puberty, no university traumas. I was happy when I got my degree. There's that picture of me with Damian, he's got that stupid lopsided smirk he did, with a dimple on one side of his face and I've got a genuine smile too, not one of those you put on for photographs. That picture doesn't exist any more. Michael tore it up in one of his fits. Not that I could have it with me here anyway. I was terribly happy the other day too, when I saw…I must stop doing that. I want to tell things in order, but it's so hard to keep everything chronological, it all jumbles together in my head, those first dates with Michael, the beatings, the hiding, the morgue, the train, conversations, nice evenings we had, it all gets mixed up.

Now, where was I? Oh yes, well Louise got me thinking, but it didn't last long, because Michael was in a strangely romantic mood that night. See he had his good moments, it wasn't all bad. He'd ordered food from somewhere. He never cooked – that's another little sexist trait I should have picked up on. So when I emerged from the bathroom he said, 'dinner's ready,' which is not a phrase he often employed and it made a very pleasant impression. He did insist that I put on a rather low-cut dress that was a favourite of his, when I could have happily stayed in my dressing gown, but at least I didn't have to put any make up on. Thank heaven for small mercies! It's surprising how many of these asinine catch phrases and sayings I come out with now, but they do so seem to sum up things and be very apt – there's a word I love, 'apt' – has a nice ring to it, maybe I'll turn my hand to proper writing once I've got this diary, journal, memory thing down.

So we had dinner – now what was it? I want to say Schechuan beef, but I'm pretty sure that was another occasion. My memory is very selective these days, which could prove a problem with trying to capture this whole saga. There was plenty of red wine, that I do recall, at least one bottle, maybe two. Must have been a Friday or Saturday because no way Michael would have drunk that much on a 'school night.' And we discussed…the O J Simpson trial, I think. Yes, it was! We had quite a debate. I thought he had definitely killed them and Michael thought he'd been set up. I worried things were going to descend to a dangerous level. (Was I already censoring myself, trying not to let things develop into arguments, because we know what that led to? Surely not, surely not *that* early on?) I think in the end I agreed it wasn't a clear-cut thing and he wasn't likely to get a fair trial with all the media exposure (it probably saved my bacon – there I go with the verbal clichés again!)

And we talked about art (must have been one of the few times). We had rarely been to an art gallery again together since that time we went to the Haywood when we'd first been courting (I like to say courting, it makes it sound like something noble though it barely lasted long enough to be considered a courtship). In fact the best bit had been walking along the river after we'd met Anna. It was a lovely evening and the ebbing light played on the Thames and I adore all those bridges along that section and the view across to St Paul's. Parts of London are so unbearably beautiful in the light of a summer evening. I miss it sometimes, I really do. I don't think I've been to the Hayward since and I totally missed the opening of Tate Modern, though I read about it. That is very sad, because I love art. I hadn't realised quite how much until I said it. Still I'm in the right place for it now. I can have all the art I want.

The Turner Prize had just been announced and was all over the papers, the winner berated and lauded in equal measure. For once Michael and I agreed, though I was tempted to disagree on principle. Damien Hirst had won with his Mother and Child Divided, which I couldn't bring myself to describe as art no matter how hard I tried.

Michael was rattled as only Michael could be about the absurdity and obscenity of modern art. 'It's a total abortion. You can't call that art. It's an abomination.'

'I know.'

'It's obscene the way... Hang on a minute, did you just agree with me?'

'Yes Michael. I love art; you know art that takes talent – Monet, Renoir, Poussin...'

'Yes, all right, no need to show off with all the painters you know.'

'Sorry. Cutting a cow in half and sticking it in formaldehyde is not what I call art.'

'Well, I'm glad we agree. It's just like the old days. Remember those talks we used to have when I met you? All about our hideous childhoods and evil parents?' Your terrible childhood, I thought, mine was fine. I never should have said a derogatory word about Louise. How had I let him suck me into his 'us and them' mentality? But I smiled and snuggled closer. 'More wine, I think. Let's toast our agreement on the state of modern art. To modern art and its complete crapness.' He raised a glass. He was uncharacteristically tipsy.

I wanted to say that I did like some modern art, that some of it had a point. I'd liked to have had a serious discussion with him about what constituted art and what didn't, but I couldn't. We didn't discuss things much any more. Michael announced, and I agreed with him. But I was relieved that we'd agreed, glad that he was happy, that we were getting along.

The more we drank, the more we got to reminiscing about the start of our relationship, though in reality we hadn't been together all that long. We had a whirlwind romance and were married before most people would even move in together. Michael liked it when I talked about my life before I met him. Towards the end of the second bottle of wine, I got out some of my university photos and was regaling him with tales of me and Sarah getting pissed up and trying pot (I came to regret that particular confession). He was lapping it all up until we got to the photo of Damian with his arm around me.

'Who's this then?'

'Oh that's Damian. He was a right laugh.'

'Hmm, he seems very friendly. Was he your boyfriend?'

'No, just a friend. We did Italian together.'

'Oh I bet you did!' Michael snatched the photo and put it up to his face to look closer as though he was short-sighted. Then he ripped it up and tossed the pieces on the floor.

'What did you do that for?'

'Didn't like the look of him.'

'Oh for goodness' sake! He was just a friend, and so what if he had been a boyfriend? It was years before I met you.'

'Oh, so now you're saying he was your boyfriend?'

'No.' The wine had made me emotional and my eyes began to well. I couldn't understand why we were having this ridiculous conversation.

'Come here,' he said, putting his arm round me. 'I'm sorry Izzy, I didn't mean to upset you. I'm such an unfeeling bastard, I don't deserve you. I just love you so much, I can't bear to think of you with anyone else.'

'But I wasn't with him.'

'I know, I'm sorry. I guess I've drunk a bit too much.' He wiped my tears away and kissed me and we laughed it off as a drunken episode.

Later, as we lay in bed (I would say post coital, but I can't stand that phrase), with candles no less, Michael said again, 'I do love you, you know.'

Part of me wanted to say, 'do you, really?' but I didn't want to spoil the mood, so I said, 'I know.' I loved it when he got all sentimental. I'm a hopeless romantic, I could go the whole hog if I wanted, that's why it's so nice now with the shoe on the other foot so to speak…sorry! I will stop doing that, I promise.

'I'm so sorry about earlier,' he said.

'It's OK.'

He kissed me then, one of those long kisses that starts ever so softly and then gets all sort of passionate and intense, and then we fell asleep with our arms around each other, and I was happy then. I remember thinking, before I fell asleep, yes, I am happy, Louise doesn't know what she's on about!

I wondered sometimes if Anna was happy. She always seemed to be in her own slightly eccentric kind of way. She had her work, a lovely flat, her bike and her gadgets – she was a bit of a gadget freak even before anything like mobile phones and iPods took off. She had her cat, Jasmine (I laugh as I remember her – we had a mutual loathing). She had her lesbian stuff, her own little world of special films and books and clubs that I never knew about, and presumably a posse of lesbian friends that I didn't know about either. But from where I stood, her life seemed somewhat empty. She worked too hard and too much, didn't seem to have many friends, and certainly not many relationships that lasted. But who am I to criticize? At least she didn't have anyone constantly undermining her, and snooping on her, and hitting her. She was very self-contained. Her parents' indifference had taught her valuable self-reliance. She knew she could always rely on Anna to keep her entertained, because she'd been entertaining herself from a young age. She didn't need people. Turns out she did like to be needed though, and perhaps she needed people more than she thought.

That's just reminded me of that weird party Anna took me to once. God knows why; I'm sure I was the only straight woman there, but it took me a while to realise that! It was at somebody's house, not that far from where we ended up living. I can't remember where Michael was, maybe he was at a squash club do or something; I know he hadn't been invited. It must have been after our insulated honeymoon period and before Michael tried to stop me seeing my friends.

Anna was strangely excited. She never normally liked parties or social gatherings that much. It's not that she was a complete introvert, she just liked people in small doses and small groups. Now I come to think of it, I reckon she must have fancied someone who was going to be at the party and she thought taking me along might make her jealous.

We walked there, and Anna kept checking a piece of paper in her pocket that must have had the address on. She'd told me to dress down as it wasn't 'that sort of party', so I was wearing jeans, and Anna was looking particularly scruffy in jeans and a sort of lumberjack shirt, with the DMs she had favoured for a time. Little did I know that was the height of lesbian chic at the time and Anna was dressed to kill.

We entered a fairly ordinary looking terraced house, but inside was much nicer, with some sort of conservatory at the back adding light and space. Quite a few people were already there, standing around chatting or sitting on the sofa. Anna handed over her bottle of wine and introduced me to the hostess, then positioned herself by the snacks and proceeded to nibble non-stop and gulp beer.

'So,' I attempted, 'what's this all in aid of then?'

'What?'

'The party.'

'Housewarming, I think.'

'Right, and why are we here?'

'Free food and drink.'

'Well that's certainly a valid reason, but how do you know these people?'

Anna seemed annoyed with my questioning, and sighed. 'They're sort of friends of friends.'

I shut up for a bit and scanned the room. It was then it dawned on me that all the guests were women. I shot Anna a look.

'What?'

'You've brought me to a lezzer party, haven't you?' I whispered.

'So?'

I rolled my eyes.

'Oh get a grip, no one will hit on you, they'll think you're with me.'

'I haven't got to snog you or anything have I?'

'No, of course not!'

She'd started on the peanuts now, and quite a few seemed to be stuck to her shirt.

'You've got…shirt front.'

She looked down, 'thanks,' she said, brushing off the detritus.

'So, aren't you going to mingle? If you just wanted to eat snacks you could have stayed at home.'

'All in good time. I have a plan.'

'Which is?'

'Currently I'm eyeing up the competition.'

'Oh, now that sounds more interesting. Who's your target?'

'The tall woman talking to the one in black jeans by the patio door.'

'What the one who looks like a shot putter?'

'No she doesn't! She looks like a swimmer.'

I was a bit confused. 'Oh, you mean the tall blonde?'

'Why don't you say it a bit louder, Iz, I don't think everyone heard you.'

'Sorry. So you've got a thing for her then?'

'A mild interest,' said Anna, trying to play it cool.

'Yeah right. You've dragged me to this ridiculous party because you're only mildly interested! She's a bit tall for you, isn't she?'

'Height's irrelevant in the bedroom.'

'Oh, I see. Perhaps I'd better leave you to it then.'

'No,' she said gripping my arm. 'I need to look like I can pull an attractive woman.'

'So I'm attractive now, am I?'

She smiled.

'Well, I'm not standing here all night like a lemon. I'm going to go outside and cadge a fag.'

'But you don't smoke.'

'I do occasionally. Anyway, the shot putter is moving away leaving the blonde free, so now is your moment to strike.' I gave her a gentle push.

I think Anna did end up having a bit of a fling with the blonde. She always seemed to get her woman if she tried, but she didn't try very often.

Anna was analytical and enquiring; I'm not surprised she went into pathology, but cutting up bodies, that seemed a bit extreme even for her. I did wonder when she went to medical school, about her bedside manner. I couldn't quite picture her in a 'caring' profession or as a GP reassuring people over their snuffs and sniffles and minor rashes. It's not that she didn't care, but she didn't suffer fools lightly and hypochondriacs even less. She was an only child, but not the spoilt kind. Her parents encouraged her every interest, bought her books, a bicycle, her first microscope, but they didn't try to mould her. Basically they left her to her own devices and Anna thrived. She had no trouble amusing herself and filling her days with explorations and projects.

At school she wasn't popular and she wasn't unpopular. She had a few friends, of whom I was the closest, or at least I like to think I was. We must have been because we've kept in touch all this time, and what she did for me, well…Mostly people thought she was a science nerd, and she was. It's a good job she didn't wear glasses then and was reasonably good at sport or the nerd moniker really would have stuck. The fact that she wasn't above helping other children with their science homework helped too.

There wasn't much overlap in our interests, but somehow we were drawn together, probably as much by the proximity of our houses as anything. I was more popular at school. I was pretty and girly and had more friends, but no one intrigued me quite like Anna. When I hung out with her I always had more fun, and did stuff I didn't do with anyone else. I thought she was a genius and I was happy to be taken advantage of to bask in her wisdom. By the time we went to high school, Anna had catalogued a huge variety of insects and analysed a number of soils abetted by her willing assistant, though I hated getting my hands dirty and as soon as we got back to her house I rushed into their downstairs loo to wash them with the Imperial Leather soap her mum kept there, accompanied by shouts of 'Isabel, you big girl's blouse,' as Anna ran upstairs with our finds to her 'lab'. Even now the smell of Imperial Leather reminds me of Anna's house.

If her mother was at home, which wasn't often, she'd give us squash and Jaffa Cakes in the kitchen. I loved Jaffa Cakes, they were something we had at home only on special occasions. I also loved the attention and the gorgeous kitchen with its big pine table with fresh garden flowers, everything neat and tidy and spotless. It felt like there should be an Aga and a litter of puppies, which there wasn't. It was the kind of kitchen I wanted when I grew up.

Anna, on the other hand, hated these distractions, itching to be alone in her room looking things up in her encyclopaedia. When we escaped, she would rush to her desk completely oblivious to my presence. I'd throw myself on her bed, fidget, get up, look at the stuff on her shelves. Without looking up from what she was doing, she'd say, 'don't touch anything.'

I'd soon get bored and reluctantly would leave, knowing that Anna was lost to her own geeky world. 'See you then.' I always hoped she'd say, don't go, but she just mumbled, 'yeah, see you tomorrow.' Part of me hated the assumption that we'd repeat the performance the next day that I wouldn't have anything better to do, part of me loved it.

Michael and I had so much in common in the early days. He used to joke sometimes that we were like twins separated at birth. I wanted to point out that would have made the sex really weird, but I kind of knew what he meant. We had an almost instant bond and for a while I felt like I didn't need anyone else. But that never lasts does it? Within a few months, I was itching to hang out with Anna again, go drinking with the girls from work and go shopping with Louise. Michael didn't see it quite like that.

We both loved reading and films, although sometimes his taste in films didn't match mine. There was that awful time we went to see *Silence of the Lambs*, which he loved and which scared me shitless. And there was the time we saw *Basic Instinct*, which I had to admit I liked despite Anna's protests about the depiction of lesbians, but it didn't capture me in quite the way it did Michael.

'That was great,' he said, as we came out of the cinema.

'Yeah, but was Stone the killer or not?'

'We'll never know, will we?'

'But we know the shrink must have killed the policeman at the end.'

'Do we?'

'Well, she was right there and Sharon Stone's character was off at her beach house or something. And, it must have been the doctor who leaked his psychological file.'

'Yeah, I suppose so, but Stone could have engineered it so that Beth did that murder for her or made us think it was her.'

'Hmm, maybe. So they have that shot of the ice pick under the bed just to put doubt in your mind at the end, so you're not sure who did what throughout the film? Or was she really going to kill him?'

'I think she was going to kill him,' he said.

I hated endings where you weren't sure what had happened. Michael liked that kind of thing. 'She was kind of weird though, hanging around with all those killers. I don't think most writers spend time with real killers to get ideas for books. And she could have killed her parents.'

'Or that could have been an unfortunate accident. You know the original title of the film was supposed to be Love Hurts which is the name of Catherine's murder novel.'

'Catherine?'

'Yeah Catherine Tramell, the character Sharon played.'

'How do you know that?' I loved that he always knew the film trivia.

He shrugged. 'And Kim Basinger, Greta Scacchi and Michelle Pfeiffer turned down the role.'

'Geek,' I said giving him a look to imply what a weirdo he was for knowing this stuff, but I was kind of impressed.

We were now in a booth at the pub near the cinema where we often went for a post film drink and Michael was running his hand up my leg.

I slapped his hand away playfully. 'You just liked it for the bit where she's got no knickers on!'

'No. It's neo-noir, it will probably become a classic,' he said in his pompous film critic voice that he often employed to distract from the fact that he could be a bit of a film bore. 'There was some great sex in it though.'

'Do you think? It wasn't very sexy. It looked a bit rough.'

'Why don't you come home with me and we'll try it. You might like it.'

'What tying you up with a silk scarf?'

His face fell slightly as though that wasn't what he had in mind at all. 'Yeah, if you like,' he said. 'Drink up.'

As soon as we were back at his flat, he pushed me up against the wall and kissed me hard. 'Let's go to the bedroom,' he said. I didn't have any objections. He forced me back onto the bed and immediately straddled me and started undoing my blouse. He was in such a hurry it started ripping around the button holes.

'Oi be careful, don't rip my blouse.'

'Oh sod the blouse. I'll buy you another one. I'll rip it off if I want.' He bared his teeth and sort of growled in a mock macho way. I giggled, but I'm not sure on reflection how much he was playing. He did tear the blouse off then. I tried to half sit up and undo his shirt. I wanted to slow things down, but Michael didn't. He pulled his shirt over his head and threw it on the floor and then deftly undid my bra. I wriggled out of my skirt and went to undo his trousers. I could see the bulge of his hard-on already, and I stroked it through the fabric. He pushed my hand away and quickly got out of his trousers and pants. Then he was in me immediately and it seemed like he barely knew I was there. It was all over in seconds.

'God, that was amazing,' he gasped afterwards as he rolled onto his back. I couldn't say that I really agreed with him, though there was certainly something about the spontaneity and urgency that had really turned me on.

On Sunday morning Anna called. 'Hi. Didn't get you up, did I?'

'No.'

'Good. So, can you come out to play today? I haven't seen you for ages.'

'Hmm, I dunno. I don't know what we have planned.'

'You need to get of bed sometime, you'll be getting bedsores! Just tell him you're seeing me. You don't need his permission.'

'Yeah, OK. What do you want to do?'

'I quite fancy pizza, you know that real Italian place in Soho. Or we could try the new Mexican place?'

I hung up. Michael looked up from the paper. 'Who was that?'

'Anna. I'm going to meet her for lunch.'

'Oh right, thanks for asking me!'

'Well, I don't need your permission to see my oldest friend, do I? I haven't seen her for months.'

'Oh, that's not true. You went out the other night.'

'That was weeks ago, and anyway I used to see her every week.'

'I suppose you'd rather spend time with her than me.'

'Of course not.' I went up behind him and tried to put my arms around him, but he pushed me away. I got a bit pissed off then. 'Oh Michael, don't be such a baby. You know I love you. I think I showed that last night.' I looked at him coyly, and I may even have blushed, 'that doesn't mean I can't see my friends too.'

He just shrugged, not acknowledging my allusion to our sex fest of the previous night. 'I thought we were going to have Sunday roast,' he said petulantly. 'We can still do that. I'll be back this afternoon and I can make a roast for dinner and we'll have a nice quiet evening together, OK?'

'OK,' he said grudgingly.

I couldn't believe how keen Michael was to move in together. None of my previous boyfriends had wanted to. In fact I'd only lived with one guy before and that had been more by default than design. He certainly hadn't asked me to move in with him within a couple of months of meeting. But Michael wasn't like other men. Now I'd say he was overly needy and clingy, but back then when I was in love with him, it all seemed perfect. Neither of us were twenty-somethings any more. It was sweet that he wanted to settle down and have children. All these years later I can see that everything was rushed, and maybe there was something not quite right about that, but at the time I was swept up in a tornado of love and the excitement of thinking someone wanted to spend the rest of their life with me. Someone intelligent and caring, and his good job and financial stability wasn't a turn off either!

One Saturday we were sitting eating lunch, as we often did, in The Lamb. It was an OK pub, though I wasn't a huge fan. However, it was relatively near Michael's squash club, and since he and his squash partner Rob had been having a post game pint there for years before he'd even met me, I'd taken to meeting him there afterwards. Michael was always in a good mood after squash, especially if he'd won, and on that Saturday he had uncharacteristically thrashed the living daylights out of Rob. He was very excited and couldn't wait to tell me all about it. Having suffered through excruciating point by point detail of the game all through my jacket potato (he and Rob were usually very evenly matched, so I suppose it was a big event – it later turned out that Rob had been coming down with the flu, but Michael didn't let that spoil his moment of glory!), Michael suddenly gave me his full attention and changed the subject.

'I thought we might go and look at some houses this afternoon,' he said.

'That's a bit sudden, isn't it?'

'I don't think so; we're virtually living together already.' This was true, but it felt like we'd only been going out for a matter of weeks. 'Where do you fancy?'

I was gobsmacked, but also ecstatic. A boyfriend who wanted to move in together? This was the stuff of Bridget Jones-like fantasy. It was a million times better than the promise of a 'mini-break' in the country. This was real romance. I tried to resist kissing him.

'I don't know, maybe somewhere round Highbury, or Stoke Newington?'

'Hmm, what's wrong with Finsbury?'

'We probably can't afford a house round here, and anyway Anna is in Highbury, and my parents are near there. It's a nice up and coming area.'

'You sound like an estate agent! OK, OK, we can look in that area if that's what you want.'

It wasn't long before every weekend was taken up with looking at houses. Michael even cancelled squash once, he was that keen. Though in the end we didn't really look at very many. Michael seemed less interested in the actual houses and more interested in the prospect of living together, which I thought was the height of romance. He happily deferred to me as I rambled on about curtains, and what we could do with different rooms, how the furniture from our respective flats would fit. 'Whatever you want Iz. I'll leave the decorating to you.' But in the end, the house we chose was more about what Michael wanted than me.

Like most houses in the area, it was a Victorian terrace, but this one had been modernised, and boy had it been modernised. The downstairs had an open plan kitchen diner, with a very modern kitchen, not at all what I'd had in mind. It had three bedrooms, though the third bedroom was pretty small and Michael immediately commandeered it as his 'office' though I don't think he ever did much actual work in it. The master bedroom was big with an en-suite shower, but the whole house had been done out in magnolia and beige carpets, apart from the tiles in the kitchen, and felt devoid of character. Still I managed to fall in love with it. I saw it as a blank canvas that I'd be able to do what I wanted with.

It seemed that to Michael a house was just a house. He favoured bland, sterile houses, where I liked the older ones with character. My favourite thing about this house was the yard. It was narrow and long with flagstones and pots and well-established bushes making it feel secluded, and it was the only part of the place that seemed at all Victorian. Michael didn't like gardening so he was pleased with the lack of grass to cut and liked the privacy provided by the bushes.

'This is more like it,' he said as soon as we went in. 'Wow, check out the kitchen, Iz.'

'It's certainly big.'

'Don't you like it?'

'I had something a bit more cosy in mind.'

'Cosy? Why would you want a kitchen to be cosy? Don't you want space and work tops and…'

I could tell he was enamoured of the sleek, masculine, graniteness of it all. The estate agent showed us into the living room.

'Nice fire place.'

'It's not actually functional,' said the agent, 'the chimney's been blocked off, but it is an original feature.'

Upstairs, and away from the agent, Michael whispered, 'I think this is it.'

'You do?'

'Yeah, don't you?' He seemed deflated as though he couldn't imagine why I didn't like it. 'It's a great location, near the high street and park.' He put his arms round me, 'and room for a baby or two.'

I ignored the reference to children and worked out in my head how close it was to Anna and to my parents. It *was* a great location, and I could decorate it the way I wanted, soften it. Michael was so enthusiastic I couldn't help but be caught up. And it was ready to move into. Some of the other houses we'd seen would have needed a lot of work, and I couldn't quite picture Michael as much of a DIY expert. 'OK,' I said.

'I'll call and make an offer.'

We were lucky, I can see that now, money was never an issue. We had no trouble securing a house that many people could only dream of, but somehow it never felt as homely as I'd always imagined it would.

As soon as we'd put in the offer, we started making plans. I remember we went back to Michael's and he opened a bottle of champagne that he just happened to have in the fridge and we talked about how great it would be to be in our very own house together. I felt so grown-up and also like a teenager. I'd had my moments at university, but I'd never really been a wild party girl, I'd always been sensible, up until now. This was more the kind of thing Louise would do – move in with someone she barely knew. She'd be green with envy. I couldn't wait to tell her.

Then out of the blue Michael said, 'I'm not sure I really like the idea of living together.'

'What? Then, why…' I was totally shocked. Why had he got my hopes up by having us look at houses then? Shit, we hadn't just looked, we'd put an offer in, which had been accepted! 'Michael…'

'I don't think people should live together unless they're married.'

'How very old fashioned of you Michael,' I said, thinking this wasn't the time to adopt prudish Victorian mores. 'Hang on, did you just propose to me?'

'Maybe.' He smiled.

'Oh Michael.' I hugged him. I was speechless, and there I was thinking he wasn't romantic!

A few days later, he confirmed he had been serious as he went down on one knee and proposed properly with a ring. I was ecstatic. As soon as I told my parents, my mother and I went into overdrive on wedding plans. Michael didn't want a long engagement, but I wanted the big fairy tale wedding, so we didn't have much time to plan. My father said, 'he hasn't got you up the duff, has he?'

'Oh Arthur, don't be so crass,' said mum, 'neither of them are getting any younger.'

'Thanks mum! It's just romantic, dad. We don't *have* to get married, we want to.' Dad went on about 'the youth of today' and how it was all very rushed, but I think he was pleased really.

Of course Anna was the first person I told about Michael's proposal, or she would have been if she hadn't been so busy. The first free moment I had at work I called her.

'Hi, it's me.'

'I know. I can't really talk right now, I'm about to go and extract a spleen.'

'Oh spare me the details. You could have just said you were busy.'

'Whatever! So is this important or did you just call to talk about clutch bags.'

'It's important. I have news, big news.'

'You're not pregnant are you?'

'No! Are you free for lunch?'

'Not really.'

'Just a sandwich? Please Anna. I can't tell you over the phone.'

'Oh all right. It'll have to be a quickie though.'

I was so excited I didn't even fall into her trap and make a joke about quickies, but I couldn't contain myself until Anna's tiny window of opportunity at 2 p.m. Next I called Louise.

'Hey sis.'

'Hey yourself. You sound very chirpy. What's wrong?'

'Cynicism doesn't become you Louise.'

'Eh?'

'Never mind. Look, are you free for lunch?'

'I am as it happens.' How did I know she would be? Louise was always free for lunch especially if there was a chance I'd pay for it. 'What gives?'

'Ooh I can't tell you, you'll have to wait.'

'I hope the suspense doesn't kill me. Usual place?'

I don't think I did much work that morning. I did a lot of photocopying with my left hand strategically placed so that anyone walking past would see the engagement ring and ask me about it. However, once at the café, I tried to keep my hand out of view. I wanted to milk this for all it was worth and keep Louise waiting, but I never was very good at that kind of thing, and I ended up blurting it out almost immediately.

'To what do I owe this unexpected pleasure?' asked Louise once we were seated.

'Oh you know, just fancied seeing my little sister.'

Louise didn't believe a word of it. 'You never want to just see me. What are you scheming? Mum and dad haven't got some big anniversary coming up have they? Oh God, you're not 40 already, are you? Have I got to organise a big party?!'

'Very funny. I'm barely into my thirties. No, way more exciting than that.'

'You got a promotion?'

'No! I said exciting?'

'OK, so spill already, what?'

I lifted my hand up then and flashed the ring at her.

'Noo! He didn't?'

'He did.'

'But, but, you've only been seeing him for about three weeks.'

'Oh don't be ridiculous, it's way longer than that.'

'It's not been long though.'

'No. But it just feels right, and it's so romantic.'

'Well, you are getting on a bit!'

'Shut up. You think anyone over twenty-five is old.'

'They are.'

Anna was slightly less enthused when I told her, shortly afterwards. 'And you accepted?'

'Yeah, why not?'

'Well bloody hell Iz, it's worse than a couple of lesbians.' I look confused. 'You know the joke – what do lesbians bring to a second date? A removal van.'

'No, not really.'

'Are you sure he's the one?'

'Yes. He's so attentive and he understands me so well.'

'But you have been in the honeymoon bubble since you met him. Don't you think you should come up for air before you commit to 'til death do ye part?'

'I love him. He clearly loves me. Why wait?'

'Well if you really know what you're doing, congratulations.' She raised her coffee mug. 'But if you think I'm wearing a bridesmaid's dress you've got another think coming!'

'You're home late,' Michael said.

'Yeah, there was a meeting at work.'

'Couldn't you have called?'

'I didn't really have time. Anyway, I'm only about half an hour later than usual,' I said, looking at my watch. 'You didn't have plans did you?'

'I thought we might go out for dinner.'

'Oh that would be lovely, but I'm so tired, couldn't we just get a take-away?'

'How come you're so tired? You're just some glorified secretary, aren't you? How tiring can that be?'

I shot him a dirty look, shocked by his sudden derogatory tone. 'What would you know about it in your ivory tower being waited on hand and foot while you do your big deals and get your big bonuses?' I said jokingly, hoping to break the tension, but he didn't get the tone and took it the wrong way.

'Don't fucking talk to me like that,' he shouted, slamming his hand down hard on the counter top. That really scared me. What was he getting so worked up about? Was he really so upset that I was home a bit later than usual? There could have been a hold-up on the Tube, or a fire alarm, or anything. Half an hour was nothing. He moved closer to me then. He brought his face close to mine so I could see the vein in his forehead throbbing and hear his breathing. 'You don't mind living off those bonuses though, do you?' He poked me in the ribs.

'I don't live off them; I pay my own way, that's why I keep my job that you so hate me doing.'

'Well that pittance hardly pays the bills! You might as well give it up.'

'But I don't want to give it up.'

'Well I want you to,' he said. 'How do I know what you're up to? I bet you're banging someone in the stationary room, aren't you? Or, or having drinks with some so called client. That's why you're late.'

'Oh don't be ridiculous Michael.' I couldn't believe that he was imagining some affair based on my being a bit late home. 'Roger called a meeting at short notice because Pete's going to be off sick longer than we thought and we have to cover his work. It ran over a bit. There's no conspiracy, no affairs. I would have called you if I'd known you'd be this upset, but what's there to get upset about? It was incredibly boring and we didn't even get any tea and biscuits!'

Michael smiled a shy smile then and took my hand. 'I'm sorry. God, I'm such an idiot sometimes. I always overreact, don't I? I don't know what came over me. I just love you so much. I can't bear the thought of you being with someone else, and when you weren't here when I got home, I started imagining all sorts.'

My heart gradually stopped pounding. He was just worried about me, that's what it boiled down to. A slightly odd way to show it, but he was just worried something bad might have happened. I gave him a hug. 'So are you going to order some food or what?'

※

My parents are traditional people. Not conservative, but not, I suppose, overly liberal. They loved Anna, but in all honesty probably weren't all out for gay rights. They supported the rights of immigrants, but probably didn't want any living next to them. They were good people in a boring middle class way, and so they were predictably ecstatic when I told them Michael had proposed, even though we hadn't been going out together that long. Well, mum was ecstatic, dad said, 'how much is that going to cost me?' but I could see he was pleased.

We didn't see a lot of my parents, but they liked Michael. He was from the right kind of background. He made the right kind of comments in conversation. He was well off financially and only likely to get richer. He was perfect. My mother in particular, despaired of Louise ever getting married, and so far she's been proved right, so all her wedding eggs were in the one basket – mine. And we were all so very careful not to knock over the basket in case it upset the alignment of the whole planetary system. Mother began making plans almost before the ring was on my finger and I can't deny I didn't participate fully in her mission to have the world's most perfect wedding. Louise was right, once we were on that yellow brick road there was no getting off it. The fact of the groom being a bit 'smarmy' was neither here nor there, and since when has that ever stopped a wedding.

Louise loved and hated it in equal measure. She loved being chief bridesmaid, but hated the attendant dressing up that was required. She thought the wedding party would be lots of fun and that she'd 'cop off' with someone from the groom's side, which I think she did, but was miffed that the attention was centred on me. But all in all, she was as swept up in the wedding plans as anyone else and eagerly joined in the discussions on cakes, dresses, flowers, and caterers. She was keen that unlike the service, the reception shouldn't be too formal or stuffy, and in a moment of total misjudgement, my mother left her in charge of procuring a band for the party. Through some friends of friends she found The Jumping Fleas, a ukulele band who played the local folk pub circuit (which, believe me, is pretty small). Now, to give her some credit, they were better than anyone expected them to be, but they were not what mother, or indeed, what *I* had in mind for the world's most perfect wedding. I thought mum might have a stroke when she saw them, but dad at least was pleased with their rates.

I was worried Louise might turn up to the church in dreadlocks and a nose ring. She was going through a particularly 'alternative' phase in the run up to the wedding and had had several tattoos done. One went from her ankle up most of her calf and mum was decidedly unimpressed and insisted that Louise would be wearing a full-length dress to cover it up. The dress did cover it up, but left the butterfly on her shoulder fully exposed. She had finished art school the summer before and was still trying to work out what to do with her life while she hung out with a rather unsavoury crowd. Still at least she was back from her round England trip in Craig's camper van. Mum had been worried the entire three months, though I don't reckon they got up to anything much more exciting than making homemade cider and having very loud sex in numerous farmers' fields. She still smoked a little weed, but overall I think Louise liked to tell a tale more than she liked to do anything really daring. I was mildly jealous of her freedom. While touring the countryside in a VW van was not my idea of a good time, my prospective married life with a city banker and a respectable job was starting to look somewhat boring by comparison. Still that was what I wanted – the man, the house, the money, the security and lots of foreign holidays. Michael had swept me off my feet and I couldn't have been happier.

Anna was the only voice of reason in the milieu, but she came at things from such a different angle that I didn't see any of her jesting and criticism as a warning against marrying Michael, only as a protest against the institution of marriage itself. But even she seemed delighted by the prospect of embarrassing me with her 'best man' speech, and despite herself she seemed to rather enjoy the party too. She drank far too much, and confessed later that she'd been sick into one of the plant pots holding decorative palms! Lucky for her I didn't see that.

I drank rather a lot myself, and danced loads, though not with Michael. I don't know where he was half the time. He invited a dreary bunch from the bank who looked decidedly disinterested through all the speeches, and didn't laugh at Anna's jokes, and then proceeded to eat and drink as much as possible and flirt unsuccessfully with the bridesmaids. Still the girls and I had a fantastic time. Sarah said it had been one of the best weddings she'd ever been to.

Anna was the star of the speeches. Dad was predictably proud, and predictably unoriginal. I can't even remember Michael's response. I can only remember his nervousness, which seemed to emanate from him like body odour throughout most of the proceedings, but Louise told me later it was 'cheesy'. The sight of Anna in morning dress kick-started a feeling of bonhomie towards her from most of the crowd from the moment she stood up. She had insisted that if she was taking on the role of best man she should be dressed accordingly, and she wasn't going to wear a dress on any account, not even for me. I remember squirming in my seat, my palms sweating lightly at the stories she might tell. Anna knew me better than anyone and had been present at many of my most embarrassing moments. However, I'd already had quite a lot of champagne by then, so was imbued with a warm, forgiving glow.

'I realise that the best man is traditionally supposed to make fun of the groom, and much as I would love to metaphorically tear Michael to shreds for stealing my best friend, I know relatively little about the man. Also, as you will see, I'm not a traditional best man.'

She paused for laughter. I groaned; this was going to be worse than I expected.

'Apart from her parents and grandparents, I don't think there is anyone in this room who has known Isabel for as long as I have, or who is better qualified to exemplify some of the finer moments of her life to date, before meeting numb nuts over here.'

I wondered how much champagne Anna had already drunk. I didn't dare look at Michael.

'Her first romantic involvement was in fact with myself.' I could hear Michael in my head saying, I told you she fancied you. 'Although she will try to pass this off as innocent childhood exploration, I put it to you, your Honour, that Isobel was in fact, on the afternoon in question, old enough to know perfectly well what she was doing.'

There were some polite titters, but some people were clearly intrigued to know what form this 'involvement' had taken. I hoped Anna wasn't going to divulge more details. I shot her a pleading look.

'I hope she's perfected her kissing technique in the intervening years, because I've had more passion from a bowl of cold porridge!'

Humour reigned, equilibrium restored, the best man was just joking, they never had a lesbian relationship.

'Isobel I know, will be relieved by the fact that we didn't go to university together, so I'm afraid I'm unable to elaborate on those years of debauchery. However,' she paused for effect, 'you'll be pleased to know that there were numerous unsuitable and unsavoury boyfriends before the eminently eligible Mr Atkins came along. How long have you got?' she said, looking at her watch.

'All night,' someone heckled.

I never have understood why a perfectly good dinner and party should be spoiled by these ridiculous speeches. But we got through it. In the end Anna was much funnier than I'd thought she would be, and managed to erase the numb nuts comment with glowing praise for the bridegroom. I wonder if she did like him back then, or if it was all just bluff, the courtesy and tradition required by the occasion. It's not like Anna to worry about tradition or what other people think, but she would want to spare my feelings. She never would have done anything to deliberately spoil my special day, even if she did have doubts about the groom.

~~~

'Don't forget I'm going out with the girls tonight,' I said to Michael as I went to the door to go to work.

'What girls? Those losers from your office?' Oh no, not another long tirade, I thought. Lately Michael seemed to complain every time I mentioned seeing Anna or Louise and I'd barely gone out with anyone from work for ages because he always made a scene about it, but it was Katherine's birthday and I was determined that I would have my social life back.

'It's Katherine's birthday and I'm going whether you like it or not. You can join us later if you want.'

Michael snorted. 'I wouldn't want to be seen with that lot.'

'Well, we can't all be merchant bankers,' I said, thinking of the rhyming slang and emphasizing the word banker. The subtlety was wasted on Michael. 'Why do you make such a fuss about me seeing my friends anyway?'

'I just think you could do better for yourself.'

'Really, and who do you suggest I be friends with?'

'You could try being more friendly with Michelle.' Michelle was the wife of Michael's boss Leonard and was excruciatingly boring and stuck up. I'd had to suffer several hours of being civil to Leonard and Michelle at the last Christmas party at the bank and I couldn't imagine anything worse than having to pretend I was her friend.

'But we have nothing in common.'

'You could try, to improve yourself.'

'I don't see how spending two hours talking about Gucci handbags and shoes is going to improve me.'

Michael rolled his eyes. 'Socially, Isabel, socially. They know so many people, the right kind of people'

'Well you hobnob with them then if you're so interested in the *right* kind of people. Personally, I want friends who like me and are fun. And I'm still going out with the girls later,' I said picking up my bag.

'Don't get drunk on Babycham,' he said snidely, adding 'and don't fall over your white stilettos,' as I went out of the door.

It wasn't just my work friends that Michael put down, he soon made it clear that he didn't like my family even though mum in particular thought he could do no wrong, and he didn't like Anna. At first he seemed to tolerate her, and was always pleasant enough when she was there, but as soon as she was out of earshot the snide comments would start.

'I don't know how you can be friends with that woman.'

'Why not?'

'She's so...manlike.'

'So men and women can't be friends?'

'Don't play stupid Isabel, you know what I mean. You know she fancies you.'

'Of course she doesn't, we've been friends since we were children. What difference does it make to you? I don't care who you hang out with.'

'It reflects badly on me.'

'What that my best friend happens to be a lesbian? How does that reflect on you Michael? She's never met any of your posh friends, or your high and mighty bank colleagues. And, for the record, not that it matters to me, she's a very eminent pathologist.'

'Eminent, ha! She works for the NHS for goodness' sake.'

'Well some people have a social conscience, they don't all think about the money they could make.'

'That's rich coming from you. You don't exactly give to charity, do you?'

'No, and neither do you, Michael, neither do you. You're all about money, and what people think of you. You're just like that ridiculous Mrs Bucket on *Keeping Up Appearances*.'

Michael went red in the face. 'Don't be so ridiculous,' he blustered, but I knew I'd hit a nail. He opened the fridge and took out a bottle of beer, slamming the door shut with a bang afterwards and nearly pulling the drawer off its rollers looking for a bottle opener.

'What's the matter with you Michael? You can't even take a joke anymore,' I said, trying to soften the blow.

'You, that's what's the matter with me,' he shouted. 'You've got no class, no ambition.'

'I don't need to, you have enough for both of us,' I said, going upstairs and retreating to the safety of a hot bath.

⁂

Ironically, given how long I spent planning it, I don't remember that much about my wedding day except Anna's speech, but the honeymoon was divine. Michael really surprised me with the honeymoon. He arranged everything to try to please me. Whenever I asked him where we were going he said, 'it's a surprise, leave it to me.' As it turned out we had very different tastes in holidays, but I didn't know that then having never been on a holiday with him. It's crazy when I think about it now that our honeymoon was our first holiday together. The longer we were together the more it became apparent that Michael didn't really like holidays at all. He liked routine, and didn't find it easy to relax. I'd organised all the wedding and he'd let me have everything, even Anna as the best man. So the only thing left to Michael was arranging the honeymoon and I couldn't take that away from him.

Still, I got a pleasant surprise when at Gatwick he said we were on the Florence flight. Florence is one of my most favourite places, and I hadn't been since the summer before my final year at university when I'd worked as a waitress, practising my Italian and spending my days off hiding from the sweltering heat in the galleries and museums. 'Oh Michael,' I gushed and kissed him, which he still wasn't keen on even if we were on honeymoon. He hated PDAs as me and Louise called them.

We arrived late, a taxi whisking us from the airport through the dark streets. I could tell just by the feel of it that we were going to the centre, to the oldest part of the city. Out of the car the night air felt warm, with just a hint of coolness. Through an unassuming wooden door we entered a small courtyard and up stone steps into an old house tastefully refurbished. The concierge was efficient, but understated with clipped English, and almost without taking in my surroundings, I found myself and my luggage in the Penthouse of J K Place. It was perfect, but so completely Michael's choice. Though the house itself was old, the interior design was ultra modern and facing the bed was a large TV, which felt incongruous. However there was the most gorgeous vase of flowers with pink lilies and a bottle of champagne in an ice bucket. Michael had told them we were on honeymoon, but had apparently asked them not to make too much fuss.

'I picked this room for the views,' he said, 'not that you can see much now.'

'It's perfect.' I hugged him. 'Let's go out.' I was too excited to sleep. I wanted to dive right into my old friend and scrape the rust off my unused Italian.

Michael looked like he'd rather lie on the bed and watch the huge telly. 'Come on,' I said, 'just a quick drink somewhere. Things are just getting going here.' I looked at my watch, it was only 11 p.m., most Italians would be barely finishing dinner.

Slightly reluctantly, he agreed. I soon found my bearings and we headed down a narrow street towards the river, walking arm in arm, and entered the first appealing bar we saw. It was busy, but there were still a few free tables. There were red candles in wine bottles making it suitably romantic and just enough of an Italian cliché. Michael caught the bartender's eye and ordered two glasses of Chianti, his lack of language just about stretching to that. I kind of liked it that he was being all masterful.

We sat down and clinked glasses. 'So, we've done it. We're married,' I said.

'Yes, we most certainly are.'

I could tell from his voice that the whole thing had been a bit of an ordeal for him.

'You did enjoy some of it, didn't you?'

'Oh yes, yes of course I did.' He smiled and stroked my hand.

'It's just you know I'm not a fan of crowds of people. You looked lovely though. And now it will be just you and me for a while. I get to have you all to myself.'

'I did look gorgeous, didn't I?!' I laughed, confident and sure of myself. 'The band wasn't great though.'

'Come on Iz, they were awful.'

'Yes, OK, I'll give you that, they were awful, but is it a proper wedding without an awful band? At least no one got too drunk, or forgot their lines, or threw up on the flowers.'

Michael smirked, 'No I suppose not. Interesting weddings you go to!'

That first night in Florence was one of my happiest memories. I'm not sure it was worth all that came later, but I'm glad Michael gave me that. Looking back I can't believe it was the same man. He changed so much.

I woke to a gloriously sunny morning, crisp white sheets, and a handsome man next to me who was now my husband. The man I'd spend the rest of my life with. I pulled back the curtains, and the view was stunning. Florence's red tiled roofs spread out below me. Michael smiled at me from the bed, smug as though he'd done something very clever. 'Breakfast?'

I nodded. Michael jumped up and naked went to the phone on the desk, called down to reception and ordered bread and coffee without bothering to even try any Italian.

He didn't normally walk around naked, but he was on honeymoon, maybe it was the start of a new era. (It wasn't, it lasted about two days.) He come over and put his arms round me from behind. 'I'm glad we're all alone now,' he whispered.

'Yes, but room service will be here soon, so you might want to put some boxers on!'

It was late when we finally emerged into the sunlight. 'Do you want the good news or the bad news?' said Michael.

'There can't be bad news on a honeymoon!' I pouted. 'OK, the bad first, get it over with.'

'We're only here today and tomorrow.'

'And the good?'

'We're going on to a farmhouse near Montepulciano for a week.'

I weighed this up. I did love Florence, and I wanted to show Michael all my favourite bits, but I had seen most of it before, and this was for both of us, and a secluded farmhouse sounded lovely, especially in my favourite wine region.'

In retrospect, I can see it was exactly Michael's idea of what he thought I would like, rather than what *I* would really have liked. A few days sunning myself at Rimini would have been nice, but still it was our honeymoon, not mine alone and he really had tried. It wasn't until years later that it even crossed my mind that it hadn't been perfect and lots of water had passed under the bridge by then, until my memory of every nice thing he'd done became tainted with thoughts of all the cruel acts. Sitting here now, I sometimes wonder if our honeymoon was the last time we really enjoyed doing things together, if it really was the beginning and the end, if after that he never quite enjoyed my company the way he had before.

***

'Hello. Michael, you home?' No answer. Good. I'd had a busy day at work, not stressful, but lots of running around and meetings and I wasn't in the mood to have to self-censor the report of my day, editing out the bits Michael wouldn't approve of. I poured myself a glass of wine and settled on the sofa with a magazine to enjoy some 'me' time, which seemed to have been sorely lacking of late. It wasn't so much that we were always doing stuff together, more that Michael always seemed to be around. He nearly always came home after me, but not by much, and increasingly he wanted his dinner ready as soon as he got in. Well stuff that, he could wait. Also more and more he hovered in the kitchen pouring wine, or criticising the way I did things, not that he'd lift a finger in the kitchen himself.

The door opened and banged and his briefcase dropped on the floor. 'What are you doing?'

I so felt like being facetious – hello to you too, have a nice day at the office – but he was clearly in a bad mood and looking for a fight. Whatever I said would be the wrong thing, and not answering wasn't an option either. 'What does it look like I'm doing?'

'Don't give me any of your lip; I'm not in the mood.'

'Neither am I,' I mumbled.

'What?'

'Nothing.' He was standing in front of me now. I could see his hands working in his pockets, clenching and unclenching as though warming up, or keeping himself in check.

'I need to go out tonight.'

'OK, so go out, no need to make a song and dance about it.'

That's when he grabbed my arm and pulled me up off the sofa. 'I need to eat first,' he said dragging me towards the kitchen.

'So fucking well get a take-away or eat out, it's not like you can't afford it.' I knew I would regret this outburst but I couldn't help myself. I wasn't going to roll over and let him control my life. This time he didn't slap me; he went straight for the stomach. The blow made me drop to my knees, retching with the pain. He still had hold of my arm, and the drop pulled my arm out of its socket sending a sear all the way down to my fingertips. He let go of me then.

'I haven't got time for this,' he shouted and slammed out of the house again.

I rolled over and felt the cool of the floor tiles against my hot cheek, as a tear rolled down and fell off my nose. In the silence I heard it drop onto the tile, like the magical huge raindrop that starts the monsoon. It felt like an eternity before I even sat up. I was numb, and scared. I didn't know where he'd gone, or when he'd be back, and if he came back if he'd carry on where he'd left off. This was not his normal pattern. (Already I was starting to consider his violence normal.) Usually we'd be having a reasonably pleasant time, when something minor would aggravate him and he'd ratchet it up into a full-blown scene that naturally required me being taught a lesson. Then as soon as he was done, he'd be apologising and trying to make up. He'd never left me in limbo like this before.

I rubbed my arm, that pain had been temporary. My stomach still hurt, but I didn't think he'd done any real damage. I pushed myself up, twinges, but overall not bad. I went back to the living room and finished my glass of wine. I don't know how long I sat there before I called Anna, but it grew darker and darker, until I had to feel my way to the light switch to find the phone. I knew I had to call her, that I wanted her there, but I didn't know what I would say. I wasn't ready to tell her about Michael's violence, but I wanted the comfort of her presence.

'Hello. Hellooo?'

'Hi.'

'Isabel, is that you?'

'Yes.'

'Are you OK? What's wrong?'

I didn't know what to say, so I didn't say anything.

'Isabel?'

'Um, oh sorry, miles away. I was wondering if you wanted to come over and watch a video or something. Michael's gone out.'

'I'm kind of in the middle of something Iz.'

'Oh. Oh, OK, well,' I half sighed, half sobbed, 'another time then.'

'No. No it's OK. I can leave this. You know what I'm like once I get into a project. I'll be right over.'

I slumped back on the sofa. I looked at my stomach and prodded the tender part. No bruise yet. I opened another bottle of wine and tried to look at the magazine again, but my hands were shaking. I needed to calm down before Anna arrived. I needed her to think this was just a normal bout of mild loneliness brought on by the absence of a husband who rarely went out. That brought me out in a sweat. Where had he gone? What if he came back with Anna there? He was never genuinely pleased to see her, but he hid that when they met, which wasn't often. I'd long ago decided it was easier for everyone if their paths didn't cross, much as I would have liked them to be best buddies in my ideal world. Or maybe not. I wanted Anna all to myself. We had a history Michael and I could never have, and Michael and I had an intimacy I could never re-create with Anna, despite his outbursts. It was best for everyone to keep things separate.

I went up to the bathroom and splashed water on my face and

tried to calm down. I'd tell Anna we'd had an argument and he'd stormed out, that was all, I wouldn't mention the punch. As well as my general distress, I was vaguely nervous. I wasn't used to lying to Anna. I'd never done it before. She was the one person in the world I thought I never had to lie to, but I wasn't ready to tell her the truth. Telling Anna meant admitting it to myself, which I kind of had, but not in the sense of acknowledging that he wouldn't stop. I still hoped this was something temporary and he would go back to the Michael I'd known before. Instinctively I knew that Anna would take my side completely, would want to protect me like a mother, would not allow for any excuses or explanations of Michael's actions. Despite the ache below my ribs I wasn't ready for that much unconditional support. I knew I wouldn't be able to take the help she would offer.

The doorbell rang. One last look in the mirror and I ran downstairs. Anna stood at the door, cycle helmet in hand, fluorescent clips still round her trousers. I wanted to hug her and I wanted to laugh at the spectacle of her. Whatever bizarre turn my life had taken at least I could count on Anna never changing. I opted for a slight shake of the head.

'What?'

'You know what. The clips. Get in, you're letting cold air in.'

'Can I bring Molly in?' She did her pleading puppy face. 'It looks like rain.'

'Oh all right.' Usually I point blank refused to pander to her obscene bike obsession and wouldn't let Molly the Moulton in the house, but I didn't have the fight left in me.

She was already having a calming effect and I knew things were going to be OK. Anna later told me that she knew from the minute I called her that something terrible had happened and fretted for days over why I hadn't told her the truth.

'Have you eaten?'

'Only snacks.'

'You're hopeless.'

I wasn't hungry, but again in a pretence of normality the thing to do seemed to be to offer, prepare and eat something. I extracted a pizza from the freezer and put the oven on.

'So this is a turn up. Where's his lordship gone?'

'I don't know. He just turned up from work and said he was going straight out again.'

'Not like Michael.'

'No.'

'Well, his loss, my gain, girls' night in, eh?' she said rubbing my arm.

'Yeah.' I put the pizza in the oven. I was starting to struggle for conversation.

'Let's de-camp to the sofa. I've just opened a bottle of wine.'

'Even better.'

In retrospect I can see that Anna was being uncharacteristically amenable and walking on eggshells. She didn't pursue where Michael might have gone, or quip that he was off with some other woman. And while she was always pleased to see me, she usually would have complained about having to leave her work to come and rescue me from some pathetic straight girl complaint. But none of that. She still ate most of the pizza, complained about my video choice, and kept her cycle clips on all evening, but she knew something wasn't right, and she was cautiously tiptoeing around the unsaid.

☙❧

I had my first cigarette with Anna, purely in the interests of science of course. She'd cadged a couple from somewhere, and matches, so at lunch time we snuck down the side of the swimming pool, an area hidden by trees, and according to school rumour the favourite spot for illicit smoking; there was no one there but us. We crouched low to the ground so no smoke would appear above the trees. Anna, of course, knew how to do it. Placing cigarette between lips, cupping hands around the matchbox, she struck the match towards her as I'd been told never to do and brought the flame perfectly to the tip. She inhaled and exhaled expertly like a fifty year veteran, while I coughed and spluttered and blew the smoke straight out, seemingly unable to make it reach my lungs. Anna smoked regularly from then, through uni, med school, and residency before she finally gave up. In sixth form she wore her nicotine stain like a badge of honour. I thought she was so cool.

I had my first kiss with Anna too. It was in the woods. I can't remember how old we were, but old enough to be interested in boys I suppose. Anna had grown out of grubbing around for bugs, or climbing trees, but we still often went to the woods, it was our secret place. Anna liked to smoke there, out of sight, so she wouldn't get in trouble with her parents. We'd spend hours sitting in the low branches of a huge oak tree, chatting, or walking kicking up leaves. Occasionally, we'd fight our way through to where the hidden blackberries were and pick loads to take home to my mum. Anna's mother wasn't into home baking even though she didn't work.

We must have been talking about some boy I fancied. In retrospect, Anna never talked about boys she liked. Maybe she already knew she was into girls or maybe she was just too into science and becoming a doctor to waste her time on teenage fumblings.

I asked her one time if she'd ever been with a man.

'Once at uni,' she said and pulled a face. 'I was drunk, thought I'd give it a go. It wasn't awful, but not worth losing gold star status for.'

'Gold star?'

'Yeah, a lesbian who's never been with a man,' she said, as though everyone should know that.

Anyway, back to the kiss. I don't know how the conversation came round to kissing, I only remember Anna saying, 'I'll show you,' in that supercilious tone she had of oh you idiot, don't you even know how to do that?

Before I could reply, she had leaned in and kissed me quickly on the lips.

'Is that it?'

'No,' she said, suddenly becoming shy. She put her hands gently on either side of my face and kissed me again slowly and tenderly. After two more little kisses, her tongue ran along my lips trying to get in. I pulled away.

'Don't look so shocked. That's what boys do, they try and get their tongue in your mouth.

'Really? Seems a bit gross.'

She laughed and shrugged. 'You wanna try it, or not?'

'OK.'

'OK, so you need to open your mouth.' Her face loomed towards mine again. She deftly parted my lips and let her tongue explore a bit. I responded, before pulling away and wiping my mouth on the back of my hand.

'So that's it?'

'That's it, except a boy will try to stick his tongue down your throat!'

'Yuck.'

We both laughed at that hideous prospect and started a frantic leaf kicking session until we fell down.

I remember the softness and the taste of tobacco. It was pleasant, but left me wondering what all the fuss was about. After I'd kissed Jason the following summer, I forgot about ever kissing a girl again.

I never wondered if Anna had engineered the kiss; now I do, especially after last night. After twenty-seven years of never thinking about kissing a woman, I was kissed by a woman again. It took me by surprise, I have to say, and its softness took me right back to that day in the woods. How I wish I could call Anna and tell her.

It used to gall me a bit that I told Anna all my secrets. All about my crushes and boyfriends and hopes for the future, and she only told me part of hers. She left out all the love stuff, the longing and desires. I can't believe she didn't have any. But she will always be the keeper of my secrets. I don't believe she ever told a soul.

***

Michael succumbed to my pleading for a mini break once. We'd been going through rather a bad patch of misunderstandings and violence. You may say our whole marriage was based on that, but it wasn't, it went in peaks and troughs. We could go for months without him hurting me, being like any other happily married couple, that's partly why I stayed with him for so long. So, I suppose he was trying to make amends. I can't remember now, but that was the usual pattern, at least at first – he'd be horrible and then he'd be incredibly loving and attentive and almost spoil me with anything I wanted and doing things he knew I would like.

'I have a surprise for you.'

'Really? I'm not sure I want any of your surprises.'

'A nice surprise,' he said hugging me from behind.

'That's not much of a surprise, we've done that before!'

He laughed and released me. 'Not that. Though since you mention it...'

I slapped his arm playfully. 'No chance.'

'Oh. Not even if I take you away for a dirty weekend?'

'Where?'

'Let's just say it's somewhere you said you wanted to go.'

'And I suppose you're not going to tell me any more than that.'

'Well it wouldn't be a surprise then, would it?'

'I don't know what makes you think I like surprises. (I didn't. I hated surprises, and the more Michael's outbursts came out of the blue, the more I hated them, even pleasant ones.) But OK, I'll play along.'

'Meet me after work tomorrow at King's Cross with a weekend bag.'

'Oh very cloak and dagger!'

'You'll like it. I promise. I know I haven't been very...I've been a bit...well crap lately.'

The big surprise was Cambridge. We stayed in one of the swankier hotels and spent a good deal of time in the hotel room, but we also did all the typical tourist things like punting along the river. This time Michael didn't attempt to impress me by punting himself, standing up in a boat was way too scary so he paid over the odds for a posh sounding student to chauffer us and give us a history of the colleges. It was a dull day and we huddled under the punt's tartan blanket though it wasn't really cold, and I remember Michael caressing my legs out of sight under the scratchy wool like naughty teenagers on a school trip. I can't remember any of the colleges, except the iconic Kings of course; I just have a sort of cinematic impression of the gloriousness of it all, the splendour and history, and I felt rather smug as we glided effortlessly past the unfortunate tourists trying to punt themselves.

On the Sunday we rented bikes and cycled to Grantchester and had a long afternoon tea under the trees at the Orchard. We read the papers and it was just like old times discussing articles and reading bits out to each other. We walked hand in hand along the Backs and through college gardens, drank riverside cocktails and had candle lit dinners. It was exactly my ideal of a romantic weekend and I fell for the *Four Weddings and A Funeral* style schmaltz and I fell for Michael all over again. A little kindness goes such a long way in the midst of unpleasantness. The terrible times almost made the good times sweeter, more cherished, more appreciated.

We re-ignited the sexual spark on that trip too, not that it had entirely gone out but it had become more of a sparkler than a Roman Candle. Michael had been tentative about sex when we were first together. After that amazing first time on the sofa, we soon dropped into a routine, and while it was pleasurable and satisfying, it could have been a bit more exciting. I'm not saying I'm a nymphomaniac or anything, far from it, but I wouldn't have minded a bit more experimentation, a bit more 'spur of the moment' passion. It soon revolved around the two, or occasionally three, things Michael liked to do, and I didn't get much say about what I liked.

But after he hit me that first time, things changed. He liked to use sex to make up. The bigger the misdemeanour, the bigger the make up, at least until he went really weird and manipulative. It was still always about him, but he cared more about my pleasure in a bizarre kind of way as though great sex would wipe clear the pain he'd caused me earlier.

He'd talk dirty, and take me by surprise, and I have to say it turned me on. I think back to those days a lot now, I have plenty of time to reflect, and some of the good times are starting to re-emerge and the violence to recede, as though my mind is trying to rearrange history into something bearable.

'Come here you little vixen,' he said, grabbing my arm quite brusquely. There was an edge to his voice and my pulse quickened not knowing if he was about to hit me or drag me into the bedroom. He shoved me against the wall, not hard, but with purpose and kissed me. I'd say he took my breath away but that would be too clichéd, but he did, I was gasping at the unexpected passion. I wanted to ask what had come over him, but I didn't get the chance. He ran his hand up my leg and into my knickers. It had the illicit feeling of doing something we shouldn't, like smoking behind the bike sheds. He pushed against me and I could feel him hard against my thigh. I unzipped him, and then it was like something out of *Fatal Attraction*, my knickers on the floor, my skirt hitched up, his trousers round his knees, pounding me against the wall.

'Blimey, what brought that on?' I gasped.

'Sometimes I like to mix things up a bit,' he said, giving me a coy smile as he zipped himself up.

❧

It wasn't long after the night when Michael had punched me in the stomach that I did finally tell Anna about Michael's 'activities'. She rolled her eyes, or am I imagining now with hindsight that she would have rolled them. 'If only I'd converted you to the dark side when I'd had the chance,' she said.

'Eh…oh right yes, your team.' I sat silent. I wasn't in the mood for humour, and perhaps somewhere deep inside me I was wishing I could have been part of Anna's gang. How much easier things would be if I loved a woman. Surely women didn't treat their wives like this? At that point I would have wished for anything to not be with Michael, or for Michael to be someone different. I brushed a tear away.

'Oh come on Izzy. I'm sorry. Come here,' she said taking me in her arms and letting me sob against her. I think it was the one and only time I really cried about it all. Most of the time it took all my strength to stay alive; I didn't have any left over for crying. 'God, what a bastard. I never liked him.'

'No, it seems I'm the only idiot who didn't see his true colours. Even my dimwit of a sister has confessed she doesn't like him much and offered to help me get a divorce!'

'Well, what are you going to do? You are going to leave him, aren't you?'

'I don't know.'

'Oh come on, don't give me any of that, he didn't mean it; he won't do it again, crap. If you do...' She dropped whatever threat about our friendship she was going to make, seeing how fragile I was. 'He will do it again. I hate to say it, but he will.'

There was a pause, while I sniffed loudly and unattractively and Anna got me a tissue. She didn't really do sympathy. I always knew she cared for me, but she kept her feelings very well hidden and was not demonstrative. She liked the smooth cool lines of science, not the messiness of human relationships. Looking back I can see her in my mind struggling with this revelation and how to deal with it. In the end she dealt with it the only way she knew how – practically. She provided her house as a bolthole, and her considerable wine stocks as my painkiller, and she thought and she thought until she came up with an escape route. I think that was the first time she mentioned the body as one of various options. There was no foolproof plan. There were far too many variables and unknowns for Anna's liking. But it was a plan, something to come back to and ponder as a possibility, and it kept me going for years through its mere existence.

'Why don't you come and stay with me for a bit?'

'He'll hate that.'

'So let him hate it. He beats you Izzy,' she said lowering her voice; 'you're not going to stand for it, are you? The Isabel I know wouldn't do that.'

Maybe you don't know me that well, I thought. It turns out she knew me very well, and I knew her hardly at all. 'And what would that be, a trial separation? I don't want to leave him, Anna.'

'So what do you want?'

'I want him to be like he used to be.'

'What, never hurting a fly?'

'Well, I wouldn't go that far, he's always had a bit of a short fuse, but yes, he never used to…you know. We were like an ordinary couple. We had fun. Even you remember good times in the early days, don't you? He was nice. He used to be kind and considerate.'

Anna sort of snorted.

'He was. He used to buy me things and take me out.'

'And that's the basis for a long term relationship, is it?'

'You can talk, you've never even had a short term relationship. Even whatsherface was only a few months.'

'Siobhan,' she said pointedly, 'was very nearly a year. But that's beside the point. You know me, I don't need people, I love my work and that's enough.'

'Don't you miss snuggling up to someone in bed, doing stuff together, sex?'

'Doing stuff together is highly overrated, and I can get sex if I want it.'

I was tempted to ask where, but I didn't think I would like the answer. I couldn't picture Anna taking enough time off work to go to a club and pick someone up.

'Nobody except you gets me. And some of the lab boys, but they're freaks. Relationships are too much hard work. I did warn you.'

'When? When did you warn me?'

'Hundreds of times, my whole life has been a litany of don't get involved, don't do long term.'

'Yes, for you! When did you tell *me* not to get involved?'

She shrugged and took a slug of wine.

'I must have done. I never hid the fact that I don't like him.'

'No, but you've never liked any of my boyfriends. You were the best man at our fucking wedding, I don't remember you saying I can't do that, I don't think you should marry him. You never said you hated him, it was just your usual dislike of any man I went out with.'

'OK, maybe I didn't. But would you have listened if I had?'

'Dunno,' I pouted. I knew I wouldn't have. I'd been so desperate to have my picture perfect wedding before I was too old, I didn't really think about the consequences. I loved him, we were happy, what could possibly go wrong? 'Maybe it's a phase he's going through. He never used to be like this. It's not happened often and he's so nice in between.'

'Is he?' she said sarcastically.

'Yes, actually.' She was starting to annoy me now. Everyone it seems had hated Michael from the start and knew he wasn't any good, but none of them had said anything. 'Since when do you know so much about men?'

'You're right. I know nothing about men and even less about women. I love corpses,' she said, 'they don't answer back.'

I laughed. The tension was broken, and at least someone else in the world knew what Michael had done. I couldn't bear to tell anyone else. I could only tell Anna, the keeper of all my secrets.

'So what are you going to do?'

'Drink more wine,' I said. I couldn't take any more deep conversation. I hadn't gone to her for a way to leave Michael, not then, I'd only wanted to share my burden.

'To more wine,' she said, clinking glasses. 'But seriously, Iz, I'm here for you, whatever you need, whenever you need it.'

<hr />

It was that night I cut my finger when something in me snapped. It had been weeks since Michael had hit me in the stomach, but I was still nervous and edgy, never knowing when he might lash out, trying to keep the peace and not upset him. He made snide remarks often, or denigrated the way I did things. 'Oh you're not wearing that skirt, are you? It makes your bum look huge.' Or, 'bloody hell Iz, can't you even chop a pepper? Look at the size of those chunks!' He hadn't actually been violent since then, but I was getting more and more wary of him. Often my phone rang at work but when I picked it up no one was there. I became convinced this was Michael checking to see if I was at my desk. At least once a week, he 'surprised me' at work on the pretext of taking me out to lunch and made a big display of greeting me in reception with a hug or a kiss and whisking me off. He had Lisa, our receptionist, wrapped round his little finger and she thought he was the greatest thing since sliced bread. How romantic that he should take me out to lunch so often, she would say. This made it difficult for me to have lunch with Anna or Louise because I was scared of what would happen if he came to pick me up and I was already out with someone else, but Anna didn't put up with that kind of rubbish. And then of course the inevitable happened.

'Where were you today?'

'At work.'

'I came by to see you.'

'Oh, at lunch time? I had lunch with Louise.'

'What did she want?'

'Bizarrely she wanted clothes' advice. Seems she has to go to some art show on Friday and she wanted something conservative. She's trying to impress a new boyfriend who is friends with the gallery owner.'

'Oh right.'

'Yeah we just had a quick sandwich and then looked round some shops.'

'I hope you didn't buy anything.'

'No, I didn't as it happens, but Louise got a lovely dress. Quite sophisticated, not like her at all. She'll probably take it back after she's been to this do in it!' I laughed, trying to make light of it all. I couldn't tell what Michael was thinking, but he didn't look happy.

'I don't really care about Louise's dress.'

'No, no of course not. So how was your day? Busy?'

'I'd rather,' he said, leaning close to me to emphasise his point, 'that you didn't go out at lunch time.'

'Well when do you propose I see my only sister? You don't like me going out at the weekend.'

'Don't answer back,' he shouted, hitting the wall next to my head and making me jump.

'Jesus, Michael, get a grip. Why don't you just call me if you're planning to take me to lunch and then I can arrange to be there?' He didn't say anything. 'Look, I love that you just turn up to take me out, it's romantic, but sometimes I have other things on.' My heart was still pounding. I needed to calm him down. 'You know sometimes I have to see Louise, or go out to get tampons or something.' He hated it when I talked about women's things so I hoped that might shut him up. 'If I keep the weekends for you, so we can spend time together, I have to fit everything else in during the week, don't I?'

'Yes,' he finally said. 'Yes, I'm sorry. You're so good to me. I really don't deserve you. It's great that we have the weekends just for us. You're right.'

Except you never give up squash with Rob to be with me, I thought, but I didn't mention that in case he did give it up in a fit of remorse and that would be another two hours I no longer had to myself. Time alone, or at least time away from Michael, was becoming very valuable as I started to wonder if the intimacy of our first months wasn't becoming rather claustrophobic.

But I've jumped ahead of myself again. I need to go back a bit, do a proper lead in to the 'knife' story. Soon after we were married Michael insisted that we both put our salaries into a joint account to pay for all the house bills. I thought this was a great idea and saved me worrying about anything. It was only once he started complaining whenever I spent money on clothes or things for myself that I wondered whether I should have an account of my own. I mentioned it one time, and he just laughed at the suggestion. 'What do you need your own account for? Just take whatever you need from the joint account, there's plenty in there.' There was no point trying to explain that made me feel dependent on him even though all my salary was in there too, or that I couldn't just take money out of the joint account because he always questioned it, but I couldn't start putting less money in because he would know. He always knew what the balance was. He studied the bank statements closely and kept his own spreadsheets of our finances. Fortunately I also got performance related bonuses at work which were paid separately to my salary so I decided to open my own account and put those in it. It wasn't much, but at least I had a bit of money in my own name to buy things I didn't want Michael to know about. But I was worried somehow he'd find out about it. I couldn't keep anything from him, at least not when it came to spending money. If I bought a more expensive brand of cereal

'It was after you pounded me senseless on it,' I said, hitting him with a cushion.

We play wrestled for a bit, then he lifted me up and carried me upstairs.

I only ended up in hospital once as a result of Michael's beatings, which is miraculous given how many I endured, but I think he wanted to instil fear rather than inflict serious injury. He loved the power, the proof that he was the man, he was the one in control, he owned me and he wanted me to know it. It was about three years into the marriage. By then the beatings had become commonplace rather than one-off events, and while I often censored my words and actions to try and minimize his anger I hadn't totally sunk into thinking that I could prevent his outbursts by changing what I did. So on this occasion, just for a change of pace, I was fighting back. He didn't like that. He wanted submission, and he wanted it quickly, followed by my forgiveness. I learnt my lesson well. I didn't fight back any more after this. It became guerrilla warfare, a war of attrition with me taking my tiny victories silently without Michael knowing about them, and giving him the impression he was very much the victor.

'I'm not going to take it Michael. You promised.' I was on the edge of tears, my voice high and shaky with anger and fear, but I wasn't going to give him the satisfaction of crying. I shoved him.

'Don't hit me. Who the hell do you think you are?'

'Your wife Michael, the one you promised to honour and respect, and not beat the crap out of.'

'Well, I didn't know you were going to turn into such a bitch when I said that.'

'Me, me?' I said incredulously. 'You're the one who's changed. You used to be so considerate and caring. What happened?' I softened my voice, trying to reason with him, even though I knew it was pointless.

'You're unbearable. You nag all the time. Do this, do that, go and see your parents, take me here, take me there. Not to mention all the time you spend with Anna.' He spat out her name like it was a swear word.

I couldn't believe what he was saying. He was the one who told me what to do and when to do it. How could things get so twisted in his head? 'Where the hell do you get that from? Nag you? That's a joke. Who cooks for you? Cleans the house? Picks up your crap, while you do whatever you want.'

'You thankless bitch.' He pushed me, hard. I fell against the bedroom door and half out onto the landing. And then, I still can't believe he did this. After all these years, it still makes my heart pound. He kicked me and for a long suspended second I saw what was going to happen. I tumbled awkwardly without being able to stop myself, and came to a huddled halt in the corner, just before the last few stairs into the living room.

I wasn't unconscious. In fact for a moment I thought maybe I wasn't hurt, just bruised. But it was like a switch went off in Michael. It was pure Jekyll and Hyde. He suddenly snapped out of his anger.

'Oh no, oh shit Iz, are you all right?' He said as he ran down the stairs and kneeled next to me. 'Careful, don't move.'

I didn't want him touching me. Every time he hit me he repulsed me, and it was taking me longer and longer to bounce back. Right then, I didn't think I was going to bounce back. I thought that was it, I was going to leave him after that, no doubt. I leaned up on one hand. 'Ow.'

'Where does it hurt?'

'My ribs. Ah, I don't know, all over.' I was having trouble breathing.

'I'd better call an ambulance.'

'Wait.'

'But you need to go to hospital. Oh God, what have I done? Oh I'm sorry.'

Sitting up, 'Don't say you're sorry,' I spat, 'you don't mean it.' He looked scared then. Just for a second. I stood up, very carefully. My legs seemed to work. 'I don't need an ambulance, I can walk. You can drive me to the hospital.'

'OK, OK, whatever you want,' he said all appeasing.

We drove in silence, but as we got near to the hospital, he said, 'you won't tell them what really happened, will you?'

'What, that I fell down the stairs?' I looked at him, with what I hoped was as much venom as I was able to project. 'No, I won't tell them, Michael. I should, but I won't. But this is it. It's over. Don't think you can kiss and make up after this.'

He sat in silence.

He pulled up at the entrance to Casualty, parked illegally, and helped me into reception, playing the attentive husband to the hilt. 'My wife's had an accident, she needs to see someone right away.'

Much of what followed is a blur. At some point Michael left to move the car and I was taken to a cubicle. I remember being relieved when Michael was gone, and not wanting him to come back. I was in terrible pain, but my mind was still working, calculating the best thing to say, and trying to work out a way to not have to go home with him. I never wanted to see him again, but at the same time I didn't want to create a scene and I didn't want to tell anyone that he'd pushed me. I knew Michael would make me live to regret that, if I lived at all. Then in a flash it dawned on me that we were at the hospital where Anna worked.

'Is Dr Green on duty?' I whispered.

'Dr Green?'

'Anna Green, pathology.'

'I don't know, but...'

'She's a friend. Could you check?'

'OK,' the nurse replied, reluctantly. 'Wait here for the doctor.'

I wondered where else she expected me to go, though technically I had walked in, so I suppose I could walk out, but I wouldn't have got far.

I think perhaps I closed my eyes for a while, because then Anna was at my side, and there seemed to be a sudden increase in activity. 'They're taking you to X-ray,' Anna said matter-of-factly and in what I knew to be her 'doctor' voice. I remember thinking I'd never seen her in her white coat before. 'I can come with you, but we can't talk much.'

Later I realised that she was warning me not to talk to her as a friend who knew everything. She thought I was going to say that Michael had hurt me, that I was going to report him, and she wanted me taken care of before I told my story. I just lay back and let them wheel me away. I tried to picture myself in ER with George Clooney, anything to take my mind off reality. Dr Ross's proposal to Nurse Hathaway was the talk of the girls at work and a pleasant distraction from Michael.

I didn't know or care where Michael was. I'd lost all sense of time and assumed he was still parking the car somewhere. The rolling of the bed made me feel nauseous. Someone had clearly deemed I was not to move more than necessary. I hated the smell of hospitals, that mix of antiseptic and illness. I didn't want to be there. I just wanted to go and lie under a very soft duvet for a very long time. We clattered through some double doors. All the noises felt blaring and seemed to be right inside my brain. I realised my head hurt and I wanted to go to sleep. I closed my eyes. Anna tapped my hand. 'Stay with me, we're nearly there.'

We went through more doors and into a blissfully dark room. 'OK Iz, they're going to take some X-rays. I'll be right outside.'

Anna left and another nurse entered. 'Hi, Mrs Atkins. I'm just going to take a couple of X-rays. Now, are you pregnant?'

'No.'

'Are you sure? Is there any way you could be pregnant?'

'No.'

'Sorry, you're not sure?'

God, it hurt just to breath without having to explain everything three times.

'There's no way I could be pregnant.'

Afterwards was the long wheel back to where I'd come from. I just wanted to sleep but there didn't seem to be any chance of that. Back in the curtained cubicle, Anna and I were briefly alone.

'He did this, didn't he?'

I was silent. I wanted to tell her and I didn't want to tell her, and I knew whatever I said wouldn't make any difference.

'Jesus, Isabel.'

'Don't. Don't make a fuss. I just want to go home.'

'Home? You're not going home with him. You're coming with

me.'

'Where is he anyway?'

'Out in the waiting area, I expect. I told reception not to let him back here. That's usual anyway until the doctor has seen you.'

'You've seen me.'

'I mean the proper doctor.'

'Well, when's he coming, this proper doctor? I want to go to bed.'

'I did try to chivvy them a long a bit. So what happened?'

'I fell down the stairs.'

'I mean what really happened?'

'I fell down the stairs after…'

'Mrs Atkins, isn't it?' The curtain pulled back and the 'proper' doctor entered.

Let's just say he wasn't George Clooney. 'Green, what'u doing down here?'

'Friend of the patient, Bill. Could you get on with it?'

'Right. So what happened?'

'I fell downstairs.'

'And did you lose consciousness?'

'No.'

And so the questions went on, while he prodded and poked me. I wished Anna was examining me, but I felt comforted by her presence and her watchful eye.

The eventual diagnosis was two broken ribs and a sprained wrist, which was duly bandaged. Nothing much they could do about the broken ribs and I was released, her colleague trusting that Anna would see me reunited with my husband and safely home.

'We'd better tell him what's happening, hadn't we?' I asked.

'I don't see why.'

'Because,' I said, as though explaining to a child, 'if we don't tell him that I'm going with you all hell will break loose. We can't just leave him waiting in the hospital, asking the receptionist what's going on every five minutes.'

She nodded and guided me back out to the waiting room where Michael sat anxiously picking at his fingers.

'Oh thank goodness. They wouldn't tell me anything. They wouldn't let me see you,' he started rambling.

I cut him off. 'I'm going home with Anna.'

'What?'

'She can look after me.'

His face turned thunderous. 'And I can't?'

I gave him a look. The look that said you got me here, I don't want any more of your care. And he seemed to shrivel up. He knew he was defeated, if only temporarily. Briefly I had control. I had the power to tell the police what he'd done, and destroy his illusion of perfect married life. And I had the power to walk away and never come back, at least I thought I did. If he wanted any hope of getting me back, he had to let me go and he knew it. Shame that feeling didn't last long.

I woke up hot and in pain in Anna's bed with Jasmine glaring at me. I briefly wondered why I was there and then I remembered. I tried to lift myself up, but that really hurt. I flopped back down and turned towards the curtains. It was light outside, but I couldn't tell from the gloom whether it was early morning or cloudy. Jasmine padded up and sat next to my head, purring. 'Get lost cat.'

Anna came through the door then, dressed in jeans and a jumper. 'How're you feeling?' She came over and picked up Jasmine, who wailed pathetically. Anna stroked her ears and put her out into the living room.

'Everything hurts.'

'I'm not surprised. You can take more painkillers, but you should take them with food.'

'OK doctor!' She smiled. 'I'm not hungry though. Maybe after a cup of tea?'

'Hmm, I see. You expect me to be waiting on you hand and foot, do you?'

'Of course! Shouldn't you be at work? What time is it?'

'Ten o'clock. I'm on call, so we get to play doctors and nurses at home.'

'Tea.' I said, pointedly, but I was glad of her banter. I lay back and listened to her clattering around in the kitchen. 'So, doctor, when are my ribs gonna stop hurting?'

'About three to four weeks 'til they heal properly, but the pain should reduce over that time.'

'Great.'

'Here, eat some toast and then you can have your pills.'

I chewed and chewed the toast, but had a hard time swallowing it. I didn't get ill very often and I was pretty self reliant when I did, so I didn't think I was going to like Anna taking care of me, though the thought of just lying there and not doing anything, of not having to think about the next meal, or whether the house was tidy, or what mood Michael would be in, was very appealing.

'I'm going to have to get up. I'll go nuts lying here.'

'OK, but take it easy.'

'Where did you sleep, by the way?'

'On the sofa.'

Anna took away the half-eaten toast and I tried to get up. As I sat on the edge of the bed I thought about Michael. I wondered what he was doing now. He would have gone to work. I knew he would want everything to seem as normal as possible. He had to keep up appearances. It wouldn't be until tonight that he missed me, or missed his dinner on the table, I thought cynically. I wondered when he would call, when he would start coming round and trying to persuade me to go back, because he would, I was sure of that.

I would stand firm I decided. With Anna's help I could do it. I could leave him, get divorced. This was it. He was never going to hit me again. I was proud of my resolve, yet I was still sitting there in my T-shirt and knickers, unable to move. Anna came back.

'Do you want some sweats?'

'Is this what I'm reduced to? Borrowing your scanky jogging bottoms?'

'Do you want to be comfortable or not?'

I nodded, and she handed me the bottoms. 'You can stop smirking,' I said, 'it's just temporary.'

I pushed myself up and looked in the wardrobe mirror. 'Oh God,' I groaned.

Anna started to laugh. 'It's not funny! And stop making me laugh, it hurts.' I dropped back onto the bed.

'It's medicinal. It will make your ribs heal quicker.'

'Liar.'
'Well-known medical fact.'

I really should have gone to the police about Michael. I had toyed with the idea of calling them many times when Michael really physically hurt me, but I never did, and then before I knew it I'd let things go on way too long. I should have been documenting every beating, getting photos of my injuries, reporting every incident, but I hadn't. At first I was too shocked, and then I thought it would just make things worse. I was always dubious that it would do any good. I knew what Michael was like, how obsequious he was, how well he came across to people who didn't know him. The police would be bound to believe him. And he was such a master of his craft – yes, there were bruises, but never any broken bones (except that once), rarely any cuts or broken skin, never any wounds to the face. I was sure that he would be able to explain away the bruises and sprains – I'd fallen, or knocked into a piece of furniture, 'she bruises very easily officer, I'm sorry she's wasted your time.' I could see it dragging on for months, or years. Me having to slowly prove my case while all the time his brutality would get worse because I'd questioned his authority, and showed him up in public by making a scene, all of which he couldn't stand.

One day though the choice was taken from my hands. I don't remember when it was – I would have made a terrible witness to any case because soon all the bad times kind of merged in to one conglomerate of 'bad Michael' and the good memories seemed to blur into one ephemeral image of 'he used to be so nice', but where was I? Oh yes, I guess it can't have been too long into the marriage because we were making a lot of noise, and as things went on I stopped fighting back and just took it because that seemed to make the violence shorter and less intense if nothing else. Preventing serious injury became more important than pointing out how ridiculous Michael was being with his latest accusation.

I was sitting on the sofa nursing my bruises. Michael was sweeping up the vase and flowers he'd smashed in the kitchen and I was no doubt preparing myself mentally for the next stage – the apologies and the making up – hoping this would start with a mug of tea or a large glass of wine, when the doorbell rang. I turned and looked at Michael, who glared at me as though I'd engineered the ringing bell. I shrugged. He dumped the flowers and broken glass in the bin and put the broom away before he went to the door.

'Oh. Good evening officer,' I heard him say.

'May we come in for a minute sir?'

'Er, yes of course. Is there a problem?'

A male and female officer came into the living room and I tried to sit up straighter. 'Evening madam. Everything all right?'

'Yes, erm, yes.'

Michael came and sat next to me, very close on the sofa.

'Your neighbour called sir. Said there was a lot of banging and shouting coming from here and she was rather worried.'

'Really?'

'Yes sir.'

'Well I'm surprised. The people on the other side have young children and you hardly hear them. And we weren't making much noise, were we Isabel?'

'No, not much.'

'But there was some noise, was there?' The officer continued.

'Well, a bit I suppose,' said Michael. 'See I'd bought my wife some flowers and she'd just arranged them, and then I managed to knock them off the kitchen counter, I'm so clumsy sometimes. The vase smashed into a million pieces. You can see we've got stone tiles in the kitchen, so…and my wife understandably had a bit of a shout, but like I say I'm surprised the neighbours could hear that. I really think you've been called out on a wild goose chase.'

The officer looked at me then and said, 'is that true madam? Are you sure you're all right?'

Well what could I say with Michael sitting right there? He'd already explained what had happened, there was no way I could contradict him. I could hear his voice in my head saying, 'you dare say anything else, just try it, you'll pay,' and my arms ached where he'd grabbed me, and there was no sign of a struggle and we both looked calm. Don't tell me you would have said different, because you wouldn't.

'Yes. I'm fine. Michael's right. He broke the vase. He's such a klutz sometimes. You wouldn't know it to look at him.'

'OK,' said the officer, standing up, 'well try and keep the noise down in future, these are terraced houses you know.'

Michael certainly kept the noise down after that. Even when he kicked me down the stairs he did it quietly.

❧❦

That first day at Anna's was fun in a way, apart from the pain. I felt freer than I had in months, in years. At the back of my mind I knew Michael would call or come round at some point, I knew I would have to see him again, but for a few hours I didn't want to worry about it. In my naivety, which I probably should have lost by then, but hadn't, I thought Michael would be reasonable, that he wouldn't object to me staying a few days with Anna, that he would recognise I needed some time apart and that Anna, as a doctor, was well qualified to care for me. I had left my mobile switched off and I wasn't tempted to check it. I'd called work and told them about my accident, explaining that I would need at least a week off work and I'd send them a doctor's note. I tried consciously to not think about Michael, but every spare moment brought the previous night's events to mind. I needed action, something to occupy me to give my mind a break from thinking about it, but my body wasn't up to much action.

'We're going to have to go to my house to get some stuff,' I said, 'I can't stay in your sweat pants for ever.'

'You could stay in them for today though, it won't kill you.'

I wasn't sure about that, catching myself in the mirror with my unwashed hair and homeless person's outfit was more than I could bear on top of everything else. 'Maybe, but Michael will be at work today, he won't be tomorrow. I don't want to see him.'

'He'll be at squash tomorrow, won't he? He never misses that.'

'True. But you haven't even got any good books to read or

magazines and…'

'If I go and buy you some entertainment, will you shut up?' That felt a little harsh. Anna certainly practised the tough love approach. I think my eyes must have welled, as she softened a little. 'Sorry, I'm in doctor mode, not friend mode, but you really ought to have at least one day of not doing anything.'

'Can I have a bath?'

'Yes, but I'd rather stay in the house in case you can't manage. I'll pop out later and pick up some things, OK?'

'OK.'

I lay in the bath and cried silently. Anna, the shower queen, didn't have any bubble bath, and I was using some kind of sporty active wash to soap myself. My whole left side was a deep purple and after Anna had run the bath and left a towel close by, I ushered her out. I was determined to manage. I didn't want her seeing me so damaged. The door was only pulled to, but I felt comfortable that Anna wouldn't enter unless I called her. It felt so different from my own home, where I sometimes had the feeling that Michael was standing right behind the door.

The door moved slowly then and Jasmine pounced up softly onto the side of the bath, making me jump. I am not a cat person and must confess I was surprised when Anna got her. There was some long involved story of a friend who couldn't keep her any more and who begged Anna to take her. Plus it's a lesbian thing apparently. Anna claims she's very low maintenance and all she has to do is open a can of food once a day, but I still didn't see why she put up with her. I didn't have the strength to shoo her away, so I let her sit there and I have to say the soft purring next to my head was quite soothing.

'Iz? Are you all right in there or have you drowned?'

I jumped again. I must have dozed off. The water was tepid and the purring had stopped. 'I've drowned,' I replied. 'I'm getting out now.'

'Need help?'

'No thank you, you lesbian pervert, I'm not that kind of woman!'

I heard Anna laughing from the living room.

'Feeling a bit better then?' she asked as I emerged. 'Want to look at the paper?'

Anna was a newshound as well as a medical journal junkie. She put the kettle on.

'Can I have tea please? I'm too weak to take your coffee.' Anna liked her coffee strong, very strong, the dregs in her mugs looked like petroleum sludge.

'Anything for my little invalid,' she said, kissing the top of my head. I briefly wondered if Anna in caring mode wasn't going to be almost as bad as living with Michael.

We were watching a video when the phone rang. 'Aren't you going to answer that?'

'No, I'm watching a film.'

'It's a video, you can pause it. What if it's work?'

'They'd page me.' She said between popcorn mouthfuls. 'Anyway the answer phone will kick on in a minute.'

It did and the caller hung up.

'See probably someone wanting to sell me double glazing.'

'Well you're going to have to rewind it anyway, 'cos I've missed a bit now.'

'But you've seen this film loads of times.' We were watching *The Usual Suspects* again, it was our fallback movie if we couldn't agree. It had no lesbians, it wasn't a cheesy straight girl rom-com, it was a good solid film and I fell for it every time even though I knew what was coming.

'You know I never remember how it all works out.'

'The…'

'Don't tell me, just rewind it and stop hogging the popcorn.'

'Argh, only because your ribs are broken, that's the only reason I…'

The phone rang again. 'This is Michael. I know you probably don't want to talk to me.'

'Damn right,' Anna interjected.

'But I just called to see how you are. I'm really sorry Isabel. I'll call again tomorrow.'

We look at each other. 'Play the film,' I said, 'I don't want to think about it right now.'

The next day was Saturday and we took a taxi to my house to pick up some of my stuff. Anna had offered to go by herself, but I knew she wouldn't be able to find the things I wanted even with instructions and she might leave the place in a mess. I planned to extract my things so carefully Michael wouldn't even know I'd been there, though I was pretty sure he would know. Michael being Michael, he would probably check my wardrobe every night to see if I'd been and taken anything and then gauge how much of a chance he had to win me back by the number of clothes I'd taken. Also, part of me thought I needed to go back and see my house before I left it completely and never went back. That's what I was thinking then – that I'd never go back.

I sat in the car while Anna went and let herself in. If Michael hadn't gone out, I didn't want to see him. She came back out and waved from the doorstep. The house felt cool and empty, not like people had gone out, but like no one lived there. It smelt vaguely of toilet cleaner, whereas I would have expected it to smell of coffee or something. Part of me wanted to walk through each room and see every detail, but the other part wanted to get out as quickly as possible and I headed for the bedroom with Anna close behind.

The bedroom was neat and tidy apart from the unmade bed. Michael was a neat freak and the fact that his wife wasn't there wouldn't cause him to leave the place untidy.

'There's a holdall in the top of the wardrobe, can you get it for me please?'

I started opening drawers and piling underwear and T-shirts on the bed. Anna started shoving them in the bag. I wanted to ask her to pack a bit more neatly, but it wasn't like I was going on holiday or something, I could unpack them again soon enough. I extracted some jeans, trousers and jumpers from the wardrobe and a pair of trainers, then I went to the bathroom for toiletries. On the way out I stopped in the living room to get some books.

'What time does he usually get back?' asked Anna.

I looked at my watch – it was 11 a.m. 'Not for ages yet.' But fear rose in the pit of my stomach. What if he hadn't gone to squash, but had only popped out for something? What if he decided to skip drinks with Rob and come home early? I grabbed a couple of paperbacks I hadn't read yet and we went out to the waiting taxi.

On the way back we picked up croissants and papers and spent the rest of the morning reading them. I didn't want to talk about what had happened or what I was going to do and Anna didn't press it. We digested the news and grazed from snacks to meals to snacks. I swear all that woman does is eat, read and work!

By lunch time I was exhausted and after we'd eaten I went for a nap. Lying in Anna's bed, I tried to think pleasant thoughts. I tried to think about what my new life would be like – getting a divorce, finding my own place, but as soon as I started to think of the practicalities I broke out in a sweat. I imagined Michael fighting me over the house, somehow swinging it so that he got to keep it and I was left with nothing, even though it was a joint mortgage. Never mind I thought, my family would help me; they would lend me money, or let me stay with them. Oh God, the thought of spending even a week back at my parents, or staying with my little sister filled me with dread. I could picture Louise's told you so attitude even if she never said the words. Although an accomplished woman in her own way, I got the feeling she thought she'd never quite match up to her big sister and liked to get playful digs in whenever possible about my age, the odd grey hair, my appalling taste in men, my lack of knowledge of the current music scene.

Well, I could stay with Anna for a while, but even that thought didn't fill me with joy. For now Anna was trying her best to be caring, but soon she would revert to her normal character. She would do anything for me, I knew that, but taking care of people was not really her bag, ironic for a doctor, huh. She didn't like people that much and I knew that while she might not say it she would soon be wanting her flat back to herself and would be forcefully encouraging me to leave my dirtbag husband and get a new, independent life. She'd wanted me to leave him when I'd first told her about the beatings, now he'd pushed me down the stairs and broken bones, no telling what she might do.

I willed myself to think of the good times with Michael, and there *had* been good times. But my mind would not be controlled. It kept flitting back to that kick, and the tumble down the stairs. To the arguments and punches; the lack of respect and constant maligning of my friends and interests; the monitoring of my movements and control of my finances. It couldn't go on. I had to leave him.

It was late afternoon when Michael called again. We didn't answer the phone. Anna's fancy answer phone that allowed you to screen calls was a Godsend. He sounded either drunk, or pissed off. No doubt he'd had a few pints with Rob and laid the world to rights, and probably complained to Rob about his useless wife and received Rob's bachelor commiserations. He was still apologetic, still almost grovelling and swearing he'd never hurt me again, but the tone wasn't quite right, and I had no inclination to believe him or to speak to him.

A while later Anna asked if I'd be all right if she went out for a bit.

'I'd rather you didn't. What if he calls again?'

'Just ignore it like before.'

'What if he comes round?'

'Don't answer the door.'

I looked glum, and while I felt pathetic I knew that the weekend would be over soon enough and Anna would be back at work. I'd be alone and would have to deal with the Michael situation by myself, although at the time I thought that would be mainly in my head, not having to physically deal with him.

'OK, I'll stay, but I'm going to have to go and pick up some work tomorrow, and goodness knows what we'll eat,' she said, going into the kitchen and holding the fridge door open as though that would magically make food appear. She closed it and opened a cupboard.

'Could just about rustle up spaghetti carbonara, I suppose.'

'Thank you Anna. You're a star.'

'Hmm. You'd better not stay here too long or you'll exhaust my limited culinary repertoire.'

We were just embarking on Anna's spaghetti extravaganza when the doorbell rang. We looked at each other. 'Expecting anyone?' I said.

She shook her head.

Then there was knocking. 'Isabel open up. It's me. You've got to talk to me sometime you know.'

Do I? I thought. Why? I moved to stand up. I was angry with him, angry at his presumption that I'd talk to him, that I'd eventually forgive him. I was going to give him a piece of my mind. Anna put a hand on my arm and shook her head.

'What?' I whispered, 'I'm going to tell him to fuck right off.'

'I think it's better to just leave it.'

There was silence from outside.

'Fine, have it your own way. But I'll be back. I've left you something.'

We waited a good ten minutes before Anna went to the door and tentatively opened it. She struggled in with a huge bouquet of flowers and a folded over piece of paper. She gave me the paper first.

It looked like it had been torn out of a diary – Michael clearly hadn't come expecting to have to write a note. I opened it: 'Isabel, I know I did a terrible thing, and I'm so, so sorry. I know you won't believe me, but it will NEVER happen again. Please let me see you. We have to talk. Michael.'

I handed it to Anna.

The flowers were gorgeous. 'Nice flowers.'

'Please tell me you're not going to fall for that.'

'No.' I looked around for a card. There didn't seem to be one. Typical Michael, he never knew what to say. Then I found it stuck between the pot and the paper. 'From all at NFU. Hope you feel better soon.'

'Ha. He didn't even buy me the flowers, they're from work!'

'Arsehole.'

We laughed. But I'd gone right off my cooling spaghetti. I needn't have worried, Anna ate hers and most of mine. I made do with wine.

I should have known the flowers weren't from Michael. He never was much for buying flowers even when we were first going out. He did it occasionally, especially if he was feeling bad about the way he treated me, and I think he did feel bad about it, but he wouldn't buy them 'just because' or as a gift for some minor celebration. If he wanted to impress, or was seeking forgiveness he took me out for a meal or bought me a book. At least half of my library must have been gifts from Michael. I thought it was great at the time. A book was so much more practical and long lasting than flowers, but the romantic in me craved a man who picked up a bunch on the way home just because they looked fabulous, or who preferred the occasional diamond to a first edition. I loved reading, but I wasn't into having books as possessions. Once I'd read them that was it. I didn't read them twice. Just as well since I didn't get to bring any with me. Now I read what I can, when I can, I haven't got more than three books that I own. I think Michael put me off books – not reading, he could never do that, but hanging onto books as memories and keepsakes.

We had an overlapping interest in certain writers that was one of the things I most liked about him in the beginning. We were always exchanging books, eager to hear the other's opinion of it. Of course he didn't like Bridget Jones, which I loved. 'Utter pap' he called it and hated my constant pleading for 'mini breaks'. He thought it was just like a girl to be hung up on romance. Why couldn't I be satisfied with a good man. 'I would if I could find one,' I retorted. I couldn't understand his obsession with the books of James Ellroy. He devoured each new one, sitting up late to read huge chunks at a time. The L A Quartet was OK, but I found them too dense and didn't like his short snappy style. Michael said I just wasn't clever enough to get them – that was Michael all over. But I'm waffling again.

Later in bed I decided I'd check my mobile while I was still angry. There were twenty texts and missed calls, all from Michael except one from Katherine at work, all saying the same thing – how sorry he was. I supposed he was sorry, but was that good enough? He'd hit me so many times before and every time he claimed he was sorry and it wouldn't happen again, and it always did. Why would this time be any different? Except, this time he had hurt me more.

I'd had to go to hospital. There would be a record of my injuries and even if I never said he'd caused them, how did he know I wouldn't tell someone or make a police report? I realised that for once the ball was in my court. I had the power and he was the one who was scared. I could tell someone what he'd done and blow his life apart. I could refuse to go back to him. He wouldn't be able to keep pretending he had the perfect life and marriage if his wife divorced him. He wouldn't be able to keep that quiet indefinitely. I smiled, even as my ribs ached, it was a beautiful feeling thinking he might be suffering in some way. Maybe I could go back to him? Surely I could play on this event for a long time. Maybe this would be the thing that made him change? Maybe this was one step too far even for Michael. I took pleasure in deleting all his texts and messages and switching my phone off without replying to a single one. I would make him pay for what he'd done. I dropped off to sleep in a happier frame of mind, especially as the painkillers had kicked in.

I did try calling the police once. It was a disaster. It was the usual kind of thing, but I remember feeling more scared that time for some reason. Something made me think Michael wasn't going to stop after one punch and that's what made me snatch up the phone and dial. Thinking about it now I don't even know how I got away with actually making the call and them arriving, but somehow I did. God, I wish I hadn't.

It started innocently enough, or so I thought, but Michael could make a scene out of the answer to any question if he wanted to. I never knew if he was going to say, 'oh that's nice' or 'what the hell are you doing that for?' I was wrapping up Anna's birthday present. I'd come across a book on the history of Moulton bikes that was just perfect for her. I'd gone to look for Sellotape and when I came back Michael was standing holding the book.

'What's this then?'

'Anna's birthday present.'

'Bet that cost a lot, a speciality book like that.'

'Not really, I got it in a charity shop,' I lied. 'I thought it was just right for her.' I always had to say too much, didn't I?

'Oh yes, I'm sure you went to lots of effort to get the *perfect* gift for Anna,' he said, dropping the book on the sofa. I felt fear rise in my stomach. I just knew he was going to go off on one. I didn't say anything. 'And I suppose you'll be going round to see Anna, to deliver this present?'

Still I didn't say anything. If I said yes, he'd be angry, if I said no, he wouldn't believe me.

'Well? Answer me,' he said, pulling my hair.

'I'll probably just meet her for lunch.' Now he pulled me up to my feet by my hair and looked me right in the eye.

'Don't lie to me.'

'I'm not.'

He hit me and I stumbled back onto the sofa. He went out of the room then, but I could still hear him talking as he walked upstairs. I don't know what he'd gone for, but I could tell he hadn't finished with me. That's when I picked the phone up and dialled 999. I whispered into the receiver. If he caught me…I heard him coming back downstairs, still ranting. I put the phone down but didn't put it back completely on the cradle, hoping the operator would hear what was going on, and praying they wouldn't say anything that Michael could hear.

He slammed the door open so the doorknob dented the wall with a bang. 'This is the crap you got me for my birthday,' he said holding up a silk tie that I'd gone to great effort and expense to find to match his favourite suit, 'a fucking tie.' He wrapped it around his hands. 'You didn't go the length and breadth of London looking for this in specialist shops, did you?'

'I just happened to see that book Michael, I didn't go looking for it, and I did…'

'Shut up bitch, I'm not interested.' He unwound the tie and snapped it between his two hands stretching it. He came closer to me and put the tie under my chin. I thought he was going to strangle me with it. 'You like silk, don't you?'

Then the door bell rang.

'Who the fuck is that?'

'I don't know,' I said, my heart beating fast and loud. I could feel the blood pounding in my ears.

Someone banged on the door then. 'You'd better answer it,' he said, releasing me. I opened the door to two police officers. I tried to convey with my eyes that they shouldn't say I'd called. They followed me into the living room.

Michael was sitting on the sofa, flicking through the book on bikes. The tie was nowhere in sight and Michael looked completely calm.

'We had a call that there was some disturbance here,' said the male officer.

'No, there's no problem here officer. Are you sure you have the right address?'

The police looked at me, but I didn't know what to say. Whatever I said Michael would contradict me and he looked so calm and reasonable. I wish I hadn't called them then. 'There's no problem, madam?'

'No, we're um…'

'We had this once before,' Michael jumped in. 'One of our neighbours seems to be oversensitive to noise. You might want to have a word about them wasting your time.'

I prayed that they wouldn't say the call had come from our house not a neighbour. They looked to me again, but I just smiled nervously. 'OK, well I'm sorry for wasting your time.'

'No, not at all,' said Michael, standing up, 'I'm sorry your time has been wasted.' He made to show them to the door. As they went out the female officer slipped a card into my hand, which I slid under the phone as I didn't have a pocket in my skirt, and I pushed the phone back down on the cradle. Then Michael was back in the room. He pushed me against the wall. 'You called them, didn't you? How the fuck could you do that?' He hit the wall behind me. I started to sweat, anticipating the inevitable, my stomach muscles tensed waiting for the punch that would come, but it didn't. He put his hand round my throat and pushed me more against the wall, leaning very close to whisper in my ear, 'if you ever do that again, I'll kill you.'

I believed he would. More than anything, I believed then he was capable of it and going to the police was not an option I could entertain if I wanted to stay alive. Alive and beaten was still alive.

※

I woke late and Anna had already left the house. There was a note in large print on the kitchen table:

'Gone to work. Will try not to be too late. Home 6ish? Help yourself to anything you want. Do not answer the phone. DO NOT OPEN THE DOOR. Do not feed the cat!'

With her office phone number.

I put the kettle on. Jasmine looked up at me expectantly. 'What do you want? Anna said not to feed you.' Oh no, I was talking to a cat. My life was officially over. I was slowly losing my mind. I sat down with my tea and took stock of my life. I was thirty-eight, reasonable job but no career as such, married to a bastard, no children and never likely to have any. It wasn't much to show for thirty-eight years on the planet. Was Michael really a monster? I didn't know what to think. I knew what Anna would say – I should leave him. He beat me and he shouldn't and I didn't have to put up with it and I didn't need a man. All of which was true, but I sometimes thought getting married had been the only positive, useful thing I'd ever done. And he was so different in between. I loved him; did I really want to leave him? Surely he'd change now? Surely any time he tried something I could just threaten to tell the police what he'd done. But that wasn't much of a basis for a loving relationship, was it, threats and coercion? I almost wouldn't be any better than him. I wasn't getting anywhere.

Right on cue the phone rang. 'Isabel, it's me. Please talk to me.' I ignored it. The phone rang about every thirty minutes for the rest of the day. He'd deduced that I'd be on my own with Anna at work. Sometimes he left a message, sometimes he didn't. The messages got progressively more pleading and desperate. In the end I couldn't stand it 142 any more. I knew I would have to talk to him sometime, even if it was only to say I wanted a divorce, so I might as well get it over with. I snatched up the receiver.

'Yes.'

'Oh Isabel, thank God. I'm so...'

'Don't say you're sorry Michael. You're like a broken record.'

Silence. 'I know. I know how it must sound.'

'Really? I don't think you're the one sitting in terrible pain with broken ribs, being constantly hounded by your abuser so you can't even get any rest.'

'I'm not hounding you.'

'So what are you doing? You've been calling constantly all day.'

'I just want to talk to you.'

'So talk.'

'I wanted to say how sorry I am, but you don't want to hear that, I realise that now. I want you to come home Iz. Let me show you I mean it. I'll never hurt you again.'

'Damn right you won't,' I said. 'I don't know if I can trust you again, Michael.'

'That's understandable.'

'I need time. I need some space to see what I want to do.'

'OK.'

'OK?'

'Yes.'

'So you'll stop calling?'

'If that's what you want.'

'It is. That's what I want.'

'OK.'

I didn't want to say I'd call him, but I didn't quite know how to end the call, so I said, 'I'll be in touch,' and hung up.

It was only 4 p.m. but I poured myself a large glass of white wine and sat on the couch. I wanted to go for a walk, clear my head, but I didn't have keys. I got up and looked out of the window. London looked grey and dreary and I was glad to be inside with nothing to do and nowhere to go. My ribs and wrist were hurting so I popped some pills and settled back on the sofa with a paperback resolved to try and enjoy the break from work and the break from Michael. Mercifully the phone didn't ring any more. I thought about deleting all his messages so Anna wouldn't know about them, but I couldn't be bothered.

By the time Anna got home, between the wine and the painkillers I was feeling quite tipsy and like a naughty schoolgirl who'd pulled a sickie.

'Not made dinner then?' Anna said, by way of greeting.

'Um, no. I didn't think. I could have. I'm not that incapacitated.'

'I'm kidding. I have curry,' she said, holding up a white carrier bag as though it were some kind of trophy. 'Ah been at the vino already? Pour me a glass.'

She stowed Molly near the door and removed her cycle helmet, and unusually for Anna, her fluorescent clips, dropping them with her rucksack near the door. 'I'm starving,' she said, setting the food bag on the counter.

'So, how was your day?' She went over to the phone when she saw the blinking light.

'Don't bother,' I said. 'There're all from Michael. You can just delete them.'

'There's ten messages on here!'

'Hmm, he's been calling all day.'

'Please tell me you didn't give in and talk to him.'

I didn't say anything.

'Oh for fuck's sake Isabel. I can't leave you alone for five minutes!'

'I had to, he was driving me nuts.'

'Sit, eat.' She motioned with her head as she put out plates and began spooning out curry and rice. It looked like way too much food, but I felt confident Anna would work her way through it.

'So what did he say? – I'm sorry, I won't do it again?'

'Pretty much and I told him to stop saying it.'

'Ooh, get you! That's promising. What else did you say?'

'I told him I wanted him to stop calling. That I needed space.'

'Very American. I would have preferred, fuck off, I want a divorce, my solicitor will be in touch, but I suppose it's a start,' she said between mouthfuls. 'Do you think he'll take any notice?'

'Dunno, but he hasn't called since then.'

'When was that?'

'About 4 o'clock.'

She looked at her watch. 'I reckon he might hold out 'til maybe eight.'

Anna wolfed more curry, while I moved rice around my plate without really eating any. 'Look,' she said after a while, 'I know you don't want to talk about it yet, and I know you need time to just think about things, but I really think you should tell the police what he did.'

'I dunno Anna. For a start it's been three days now, they're going to ask why I didn't report it straight away.'

'Maybe, but you can say you were in shock and in too much pain. I can back you up, that needn't be a reason, it happens all the time that women don't report things immediately.'

'But I don't want to press charges. It won't do any good, and I just want to move on.'

'Well you know we don't exactly see eye to eye on that, I think you should press charges and get him arrested and let everyone see what a vicious bastard he is...' I started to interrupt, but she held up her hand to continue, 'I can understand how that may not be in your best interests and it's going to be easier to just stay away from him, but I really think this should be on record even if you don't press charges. What if he comes after you again? What if sometime in the future he tries to get back together or whatever? If this is on record at least you've got a little ammunition to fight with, you can prove that he was violent at least one time. And it won't hurt when you get divorced either.'

I thought about what Anna said, it made a kind of sense, and then I remembered how Michael had been the one and only time I had called the police and it made me feel sick. 'But what if he finds out? You know what he was like that one time I called the police to the house, he went ballistic. I was more scared than I've ever been after that. It just made things worse.'

'He won't find out.'

'That's easy for you to say, but you can't be sure.'

'The police are much better about these kinds of things now. If you tell them you're afraid of how he'll react and you don't want to press any charges they'll leave it at that. I can go with you, as a doctor and as your friend.'

'OK, well I'll think about it.'

It didn't take me long to realise Anna was right. We went and saw the police together. They took their report. They took their photos and got information from the hospital, but at my request they didn't question Michael or take it any further.

Anna was wrong about Michael calling. He didn't call for a whole two days. I was starting to miss the attention. Even then he didn't start again with the phone calls. He started sending me 'love' notes by text. Things like 'I miss you, call me.' 'Whatever you want, I'll do it.' It was kind of romantic, but I tried hard not to be suckered by it. Every time I moved, I was physically reminded of what he'd done to me. A few sweet texts weren't going to fix that.

On my fourth day at Anna's, a package arrived for me. It was the new Michael Connelly in hardback with a note – 'Thought you might be hard up for things to read. Would have sent flowers, but it seemed too clichéd.' Clichéd? I wondered if the man was getting coaching from somewhere. It reminded me of when he was first trying to woo me.

I stayed two weeks with Anna, which may not sound like long, but it is when you're constantly battling with what is the best thing to do. Anna was at work most of the time and I was left to feel lonely and miserable and have too much time just thinking and weighing up the pros and cons. Nightly, Anna told me what a loser Michael was and encouraged me to call a solicitor about a divorce and start looking at flats. Daily, Michael sent me love notes and gifts and promised his undying love. I think I've said before I'm an incurable romantic. It was only a matter of time...

I don't want to dwell on the details. It embarrasses me now with all that's happened since that I fell for his charm and his lies, but he wore me down. Yes, I wanted the violence to stop, and I thought it would. This time had been different, I'd proved I could stay away from him and I had the report to the police as my secret back up. I missed him. Eventually I moved back in and agreed to give Michael another chance.

'I think we should have kids,' Michael said one morning as we lay in bed.

'Really? But we've only just got married.'

'Don't you want children?'

'I don't know, there didn't seem much point thinking about it when I didn't have a man.'

'Well, you have a man now,' he said, snuggling close to me.

'Mmm, and don't you want to keep me all to yourself a bit longer?' He was running his hand up my leg. 'There won't be much of this with a baby crying to be fed, or if I've been up half the night.'

'I'd help.'

'You'd have a problem feeding it,' I laughed.

'We could give him a bottle.'

'Oh I see, it's a boy now, is it? Anyway, breast feeding is better.'

'OK, well you could sleep during the day. You wouldn't be working.'

'Wouldn't I?'

'No, of course you'd give up work if you had a baby.' I let that go, since as far as I was concerned this was a pretty hypothetical discussion. I hadn't even thought about having children at that point, and I couldn't see myself being ready any time soon. 'I'd support you both.'

'I should hope you would!'

'Go on, let's try for one,' he said fondling my breast.

'If this is just a ploy to have sex, you could just ask, or bring me a cup of tea, that might improve your chances!'

He lay on his back with his arms under his head and pouted a bit. 'But I want children.'

'And maybe we'll have them someday, but I'm not ready to think about it yet Michael. We're barely back from honeymoon, let's enjoy each other and the house a bit, before we think about that.'

He turned back on his side and looked at me, running his fingers up and down my stomach. 'Couldn't you stop taking the pill and see what happens? I've heard it can take quite a long time to conceive after you stop, so you might not even get pregnant for ages.'

'I'll think about it.'

'OK, but you don't want to leave it too late.'

'What do you mean, I'm only 33?'

'That's already kind of old for a first baby.'

'And how many do you want?'

'Oh lots. Three or four.'

'Three or four?! And don't I have a say in it?'

'Yes, of course you do,' he sounded exasperated, 'I'm just saying, I'd like more than one and you're not getting any younger.'

'Thanks!'

'Oh come on, I don't mean it like that, I love your crow's feet, but we need to bear it in mind.'

'I don't get you sometimes Michael.'

'What?'

'Well you can't stand your own family, and you're always fobbing off my parents because you want me all to yourself and yet you want loads of children.'

'Yes, but we wouldn't make the mistakes our parents made. We'd be great with children.'

Would we, I wondered. I didn't really see Michael as a family man, but neither of us had nephews or nieces or friends with young children so I'd never seen him with babies, maybe he would make a great dad.

He broached the subject a few more times and it always ended with me promising to think about going off the pill, but I never did.

<hr>

'Let's go away somewhere. Anywhere you want to go. Just tell me.'

It was a few weeks after I'd moved back in with Michael that he suggested a holiday. He had been Mr Perfect Husband since I'd returned from my stay at Anna's. He'd agreed to all my ground rules. He hadn't said a thing about me seeing Anna, or any of my friends from work. Anna had been round a couple of evenings and he'd been perfectly civil to her and had thanked her for taking care of me. We'd even had my parents and Louise over for Sunday lunch. There had been no harsh words, no arguments, none of his moods. It was still early days, but I was starting to think that maybe Michael had changed. Maybe the staircase incident as I'd come to call it had finally made him see the light. But things weren't entirely right. I was incredibly wary of him, always alert to any sign of him losing his temper. More than once I'd flinched when he made a sudden movement just in my field of vision, thinking it was an approaching blow. And while we'd had sex, there was something different about it. I find it hard to sleep with someone I don't trust and I just didn't trust Michael anymore. I never knew how he was going to react to anything. He'd kicked me once, and he could do it again and while he tried his best to start a clean slate I couldn't let myself forget it, or forgive him. Anna still liked to refer to him as 'the bastard' and continued to counsel me to leave him – a leopard couldn't change his spots and all that, but even she noticed that he seemed to be genuinely making an effort.

I definitely needed a break. I felt like I never fully relaxed anymore even when I was asleep. A holiday alone or with a female friend would have been better, but the thought of lying in the sun with nothing to do and nothing to worry about, even with Michael next to me, was very appealing. Let's go somewhere hot and sunny with lots of water, I thought. That will test him. Although I loved Italy, and could have happily gone there every holiday for the rest of my life, I also loved trying new places and had been hankering to try a Greek island or two. It's hard to say now, after so much time whether that was why I suggested Greece, or whether I chose it to punish Michael. I knew he wouldn't like a beach holiday. I knew he wouldn't like the heat or the food and I suspected he wouldn't much like the culture either. Insofar as he liked holidays at all, which he didn't really, he liked hiking in Scotland or the Lake District, far away from crowds, and if it rained it didn't bother him. But so what? He could read. He could just sit on a lounger and read for two weeks if that's what I wanted. After what he'd done to me he should damn well take me on the Orient Express, or trekking in Nepal if that's what I desired. A week or two on a Greek island wouldn't kill him!

'How about one of the Greek islands?'

I could see him wanting to pull a face, but he didn't. 'Yeah, if that's what you want. I thought you'd fancy Italy. Or maybe Madrid or Paris?'

'No, I think I fancy just lying in the sun for a couple of weeks doing nothing. Maybe some swimming and snorkelling. Shall I pick up some brochures?'

'Yes. We can look at them at the weekend. Make a plan,' he said, though I knew what he really wanted to say was swimming and snorkelling? But you know I can't swim.

We settled on Mykonos, me elatedly, Michael begrudgingly, but knowing he had to make an effort if he was going to save his marriage and win back any of my trust.

The first day I managed to lie near the pool most of the day. Michael tried to settle with a book, but I could tell he was struggling, even though I tried my best to ignore him while flipping through my holiday magazines. Late morning he gave in and went off exploring. It was so blissful, snoozing in the warmth of the shade, a slight breeze rustling the leaves. He came back far too quickly, but he had bread, cheese, olives and wine. He went off again after a siesta and came back full of the walk he'd had, keen for me to go on a similar expedition with him. I hadn't gone to a Greek island to hike around hot dusty trails into the hills, I had gone to lie in the sun, to relax, to swim, and frankly to try to forget that I was married to Michael, or at least to try to forget a little what he'd done to me. I was perfectly happy for him to go off and do his own thing and leave me in peace.

For a few days we followed the same pattern of pursuing separate interests, coming together for light lunches in the cool of the villa and evening promenades through the Chora and dinner at a taverna near Little Venice. Michael had found it on his first trip into town and ever the creature of habit he wanted to return every day. I would have liked to try other places, but as long as the food was good and the wine abundant I didn't really mind. The more I relaxed, the more Michael seemed to get frustrated. He had soon explored most of the island and needed new adventures. He also seemed to think we should be spending more time together, like this was a second honeymoon or something, rather than a last ditched attempt to save our marriage after he'd done something unforgiveable. He seemed to think I should have already put that behind us.

His solution to my intransience was to throw money at the problem. Since he couldn't get me to go walking with him, he chartered a boat to take us round some of the islands. I had to admit it was a great idea. Everything was arranged, including picnic style lunch served on deck. There was plenty of opportunity for me to swim while Michael gazed adoringly on. The second day he even hired a local to take me snorkelling while he waved from the boat, sipping Campari and soda under his Panama straw hat. The crew must have thought we were rolling in it and blissfully happy, which pleased Michael – that's exactly what he likes people to think. I couldn't claim to be blissfully happy, but it went a long way to making amends. I sometimes gag now to think how easily bought off and seduced I was.

※

I should have been the happiest woman alive after those two weeks, and maybe I would have been if Michael hadn't started some petty argument not long after we returned. I was hoping things would be different. Michael had been so sweet and caring since I'd been back from Anna's and overall the holiday had been good, though with hindsight I suspect the fact that we'd done separate things for much of the holiday only proved to Michael that I'd never be entirely under his thumb. As usual he picked some pathetic quarrel over nothing, but when he raised his hand to strike me, I took a step back.

'I wouldn't do that if I were you. I could always tell the police about you pushing me down the stairs.' I was reserving telling him that I actually had made a police report. I wanted that as my trump card for when I really needed it.

'I'd just say you fell,' he retorted. 'It would be your word against mine. And who do you think they'd believe – the successful business man or the hysterical woman?'

'You wouldn't like it though, would you? Them asking questions. There being a record somewhere that questions had been raised about my *accident*.'

That shut him up, momentarily at least. He stormed upstairs and I heard him throwing things around. Then he came down in shorts and trainers. 'I'm going running,' he declared and slammed out of the front door.

I lent back against the kitchen counter. I felt great that I'd stopped him hitting me, and totally defeated that it was starting all over again. The relaxation of the two weeks holiday was completely erased. Tears rolled down my cheeks as I gave into the realisation that my marriage was a farce and I had to end it. My body began to tense as I thought of the way Michael had just gone back to the way things were before, as though me staying at Anna's and our holiday had never happened. Now my evening would be ruined even without the violence. I didn't know when he'd be back, what mood he'd be in, if he'd kick off again, or try and pretend nothing had happened. I remembered the card the police woman had given me that I'd stuck under the phone. That felt like so long ago. I picked up the phone, but it wasn't there. I knew I hadn't moved it and Michael never did any cleaning. Where could it have gone? Oh well, that was months ago, I reasoned with myself, maybe I had moved it. It didn't matter anyway. I knew I wasn't going to call the police again. I took a long bath, but it didn't help me relax.

Michael apologised the next morning with his usual platitudes of he didn't know why he did it, he loved me, being back at work was stressing him out after such a wonderful break. I didn't believe any of it, but I played along to make things easier on myself. As soon as I got to work I called a solicitor I knew and made an appointment to discuss getting a divorce, but she couldn't see me until later in the week. I had to keep my momentum going or things would just stay the same. Michael would be all nice and apologetic, things would be fine for a few weeks and I'd be lulled into a sense of complacency – things weren't really that bad. So later that morning I called Anna to see if she was free for lunch. I wanted to talk things through and I knew she'd encourage me. She thought I just wanted to tell her about my holiday.

'Sorry Iz. I'm up to my eyeballs here. You wouldn't believe the rush I've got on, a whole load of people seem to have got themselves killed one way or another.' She laughed. Her mortuary laugh I used to call it. It was a throaty, slightly macabre kind of laugh she had for her jokes related to body parts.

'But I really need to talk to you.'

'And I want to hear all about your holiday. Did Michael behave himself?' I didn't reply quickly enough. 'Iz? What's up? What's he done?'

'Noth...Look I can't say just now.' Katherine had come back from the photocopier and I didn't want her hearing my conversation.

'Can you come round tonight?'

I thought about the fuss Michael might kick up, now that he was obviously back to his old ways, but if that was the case he was going to hit me whatever I did or didn't do, so what the hell. 'Yes, OK.'

'Good. Come round about 8 p.m. I'll open a bottle.'

It didn't take me long to stop beating around the bush with how great Greece had been and get to how Michael was back to his old self.

'I know, I know, you told me he wouldn't change, but he was so nice when I moved back in, even you said so.'

'He was only doing that to get you to stay. He can't live without you, you know that, don't you?'

'Of course he could,' I said, not believing it myself, 'he might not like it, but he'd get over it. He'll just find himself a younger more pliable model.'

'I don't think so Iz. He won't let you go. You're going to have to have a damn good plan if you try to leave him.'

'So what about a divorce? I'm meeting a solicitor later in the week to discuss it.'

'I don't know. I mean, yes, that's good that you're going to talk about it, but I have a nasty feeling even that won't work. He's built up a pattern over years. He wants complete control over you. He won't give up without a fight, and I don't just mean about the house and money stuff. I reckon you'd have to move out once he knows you want a divorce. Maybe you should just leave him without saying anything?'

'But then I'll never be free of him. If we're still legally married…'

'You could still divorce him. I just mean get away first.'

'That didn't work too well when I stayed with you.' I was getting despondent. I wanted a more immediate answer, but everything was going to take so long and Michael would be baiting me the whole time, trying to get me to stay with him.

'But you're stronger now,' she said, 'more determined. You weren't ready to leave him before.'

I sipped my wine.

'What about a women's refuge? It might be worth considering.'

'Oh no, Anna, not that. They're horrible, aren't they?'

'I don't really know. I suppose they're not the nicest of places, but they would protect you.' Anna thought for a bit while she drank her wine. 'OK,' she said, 'why don't you try going to a hotel? Don't tell him, obviously. He won't be able to find you easily. It would give you a break while you sort stuff out.'

'Maybe.'

'Have you got any money? I can lend you some.'

'I haven't got too much, just some of my bonuses that I've been putting in a savings account, the rest goes in the joint account.'

'You need to start saving more of your own money.'

'Easier said than done! If I start putting less in the joint account Michael will wonder why. He's always checking the balance. He already complains that they don't pay me much. He doesn't know about the bonuses.'

'OK, well we'll come up with something, but for now squirrel away anything you can. If you get a raise any time put the difference in your account and anything you can save on the housekeeping. You know he can put a hold on the joint account so you can't use it?'

'Really?'

'Yeah, I think so. It happened to someone I used to work with when she got divorced, or he moved all the money to his account or something. You've got to be aware of the possibility, Michael's so good with financial stuff it will be a piece of cake for him to make sure you're penniless.'

'Bugger.'

'Just don't use the joint account for anything that might make him suspicious.'

'Well that's everything then!'

※

I saw Carole, my solicitor a few days later and tried to explain the situation, but I didn't really want to give her too much detail. Up until then I'd only talked to Anna about what Michael was really like. I was embarrassed about the violence and thought people would think it was my fault. Maybe it was my fault? I often speculated on whether I provoked him. Anna was always firm in her support of me and told me all the time it wasn't me, Michael was the only person responsible for his actions and what he did was wrong. But while I trusted Anna with my life, I couldn't entirely trust her judgements on Michael. I knew she didn't like him, but in general she didn't have much time for men. She wasn't anti men, she just didn't need them in any way. And she loved me, I knew she'd do anything for me. Maybe she just said it was all Michael's fault to make me feel better, because she was incapable of seeing it any other way?

'So he's violent towards you?' Carole asked.

'Well…'

'Isabel, I don't expect you to give me all the details. I know this kind of situation is hard, but there are legal ways I can help you if I know the facts, and if you decide you want to proceed with a straightforward divorce any evidence of violence or abuse will make negotiation easier.'

'You said there were legal ways you could help? What do you mean?'

'Well there are various injunctions we could try for.'

'Injunctions? You mean like he can't come near me or something?'

'That kind of thing, yes. You can apply for what's call a non-molestation order.'

'But would that be for if we're still living together?'

'Yes, it can be.'

'I don't see how a bit of paper is going to stop Michael doing anything he doesn't want to do.'

'It can have a power of arrest attached to it, that means the police would arrest him if he breaks the terms.'

'Hmm, I've tried calling the police before and that just made things worse.'

'Well it's something to think about. Like I say it can be rather complicated and may not be the best option, but it's something to consider. I'll give you some information on it.'

I was with Carole for what felt like hours. She went through everything clearly and succinctly but I came away more confused than before. I felt overloaded with information, which made it hard to make any kind of decision. I went back to the office and locked all the papers from Carole in my desk drawer. Even that didn't feel safe. I had the feeling that somehow Michael would know where I'd been and what I'd been considering.

True to form, it wasn't long before Michael hit me again, before I'd had time to really consider my options and decide what to do. I tried bringing up the hospital again and saying that I'd report it to the police, but this time he wasn't having any of it.

'Don't give me that bollocks about going to the police. It's too long ago. You've no way to prove what I did.'

'There's the hospital records. They show what injuries I sustained.'

'Exactly, what *injuries*, but not how you got them. It only shows you carelessly fell down some stairs.'

I was just about to go for it and drop the news that actually the police already knew he'd caused my accident, that they had it all recorded with a report from the doctor and photographs, when he came right up close to my face and tugged my hair hard from the back of my head. 'I can do anything I want to you, and don't you forget it.'

This scared me much more than him hitting me. Just like when the police had come to the house and he'd threatened to kill me, his threats put the greatest fear in me. It was something about the menacing tone of his voice, and the look in his eyes, the way he spoke right next to my face so I could feel the heat of his breath and the pinpricks of spittle hitting my skin. Before I could always make myself believe that he hadn't really meant to hurt me and that at least he was sorry afterwards, but the look in his eyes then was so, well, dangerous, I didn't know this man any more.

I knew then he would never change; things would only get worse. I knew I had to get away from him quickly and I had to do it properly. A divorce wasn't going to work. It would take too long and as soon as he knew what I was up to things would escalate. Divorcing him would be a public embarrassment he couldn't stand. I thought about what Anna had said about him not wanting to let me go. I had to find some way to get away for good.

The next day at work I tried surfing the Internet looking for women's shelters, just to see what they were like. I really didn't want to go to a place like that. I was a snob, I'll admit it. I thought shelters were for poor women with alcoholic husbands who beat them and their children daily. I had a horrible stereotype in my head of women who were not well dressed, who were on the dole or had cleaning jobs, with two or three bedraggled, snotty children in tow. For some reason I thought I was the only middle-class woman to have ever been beaten up, at least by a sober man. I can't believe myself now when I think how I was – how ignorant and prejudiced; how much in denial. I didn't want to think I was as desperate as them, maybe I wasn't then, but I would be. I didn't realise the lengths Michael would go to, I didn't plan as I should have, though every failure brought me a little closer to success. But I'm getting ahead of myself again.

The Internet was still young and Google was in its infancy, so I didn't find out too much, though reading about other women in similar situations did make me feel a little less like a freak, less alone, but it didn't really help with the immediate practicalities. I sat tapping my pen on my desk until Katherine said, 'what's up with you lately? You don't seem to be with it.'

'Oh sorry. Lot's of stuff on my mind. I think I'll go down the road for a coffee, clear my head a bit.'

Anna called me later with the phone number of a women's refuge she'd found. She said I should call, just to see what they said. She thought they could give me good advice even if I ended up not going there.

'I'm not sure I want to do this.'

'Listen to me. You have to think about it. You tried staying with me and that didn't work. He'll only talk you into going back to him if you're with someone he knows. I know it sounds drastic, but I think you need a clean break. He's only going to get worse. It'll be fine. They'll support you. Look on the bright side, you haven't got children. You can get away now before he really does something serious. I'll do whatever I can to help, you know that. Just call them.'

'OK. I'll call you later.'

I went outside and walked around a bit, trying to summon up the courage to call. Somehow it seemed a much harder thing to do than to put up with Michael. I decided, perhaps against my better judgement, to talk to Louise before I did anything else. It wouldn't hurt to talk it through with someone else. So far Anna was the only person close to me I'd confided in, but if I was going to leave Michael and hold up in some shelter or even in a hotel my family were going to have to know, if only to ensure that they didn't tell Michael anything I didn't want him to know.

I met Louise for lunch at one of our usual hangouts. I wasn't remotely hungry and pushed the panini around my plate taking the occasional nibble.

'So what's all this in aid of? Not like you to want lunch with your little sis' on the spur of the moment. And you clearly didn't come for the food,' she said, looking at my plate. 'Oh, you're not pregnant are you? I'm too young to be an auntie!'

'Yes you are. And no, I'm not. I'm about as far from being pregnant as it's possible to be with a pulse and a womb.'

'Oh.' Louise was clearly dented by my tone and my sarcasm. It wasn't her fault; she didn't know what was up.

'Sorry. It's just, well things with Michael have got really bad.'

'What do you mean, got really bad? I thought it was all hunky dory in the love shack?'

I loved the way Louise came up with these bizarre hippy phrases as though she'd lived through the 60s or something. 'I hadn't wanted to say anything, because, oh I don't know, it's kind of embarrassing, and I thought people wouldn't believe me.'

'Believe you about what? Get to the point would you?'

'Keep your voice down,' I hissed as the middle-aged couple next to us gave her a dirty look. 'He hits me.'

'He what? The fu, the dirty lowlife scumbag. How long has this been going on?'

'Um. Quite a while.'

'Oh shit, Isabel. Why didn't you tell me?'

'And what would you have done?'

'Had him beaten up. Had you stay with me. I dunno, anything. What do you want me to do? Come and stay with me now. Just go home for some stuff and come to my place.'

'That's sweet of you Louise, but it won't work.'

'My housemates won't mind. It'll be cool.'

I smiled. Louise's 'house-share' was like some kind of bohemian, art student's wet dream, rather than the first home of young professionals it purported to be. 'It's not that. He'll find me there. He'll just come and get me back.'

'How will he know, if you don't tell him?'

'Trust me. He'll work it out. He'll try Anna's and then mum and dad's and then you.'

'Do mum and dad know?'

'No. And I'd rather you didn't tell them.'

She looked perplexed as though she couldn't work out why on earth I wouldn't tell them, but tapped her nose, 'mum's the word.' If nothing else, seeing Louise was cheering me up with her child-like solutions to the problem.

'So what are you going to do?' she asked.

'I'm thinking about going to a women's shelter.'

'Shit, has it got that bad?'

I nodded. She seemed about to start into to her 'why didn't you tell me' routine again. 'I can't see another way out right now. I don't want to, but every time I think he's going to stop it starts again. I've tried staying with Anna and he talked me into going back to him...'

'Have you tried talking to him?'

'Not for years.'

'Years?! Bloody hell, Iz. It's been going on for years?'

'Soon after we got married,' I finally admitted.

I'd stunned Louise into temporary silence. Then she signalled for a waiter and ordered a bottle of house red.

'Make that Pinot Grigio,' I said. 'Very chilled. It's all right, I'll pay. I can't drink red wine at lunch time.'

'So, have you found a place?'

'Not sure, I've got a number to call, but I can't quite...'

'Maybe you should try talking to him again.' She held up a hand to stop me interrupting. 'I'm no fan of the guy, you know that, but maybe he doesn't realise how bad it's got. Maybe if you told him you were going to leave, he'd make an effort?'

'I don't know. I don't think he will. I've tried it before.'

She looked at me doe-eyed and innocent, gulping her wine.

'You know when I fell down the stairs. Well I didn't fall.'

'Oh shit.'

'I told him I was leaving then, that's when I stayed with Anna and he talked me into going back.'

'Didn't you tell the police?'

'No. I thought it would just make things worse.'

Her face showed that she couldn't grasp the concept and I admit it sounded stupid to me too. I didn't want to get into the fact that I had actually told them, but hadn't pressed charges. I was beginning to think that having reported it at all had been a complete waste of time, I hadn't been able to make use of it.

I popped back to the office, grabbed some files and told Katherine I had an appointment with a client and would be gone the rest of the afternoon. I think she suspected this wasn't true, but she didn't say anything. Then I headed for the South Bank. Walking by the river always soothed me and I needed to think and work out my next move. I really didn't like the thought of going to a shelter. I didn't want to be with other battered women. I hated that word, it sounded so vicious and violent, like getting a pounding every single night. I didn't think of myself that way. What Michael did was horrible but it was sporadic and he was still mostly good to me in between, but his increasing threats really frightened me, along with the fact of never knowing when he would fly into a rage, of not knowing what set it off, of not knowing if there was anything I could do to prevent it. It all left me in a permanent stressed out state. I felt like I could never relax. But I could cope with it in a way, it had become so commonplace by then that I was used to it. Could I cope with being in a shelter, maybe not being able to see Anna or my family, maybe not being able to go to work? No, I couldn't give up work that was my lifeline and my only source of an income to survive without Michael. And how could I get my share of the house if I wasn't living there? He'd swindle me out of everything.

I eventually talked myself out of moving out and decided to have one more go at reasoning with Michael and convincing him his behaviour had to change. I figured that if he really wanted me as much as he said, and if he couldn't cope without me, then he'd be willing to try to be better. I pushed out of my mind the memory that he'd promised to see a therapist back when it all started and he hadn't, that he promised he'd never hit me again and always broke that promise. I thought I owed it to myself to try. I'd spent over five years of my life in this marriage and I didn't want them to be completely wasted. I just wasn't ready to up and leave and live hidden away, even if it was temporary. Rather ironic really, given what I've ended up doing.

I called the number Anna had given me, not to ask for a place to stay, but to get details of a counsellor for abusers. This time I wouldn't leave things to Michael. I would make the appointment myself and take him to it, and if necessary sit outside to make sure he stayed there for the session. If Michael had changed once from nice to bad, surely he could change back again, couldn't he?

Much as I wanted to have this conversation at home, I knew I'd be safer having it in a public place so Michael couldn't just shout and storm out or hit me. It had to be somewhere quiet, but busy enough so that others wouldn't be able to hear the detail of our conversation. Bacio was perfect. I was reluctant to use the scene of so many happy occasions for this most difficult of situations, but I had to, and it had the added benefit that we were known there so Michael would be even less likely to do anything that might draw attention to us or cause him embarrassment.

I put on one of Michael's favourite dresses and fixed him a strong gin and tonic. As soon as he came home I made my proposal. 'Shall we just go to Bacio's tonight? I'm pooped, and we haven't been for ages.'

'OK, why not. I'll just go and change.'

I kept the conversation light and chit chatty until the food arrived. He seemed in a good mood, regaling me with stories from the office. My stomach was churning with nerves but I had to eat, I needed a drink and I didn't want to get drunk. I had to be in control tonight, of myself and of Michael.

'Michael.'

'Hmm.'

'We really need to talk about some stuff.'

'Do we?'

God, how was I supposed to tell him this? 'Yes. Look, things can't go on as they are. Greece was great, but since we've been back, you've just gone back to the way you were before. The way you treat me, it's not right, and I'm not going to put up with it any more. If you don't do something about it, I'm going to leave you.' It all tumbled out in a rush and I wondered if any of it had been intelligible.

'OK,' he said mildly, swirling spaghetti and not looking up from his plate.

'Don't just say OK. I mean it. I will leave you and I'll tell everyone what you've been doing.'

Now I had his attention. Now he looked up. 'So what do you want me to do?' he said through gritted teeth.

'I want you to go to counselling. I have the name of someone, specifically for, well for this kind of situation, and I want you to go regularly until you work out why you do it and stop.'

'And if I don't?'

I couldn't believe how blasé he was being about the whole thing. 'I've already said, I'll leave you.'

'Well you kind of tried that before, when you went to Anna's, didn't you?' he said smugly, but I could tell he was thinking things through. You could almost see his mind working, trying to see if there was a way round this, a way to keep me without having to go through any ridiculous counselling.

'Yes, but believe me, I won't fall for your seduction techniques any more. I've had it, Michael. If you don't agree to this, I'm filing for divorce. I've already spoken to a solicitor.'

Now his mouth fell slightly open, as though he couldn't believe I really would have done that, as though he wasn't sure if I was bluffing or not. 'OK, fine. I'll see this fellow. Give me the name and I'll call tomorrow.'

'Not so easy. You've broken too many promises before. I'll make the appointment, and I'm going with you to make sure you go this time.'

We finished the rest of the meal in silence and walked home. 'I'm going to watch some telly,' I said. I didn't care what was on, I just didn't want to be with him. I'd made my case and I didn't want to talk about it any more. I didn't want him trying to talk me out of it, saying he could change without seeing anyone.

It was late when I went up to bed, but he was still awake. I got into bed and lay on my side facing away from him. He put out the lights and spooned me, his arm over my stomach, his mouth near my ear so I could feel his breath on my neck. 'I've been terrible haven't I?'

I said nothing.

'I'll try this,' he said. 'I really do love you, Iz. I'll try, OK?'

'OK.' I whispered, but I'd been fooled too many times to trust him. I needed proof in actions first.

I never thought I'd have the feeling of love any more, or even of lust. I couldn't imagine another man touching me after Michael. I just knew that it would remind me of him and I wouldn't be able to stand it. I resigned myself to a lonely life, without love. But when Alessandra just touched my arm in that casual way Italians have it sent a shock of electricity right through me. My stomach is fluttering, and even though it's been so long, I know that feeling. It's all sensual and not logical. No part of my brain can work out why I might be remotely attracted to a woman at least ten years younger than me, but I know I want her to touch me again.

I watch her from behind the safety of my sunglasses. Those dark, dark eyes so full of mystery. I just want to watch her all day.

'You look so serious,' she says.

'Just thinking about things.'

'Well don't,' she laughed. 'Let's go in a pedalo.'

'A pedalo?'

'Yes, why not?'

I couldn't think of a single reason why not. So we did.

It harkened back to a lake years ago and Michael trying to impress me with his rowing, but I pushed that out of my mind. This was completely different. Maybe this could be a new friendship like me and Anna. Well no, nothing could be like that. No one would ever touch me like Anna had. We'd had something beyond words, beyond physical attraction. I thought back to those last few days and...

'Hey, *dove siete*? Where did you go?'

I snapped back. 'I'm right here.'

She shook her head. 'Don't leave me like that. You've got to live for the moment, you know.'

And I did know. And I tried, because that was all that was left – the moment.

The first few times Michael went to counselling he seemed quite keen. I always went with him and watched him enter the very ordinary looking house. There was a small park across the street and I sat there with a book and a view of the door and made sure he didn't come out until an hour was up. The first time I told him I'd be watching, after that I didn't, I wanted to know what he'd do if he didn't think I was there.

When I made the fourth appointment I asked Dr Abrams how it was going.

'I can't discuss it with you.'

'I know. I don't want details. I just want to know if he's talking, if he's really taking it seriously.'

'These things take time, Mrs Atkins, but I wouldn't get your hopes up too much. I would be prepared for what you would do if this doesn't work.'

'Would it help if we had a session together?'

'I don't think that would be good for either of you,' he said, 'but you should be seeing someone separately.'

I thought he was rather offhand given that I was the recipient of Michael's problem, as it were. I had the biggest stake in whether he changed or not. I hadn't really thought about counselling for myself. My priority was making sure that Michael went. I wasn't big on therapy in general; I thought it was all self-indulgence for rich Americans and film stars with addictions, but I was willing to try anything if there was a hope it might make the violence stop.

Meanwhile, life at home proceeded tentatively and tensely. Michael hadn't hurt me, or provoked an argument since he'd started the sessions, but his behaviour seemed strange. He took to often meeting me after work, as well as his impromptu lunch visits, always on the pretence of wanting to spend more time with me, going for a stroll, or a drink, or dinner, but I got the feeling it was more about checking up on me.

He took to calling me two or three times a day at work rather than a few calls a week, 'just to see how you're doing' and if I questioned him about it he'd say, 'I'm really trying to be better and show you how much I care,' but it just felt claustrophobic. If I was out of the office when he called he often gave me the tenth degree later wanting to know where I'd been. And more and more he started talking me out of seeing other people. At first this seemed innocent. If I said I was going out with the girls he'd say oh but, 'I've booked a table', or 'I've got tickets for a show', or 'can't we have a quiet night in just the two of us?' and I'd agree and then regret it. After a few of these I realised he just didn't want me out of his sight. Either he thought I wouldn't come back, or this new power trip was the only way he could deal with not hitting me any more.

When he went to the sixth session I made a big show of having to dash back to the office for an important meeting. I hid behind some bushes in the park so he wouldn't be able to see me and waited. Sure enough, ten minutes later he emerged from the house, looked around guiltily and headed towards the Tube station. I was livid. In fact I suppose I should have been surprised he stuck it out that long.

I decided not to say anything and see what happened. The following week, on Tuesday morning, he said, 'no need to meet me later. I can't make today's session, I've got a big meeting with some investors.'

'Oh, OK. When shall I re-arrange it for?'

'It's all right; I've booked it for tomorrow. In fact Iz, I'd rather you didn't come with me, it makes me feel like a naughty schoolboy. I know you want to make sure I'm going, but you have to trust me a bit at some point. I'm really committed to this. I don't want to lose you.' He kissed me.

As soon as I got to work, I called Dr Abrams office. Michael hadn't made an appointment for Wednesday. I felt crushed. I knew I probably should have been expecting it, but I just couldn't believe Michael had given up.

That night Michael was out with colleagues and I spilled my guts to Anna.

'I know you keep wanting to see the good in him, but I think you just need to get away from him before he does anything worse. Just leave. Go and stay with a friend, or go to a hotel, anything.'

'I wish it were that simple, but it doesn't seem to be.' I took a glug of wine. 'Don't look at me like that. I know you don't know why I'm wasting my time trying this counselling and stuff, but it's not you that has to totally change your life and lose your friends and who knows what else.'

'You won't lose your friends,' she said touching my arm, 'but you might lose more if you don't leave him.'

'What do you mean?'

'Men like Michael can't cope with being left. I bet he'll try anything and everything to get you back.'

'So what's the point of leaving then, if he's going to track me down? What are you saying; he'll stalk me or something?' She raised an eyebrow. 'Oh come on, this is Michael we're talking about, he wouldn't do that.'

'Wouldn't he? Hasn't he already started checking up on you, wanting to know where you go, who you see, trying to stop you going anywhere without him?'

He had, it was true. 'Yeah, but at least he's stopped beating me up.'

'And do you think that will last now he's stopped going to the sessions?'

I shrugged, but I think I knew the answer then.

'OK, so you don't like the idea of a women's shelter. What if you move? Your company has branches elsewhere, you could ask for a transfer, couldn't you?'

'Maybe.'

Anna sighed. 'How about you just kill him? Say it was self-defence. You probably wouldn't get that long.'

'Thanks Anna, really helpful!'

'I'd visit you.'

'Very decent of you.'

We laughed and drank more wine, not that it really helped the situation. I was still clinging to the fact that Michael had temporarily stopped hitting me even though he was behaving strangely, maybe things would somehow get better.

'I've got it!' exclaimed Anna with that look on her face she used to get when we were children and she'd made some scientific discovery. 'You pretend to die.'

'You what?'

'Next time I get an unidentified body in, we say it's you, and you slip away as someone new.'

'And how many unidentified bodies do you ever get?'

'Um, well, one…no we eventually found out who he was, so um…but it's got to happen sometime.'

'And they'd have to meet my general description?'

'Well, yes I suppose so.'

'And would that be kind of illegal?'

'What, falsifying the identity of a body? Yeah, technically. It's a victimless crime though, isn't it, if we don't know who they are anyway.'

'So you wouldn't mind being struck off?'

'OK, well it was a thought, you know, I bet that sort of thing happens a lot in those crime books you like to read.'

'Not that much actually. It's more sort of serial killers and loads of mutilated bodies.'

'Ooh, I like a good mutilation!'

'Oh do shut up, you freak. You're not really helping.'

Anna pouted. I could just imagine her and her 'boys' with their mortuary quips and gallows humour.

'OK, back to my original idea then Iz, go to a hotel, or a friend in another town, anything, because Michael is not going to change.'

༺༻

Most of the time I was glad I never had children. Oh every now and then I thought it would be nice. I always liked babies. I loved Louise when she'd been a baby, all chubby and smiley. Whenever people I knew had babies I liked to hold them and coo over them as much as anyone else, but somehow I couldn't see myself raising a child, looking after another person completely for at least eighteen years. In the early days Michael talked a lot about wanting children, but I was never completely convinced that he really appreciated the consequences. I think he liked the ideal of children rather than the actuality of them. I could imagine him leaving me to do all the work and he'd be the sort of man who'd come home late from work and wake the children up so he could play with them just as you'd got them off to sleep after a day of tears and tantrums.

After a couple of years he stopped talking about children, but I do remember one row we had before he completely gave up the idea. Mostly when we talked about it I promised to go off the pill, but never did. Eventually I did stop taking them, not because I wanted to get pregnant, but because I thought the coil would be easier.

We were lying in bed one Saturday. I wasn't fully awake, more sort of dozing and contemplating getting up. Michael had his arm over me and he snuggled closer and whispered in my ear, 'shall I make you pregnant?'

Here we go again, I thought, but I wasn't adverse to a little morning sex if that was what he was after. I turned on my back and looked at him. He pushed the hair back from my face and kissed me surprisingly gently. He could be such a charmer. He made love to me then, slowly and attentively, taking care to satisfy me. Afterwards I lay with my head on his chest enjoying him holding me. Michael was not usually a fan of post sex cuddling.

'You ought to put your legs up,' he said out of the blue.

'You what?'

'Put your legs up. It helps the sperm, you know, aids fertilization.'

I laughed. 'That's an old wives tale. You don't seriously expect me to stand on my head now do you?'

'That was kind of the purpose of the exercise.'

I raised myself up on an elbow and looked at him. 'I thought you wanted me.'

'I did. I do, but I said I wanted to get you pregnant and that's what I meant'

'You don't even know if I'm ovulating.'

'Don't I?' he said, raising an eyebrow. 'I know what those dots and ticks in your diary mean.'

I was appalled. The sneaky bastard. 'You've been looking in my diary?'

'Not deliberately. You left it in the lounge last night. I was just flicking through.'

'What gives you the right to…'

'Hey, don't get your knickers in a twist. I'm sure there isn't anything in there I don't already know.'

He was probably right, I put very little in my diary, just birthdays and family occasions, I didn't for example ever put when I was meeting Anna, or if I was meeting people for lunch, those were in my work diary, but that wasn't the point. 'Except when my period is, apparently!'

'Well, I know that anyway. Now, put your legs up.' He grabbed hold of my feet then and tried to pull my legs round.

'Get off Michael, you're hurting me.' I wriggled away and got to the edge of the bed. I got up and put on my dressing gown.

'Don't you want children?' he shouted. 'You've been off the pill for months, something should be happening by now.'

'Sometimes these things take time,' I said, sitting back on the bed.

He took my hand. 'Maybe we should go and see a doctor or something.'

'Let's not rush into anything,' I said trying to sound calm, but feeling myself getting nervous. We couldn't go to a doctor together, he'd find out I hadn't stopped using contraceptives. I'd have to go to the doctor alone and then get her to lie for me? Or get the coil removed and take my chances? I couldn't believe how my mind was spinning. What was I doing deceiving my husband anyway? Why couldn't I just talk to him? Decide together that it was OK to not have children? 'I don't…, I mean, maybe it's not meant to happen. Maybe we started too late.'

Michael looked crestfallen. 'But, you're still young enough. Lots of women have babies in their thirties.' Unconsciously I was gripping my gown with my free hand. I was sweating. My mind was still struggling with what I'd do if he pursued things, if he made us go to the doctor or to fertility clinics. How could I tell him that's not what I wanted? 'Hey, are you all right? You've gone all white. Here lean back against the pillow. Your hands are all clammy. You're not coming down with something are you?'

'I don't know. I do feel a bit funny.'

'Probably all that exercise on an empty stomach.' He smiled. 'I'll bring you some breakfast.'

It wasn't too long after that that the 'stair incident' happened and the question of children became moot. Just trying to stay together without him killing me seemed more than enough for both of us, though he liked to get a dig in when he could about my lack of fecundity.

***

I'm not proud of how I let things drag on, but I think it's understandable. Although Michael wasn't going to the counsellor anymore and I hadn't challenged him about it, he hadn't physically hurt me for weeks. This was the longest period for years without violence and I was fooled by it. He increasingly liked to keep tabs on me, but it wasn't totally obsessive and debilitating yet. I could get on with my life, and though my circle of friends began to dwindle I didn't really miss it as long as I still had Anna and work. Life may not have been great, but it was manageable. There was hope of improvement, and certainly not enough fear or pain to leave Michael. He even seemed to have relented a bit on his reluctance to spend time with my family and we occasionally went to Sunday lunch with my parents.

On one visit I was in the kitchen with mum clearing up, while the men sat in the living room reading the paper, the typical conservative picture – it could have been the 50s, when mum said, 'What's this I hear about you and Michael having problems?'

'What?'

'Louise mentioned something.'

'Oh, I might have known it would be Louise, that little tell tale.'

'Now, now, she's only worried about you.'

'Like he...like heck she is!'

'So you are having problems then?'

'If we were, it wouldn't really be anything to do with you or Louise, would it?' I snapped.

She gave me one of her, 'don't talk to your mother like that' looks. 'Well, we're only concerned about you. Michael's so lovely.'

I wanted to say if you think he's so lovely, why don't you live

'Maybe not for you, Miss Butter Wouldn't Melt, but I'm not like you. I don't keep everything in like you do.'

'Oh, so if your husband was beating the crap out of you, you'd tell the whole world, would you?'

'I'd tell somebody.'

'I did tell somebody and look what happened.'

'Well what did mum say? Anyway I didn't tell her that, it was very vague, and she wheedled it out of me. I wouldn't just tell her something like that, when have I ever grassed you up?'

'A million times Louise. You used to dob me in it on an almost daily basis for years.'

'I did not!'

'Whatever,' I said, throwing one of her favourite phrases back at her.

'So what did mum say?'

'Oh that Michael's the greatest, he's so lovely, we're perfect together, they're just worried about me.'

'She didn't?'

'More or less.'

'Bugger. Did you set her straight?'

'What would be the point?'

Although we were united in a brief sisterly contempt of our parents, something in me couldn't quite forgive Louise for having broken a confidence, however vaguely, and however much mum may or may not have turned the screw. I didn't see her for ages after that, which probably only made me more vulnerable when... but I'll get to that later. I'm sure she meant well, but it irked me that she'd said anything to mum when I'd asked her not to. Now I couldn't trust her or my parents. I really only had Anna. If things got bad, she'd be the only person to help me. And they did get bad.

I was standing in the kitchen preparing dinner when Michael came in and opened a cupboard door, banging it into hard into my leg.

'Ouch, watch it!' He looked up from his crouch in front of the cupboard and just glared at me. I tensed, but said nothing. He closed the cupboard and went off again.

A bit later he came back and opened an eye-level cupboard and

with him, but I didn't want to give her the satisfaction. Cl
Michael was perfect, and if there were any problems it wa
fault. So much for the parental support. I was so relieved I h
told them anything about Michael, no doubt they wouldn't
believed me.

She gave me one of her little hugs. 'So will you be making
grandma soon? You don't want to leave it much longer.'

I laughed, but inside I was seething, 'No mum, I don't thin

The whole thing was just so predictably like my parents it v
true. Dad sitting in the lounge saying nothing, while mum p
me apart in the kitchen. Nothing was ever good enough for t
No that's not it; *I* was never good enough for them. It wa
nothing I did before Michael mattered – the respectful childl
the good degree, the well-paid job, my own well-tended fla
lack of debts or ever asking them to rescue me from sci
Sometimes when I was having a childish moment I thought
loved Louise more because she needed them more. I a
managed, I always made good on my own. It seemed that
gone up in their estimation by snagging a man like Michael.
I was complete, and naturally the two point four grandchi
would follow to make their lives perfect.

Thinking about it now, I can be more generous, knowing
they must have gone through. I make myself believe that if I'd
them the truth, if I'd gone round and showed my mum son
the bruises and really told her the truth, that they would
helped me, that they would have seen Michael for who he
was. But back then I just felt rejected and alone and determin
never turn to them for help.

Not long after that I had words with Louise. Me being me,
couldn't let it alone.

'What the hell did you tell mum for?'

'Tell mum what?'

'That Michael and I were having problems.' I did quot
marks with my fingers around the 'having problems' while g
her an evil look.

'I didn't mean to. It just slipped out.'

'That's not exactly the kind of thing that slips out.'

hit me in the face with the door. 'What the fuck, Michael?' I shouted, rubbing my face. 'If you want to hurt me, why don't you just hit me like you usually do?'

'I don't know what you're talking about. I haven't hit you since you made me go to that ridiculous counselling.'

'Which you haven't been going to.'

'Of course I have,' he stammered. It was obvious he was lying. I'd caught him off guard and he didn't have a snappy answer.

'Don't treat me like I'm stupid,' I said, 'don't think I don't know you haven't been for weeks.'

He grabbed my arm then and pulled it violently behind my back, twisting it at the same time. He pulled me towards him so our faces were close. The pain in my wrist brought tears to my eyes. 'Listen bitch,' he spat, 'I'm the boss, and I'm going to do what I want. And I won't be going to any more of those wanky shrink sessions, so get that straight.' He released me then, but just as quickly he squeezed me back against the worktop, so my injured arm was squashed and I cried out in pain. Then he left.

Within hours my wrist had ballooned to twice its size and I was sitting on the sofa with it on a cushion topped by a bag of frozen peas. This time he didn't try to make up, not that night or the next day, but continued to glare at me as though I was a stranger. I went to the GP the next morning and got my sprained wrist bandaged, claiming I had tripped up, and when I got to the office I called the women's refuge in-take counsellor.

I explained what had happened, and that there'd been no violence for a while, but that he'd stopped going to counselling. She was sympathetic, but said they had no free places at the shelter. She recommended that I find somewhere else to go, a friend or relative and that I didn't go to work because he'd be able to find me there.

That evening I took the bus home instead of the Tube and looked out of the upper deck window, searching for a hotel that might be reasonable to stay in. I saw a couple that looked OK and jotted down their names on a scrap of paper that I put in the inside pocket of my coat.

The atmosphere at home was tense. I tried to act as normally as possible, cooking for Michael, saying little, pretending my arm wasn't bandaged and aching. Pretending that I wasn't planning to leave him the next day and move out.

I dressed for work as usual. Once Michael had left, I looked out of the bedroom window, making sure he was walking to the train station, then I got changed into jeans and a jumper. I packed a small bag with clothes, some books and toiletries and put it in the bottom of the wardrobe. I called work and told them I wasn't feeling well, then I set off to check out the hotels I'd seen.

The first was a B&B which was nice and not too expensive, but the owner was a very chatty lady. She seemed lonely, maybe a widow, and she lived on the premises in some rooms on the ground floor. I thought she might be too nosey. I didn't want anyone chatting, however innocuously, about what I was doing, and why I was staying there. So I said I was looking at the place for a friend who was coming to London and I'd get back to her.

The second place was somewhat worn-out. It had certainly seen better and more fashionable days décor wise, but the rooms were nice enough and an en-suite was still within my budget, and best of all it was impersonal. The girl at reception seemed like she didn't really care who came or went and that she wouldn't notice whether I was there or not, never mind be able to describe me to any charming and smartly dressed men who might come looking for me, not that I expected for a minute that Michael would find me there. It was perfect. I booked for a week and paid a deposit in cash.

Going back out to the street, I almost collided with a woman jogger, we stared at each other for a second before both apologising. She looked rather like me. I turned and watched her run off, then walked slowly back home to collect my bag. My room wouldn't be available until 2 p.m. so I had plenty of time to kill.

I called Anna and told her I'd checked into a hotel.

'That's good. Don't tell me where it is. Michael is bound to come straight to me once he realises you're not coming home and if I genuinely don't know where you are it will be easier.'

'OK, I'll call you later.'

Walking back to the hotel, I stopped at an off licence and bought gin, tonic, a couple of bottles of wine and a cork screw. I intended to enjoy my new freedom with a few drinks and a good book. I hadn't thought what I would do long term. I wasn't planning to give up work, but for now I was off sick for a few days and away from Michael. There wouldn't be cupboard doors slamming into my face tonight.

I stashed my haul of goodies in the wardrobe, poured myself a stiff gin, and ran a deep bath.

Within a couple of days I was bored of day time TV, magazines and books. I went out shopping, but I was nervous. Every time I went out I felt like Michael would be looking for me, that somehow he'd find where I was. I wore headscarves and sun glasses. I bought myself a ridiculous hat that I'd never normally be seen dead in, but it made my head itch. I tried to enjoy the freedom of being able to do whatever I wanted, but I didn't feel free and I didn't feel safe and I couldn't afford to buy anything. I couldn't take any money out of the joint account in case it gave Michael a clue where I was, and I had to be sparing with my own money to cover the hotel and food. I spent much of my time brooding over whether Michael would be able to track me down and whether I should move to a new place after a few days, but I didn't want to feel like a fugitive on the run, it was bad enough being stuck in that scummy hotel without having to move every week too.

I called Anna and we picked a brand new place to meet where we'd never been before – The Natural History Museum. I'm sure I don't need to say it was Anna's choice, but it was inspired. Michael would never think of looking for me there.

'So, how's it going?'

'It could be worse, but I'm already bored out of my mind. How's life in the real world?' I was desperately trying to make light of it all for fear that otherwise I might break down at the realisation of how my life had turned to complete shit.

'You're still in the real world.'

'No, I'm not. It feels like some parallel universe! I'm scared to go out in case Michael sees me, I'm scared to go home in case he's there. I can't go to work and I don't know what I'm going to tell them.'

'Think of it as a holiday. Reading, TV, long baths, no Michael questioning your every move. It's only been a couple of days.'

'Hmm. So what's new with you?'

'Nothing. Same old thing. People die, I cut them up, do some microscope work.'

'No love interest then?' I wanted gossip. I wanted vicarious entertainment.

'What do you think?'

'Couldn't you find another nice gay scientist geek and you could huddle over a microscope together? Even Sam Ryan gets laid sometime.'

'In case you'd forgotten, Isabel, that's television.'

'Oh, it's not real?' I said in mock surprise. 'You mean you don't solve all the mysteries for the police while up to your elbows in internal organs?'

She kicked me playfully under the table. 'I have had some unwanted attention though.' I looked at her. 'Michael.'

'Oh.'

'Predictable, I suppose. He called me the day you left, wanting to know if you were at mine. Of course I said no. Then he called me two or three times later in the evening. He couldn't believe you weren't with me, and even less that I didn't know where you were. Then when I got home yesterday, he was waiting for me. He demanded that I tell him where you are.'

'Oh shit, he didn't get violent, did he?'

'No, he was really angry though, he was shaking. He just kept saying how I must know where you are. Eventually I said, "I don't know, and if I did I wouldn't tell you, you bastard, and if you don't leave now I'm calling the police," and I got my mobile out of my pocket and starting dialling. He stormed off then, shouting something about how he'd track you down.'

'I bet he'll try as well. He won't be able to find me though, will he?'

'I hope not. I suppose he could go to the police, report you as a missing person.'

I took a slug of my now cold cappuccino. 'Would he go to the police though?

That could backfire. If they find me and I tell them I left because of him.'

'Yeah, but you just never know with that arsehole. He's almost arrogant enough to think he could talk his way out of it. You really need to lay low though. You'd better stay in the hotel as much as you can.'

I made a face.

'Iz, I'm being serious. I've no doubt he'll do everything he can to try and find you. You can't go anywhere he might think to look.'

'Better live it up while I can then. Do they have any wine in this place?'

We went shopping then and Anna bought me loads of books to help me survive and gave me some money for meals.

The weekend was worse. Because I knew Michael wouldn't be at work and could be out looking for me, I was reluctant to go out. All of Saturday I stayed in, scared that he might be roaming the streets, thinking that even if I went to parts of London I'd never been to before, I might somehow bump into him. By Sunday afternoon I was climbing the walls and I went out anyway. I took the Tube as far as I could and walked around a distant park. But even then I couldn't relax. I turned up my jacket collar and pulled my itchy hat down over my face and I felt like a criminal on the run rather than a thirty-something woman taking a Sunday afternoon stroll in the park.

On Monday I called in sick again. I knew that sooner or later I would have to tell my employer what was going on, but I wasn't ready to make things that public. As the day went on I grew more and more despondent. OK, I was safe. I wasn't with Michael, and there was a real relief in that, but I felt like I had lost too much in return. I was stuck in this tiny room, with awful wallpaper and when I did go out I was permanently scared that Michael was waiting around some corner ready to grab me. I went to a phone box and called Anna at work. We arranged to meet later. She said she'd take me to somewhere Michael would never think to look.

It should have been obvious, but it didn't cross my mind that the last place Michael would look for me would be a lesbian bar.

'*Voila*,' said Anna, holding open the door. I went in. It was dimly lit, much like any other bar or nightclub, not that I was a connoisseur of nightclubs, Michael didn't like going to that kind of place, and I wasn't a huge fan myself. It wasn't until we were seated at a table with drinks that I realised there wasn't a man in the place, not even behind the bar. Anna gave me a knowing smile.

'Cunning,' I said.

'Linguist,' she retorted and laughed a dirty laugh. I elbowed her hard.

It also then dawned on me that Anna was very well dressed, well for Anna, in black jeans and a white shirt, crisply ironed. 'I hope you're not on the pull. I have serious issues to discuss you know.'

'I know,' she said, laying a hand on my arm, but you have to dress the part in these places. Thank goodness you didn't wear a skirt.'

Anna downed a third of her pint in one, while I knocked back my white wine. And for a while we just sat.

'Not many people here, are there?'

'It's way too early yet. Nothing gets going until after ten,' Anna said.

'I can't take much more of that bloody hotel. I feel like I'm going out of my mind. I'm going to have to go back to work.'

'But he'll find you there.'

'Not if I'm careful. I'll go in early or late and leave at different times every day.'

'I don't know,' she said, 'I reckon he'll pick that as the best place to find you, unless he thinks by now you've done a runner to somewhere else completely. He must be going spare.'

'I know. Has he called you any more?'

'Yeah he keeps calling, but he's down to just asking me to call him if I hear from you. I think he's decided I really don't know anything.'

'I wonder if he's called mum and dad and Louise. I bet he has. Oh God, now they'll all be worried.'

'I don't know. I'm not sure he will. He won't want to draw attention to the fact that he doesn't know where you are. That won't make him look good, will it?'

'That's true, and he does care about appearances.'

'And it's not like you're really close. You don't see them that much, or call them every week or anything. It's not like they're going to wonder where you are, not for a while, anyway. I take it you haven't told them?'

'No way. They just wouldn't get it. You know what they're like. They think Michael's God's gift.'

We sat in silence for a bit, drinking, and I enjoyed Anna checking out women as they went to the bar. She didn't even know she was doing it.

'I still think going back to work is a risk, though.'

'Well it's a risk I'm going to have to take or I'll lose my mind. He can't sit and watch my office 24/7. He has to hold down a job too.'

Going to that club reminded me of Anna's one and only long-term relationship – Siobhan. In so far as Anna had a 'type' she tended to like very feminine women, who while intelligent, had nothing to do with medicine. In fact they were often sporty, blonde, and...to put it bluntly, well endowed, which always struck me as odd because I would have thought Anna would want someone she could have a serious conversation with. But it seems that I never really understood what she wanted. Not that we talked about it much. She liked to keep her love life private and most of the time she seemed perfectly happy on her own.

I'm sure there were more flings than I ever got to know about, but none of them lasted very long, except Siobhan. She was different, which is perhaps why she lasted longer. Siobhan was feminine in a superficial kind of way – she wore skirts and make up, but she was definitely a strong independent woman. In fact she had a hint of the Margaret Thatcher about her! Not that I disliked her, I thought she was good for Anna in a way, but I suppose I never entirely warmed to her, probably because Anna spent less time with me while she was with Siobhan.

Anna never went all gooey and sentimental over her, she didn't have a romantic bone in her body, but it was obvious she was upset when they split up, and she didn't go out with anyone else for ages after that.

I knew it was serious when Anna asked me what she should get Siobhan for Valentine's Day.

'But you abhor Valentine's Day,' I said, shocked.

'I know. I do. But she'll think I don't care if I don't get her anything.'

'And you care that she'll care?!' Anna gave me a look that said I was on thin ice.

'Hmm, OK. You don't have to buy her anything, you could cook her dinner or something.'

'Yeah, I suppose so. It doesn't seem that original though.'

'I don't know, your spicy bolognaise is pretty original. Of course it might kill her, but it's original.'

'Very funny. Like you're a culinary genius.'

'I wouldn't say genius, but it's mostly edible.'

'Well, my food is *mostly* edible.'

'What about a diamond encrusted cycle clip?'

Anna gave me a withering look. 'That's what she should be getting me!' She quipped.

I think in the end Anna did plump for cooking her dinner, and it went down rather well. For a while it was all I heard about – Siobhan this and Siobhan that – most unlike Anna. Is that how I was when I'd first been going out with Michael? No wonder Anna got sick of it.

Siobhan was quite like Anna in a way, but less geeky. She was some kind of skin expert. They'd met at a conference and Siobhan's paper on the latest techniques in getting fingerprints off human flesh had made Anna go weak at the knees. Well, whatever lights your candle, I suppose. Siobhan was surprisingly attractive. I don't want to sound mean, but a lot of lesbians, just aren't, well they're not that feminine or appealing, but Siobhan was – glossy hair, lipstick, brilliant clothes sense. I suppose she was Anna's type apart from the fact that she had a brain as well. I don't know why they split up, Anna mumbled something about commitment issues, but I always suspected Siobhan dumped her and broke her heart. Anna would never admit to having such emotions. Secretly, I wasn't unhappy that they split up, because I saw so little of Anna while they were together. I know it sounds selfish, but I'm glad Anna didn't have anyone serious on the go when I really needed her. It was almost like the breakup with Siobhan prevented her from getting close to anyone else, but she didn't like to talk about it once it was all over. But after Siobhan it was just work, Molly, the odd fling and saving Isabel.

❦

I stuck it out at the hotel one more day and on Wednesday I went back to work. I didn't get there until ten and all the while I kept alert. I checked behind me. I went totally out of my way, walking some of the way and taking a Tube and a bus instead of going directly and I didn't loiter in reception. By the time I got to my desk I felt exhausted, but elated. I'd made it. Now I was in the building I was safe, though I was going to have to think of some story to tell reception to make sure that if Michael came asking for me they wouldn't let him in or tell him I was there. In hindsight it would have been easier and safer to tell everyone the truth, but I didn't want them to know. I didn't want everyone muttering by the photocopier, speculating on my domestic situation and I didn't want them thinking Michael was some kind of a nutter.

'Oh, you're back,' said Katherine. 'How are you? You don't look great.'

'Thanks!'

'I didn't mean it like that; I just mean you look tired. We've been worried about you. It's not like you to have so long off work.'

'I know, it was the flu, I still feel a bit weak to be honest, but I was going stir crazy. Anything urgent I need to know about?'

'Not really urgent. I've tried to keep on top of it, but,' she pointed at my in-tray which was bulging.

'Right. Is Dave in?'

'Yeah.'

'I'd better have a word then.'

Dave was my boss. He was pretty laid back and not too demanding, like he just happened to be head of our section rather than our boss. He expected us to get on with things, and he didn't want us bothering him unnecessarily, but I was going to have to tell him something, especially if I was going to be coming and going at unusual hours. I knocked on his glass door and went in.

'Hi Isabel. How are you feeling? Raring to go?' he gave a nervous laugh. He was a nice man, but not as adept as he could be at the social skills and he had to make a conscious effort to be the caring, sympathetic boss he hoped he was. 'Yes. I was going nuts at home. The flu, it really knocked me for seven. I'm still feeling a bit weak in fact, so I may have to come in late and leave early for a few more days. See how it goes.'

'Fine, fine. You know we're on flexi-time here. I'm sure you'll get on top of things soon.'

'And, well, there's another thing. It's Michael. He's had a bit of a health scare. He's having lots of tests and things, and so I might have to work round that too.'

'Oh dear, that sounds serious. Do they, um, well, you know, do they know what it is?'

'Not really.'

'Oh. Never rains, but it pours eh?' He laughed nervously again. 'Take whatever time you need Isabel. I'm sure we'll manage. Keep me posted.'

The rest of the morning flew by. You wouldn't believe how absorbing messages and filing and paperwork can be after over a week of doing nothing. We each had our own private voicemail that no one else could listen to. We usually forwarded our calls if we were on holiday, but that hadn't been done with me being off sick. Needless to say many of the messages were from Michael. They started out reasonably calm:

'Iz, where are you? You can't be working this late. Call me.'

'Where the hell are you, I'm worried.'

They got progressively more angry and distressed, until the last one was along the lines of: 'Listen you bitch, I don't know where you are, but you'd better come home soon or there'll be trouble. I will find you, if it's the last thing I do,' and the phone slamming down. There were emails too. I deleted them all and tried to put

Michael out of my mind. I knew that he'd be coming to the office after work to look for me, but I was confident I could avoid him if I was careful.

I stayed later than usual, and fortunately Katherine was there too on a conference call, so we left and walked to the Tube station together. I tried to be nonchalant and not keep looking around me, but I was scared, I won't deny it. Once we'd parted company in the station, I doubled back and went out of a different exit and again made a circuitous journey back to the hotel, constantly checking that no one was following me.

The next day passed in much the same way and by Friday I was starting to relax a little. I arrived super early, before anyone else, and got loads done in the quiet of the office. Early afternoon, my phone rang and I must have sounded cheerful when I answered it. There was silence, and I knew. I knew it was Michael. I hung up, my hands shaking. I tried calling Anna, but she wasn't available. I drank way too much coffee, trying to calm myself down, but it only made things worse.

Eventually Anna answered. 'Hey, how's it going?'

'I'm, he's, I...'

'Calm down. You're back at work?'

'Yes, been here since Wednesday. But I had this phone call earlier. He didn't say anything, but I'm sure it was Michael. He knows I'm here. What am I going to do?'

'OK. OK, let's think this through. Does anyone there know what's going on?'

'No.'

'Bollocks.' I heard her tapping a pen in the background. 'Um, are there people you can leave with? Can you leave now?'

'I guess I could, but it's still early. It would be better to leave with other people wouldn't it?'

'Yes, I think so. I can't get away right now. It's Friday; do people usually go for drinks after work?'

'Yes, yes the finance boys do and sometimes some others.'

'Good, OK so leave with them and go to the pub and then call me and I'll come and meet you.'

I wasn't entirely convinced by our plan, but it seemed workable in theory. If I was always with people Michael wouldn't do anything, but he was clever, I knew he'd bide his time until he found an opportunity. I was so stupid. What made me think I could go back to work and he wouldn't find out? I didn't get any work done that afternoon worrying about what would happen, and as soon as Phil asked if anyone was going to the pub I was on with my coat and heading out the door with them, trying to put myself in the middle of as many guys as I could.

The pub was Friday afternoon busy. Plenty of places for Michael to hide and watch me, if he'd wanted to, but I tried not to think about that. I had one gin and tonic to calm my nerves and then switched to soft drinks. I needed to be totally on my guard. I half listened to the office gossip and sports trivia and plans for the weekend, but mostly I was looking around me. I held out until around 6 p.m. when I thought Anna might be free to come and meet me and headed off to the toilets and pay phone. When I came out of the loo, an arm went round my waist and stubble brushed up against my ear.

'Cause a scene and I'll kill you.' It was Michael. It sounds bizarre, but it was almost a relief. The inevitable had happened and now I no longer had to worry about it happening. He took one of my arms and pulled it tight behind my back. 'Do you understand me?'

I nodded. He released his grip, but kept his hand on my hip turning me round to face him. He looked terrible. Unshaven, hair flopping greasily over his eyes, his shirt unpressed under a suit that looked like it had been slept in. 'I've missed you Izzy. Where have you been? I've been going crazy with worry.'

'I, well, er...' I didn't know what to say. What could I say?

'Never mind,' he said. 'I've found you now, that's all that matters. Let's go home. I won't hold it against you. I'm just glad I found you.'

His reaction was so bizarre, it took me completely by surprise. It was as if I'd been kidnapped, or shipwrecked, as if he thought I was dead and now he'd found me. He seemed to have no realization that I might have left because of him. He'd gone from psycho wanting to kill me to lost little boy in a matter of seconds.

'I'm here with some friends. I'm not sure I want to go home,' I said, testing the water while we were still in public and I could summon help.

He put on a pained expression. 'I don't want to hurt you, I really don't, but you need to come home now Isabel. You can't keep on hurting me. You need to come home.'

Looking back now, I don't know why I went with him. Did I feel sorry for him? Was I scared? Yes, I was afraid. I believed then and I still do that he was capable of killing me if I pushed him too far, if the situation went out of his control. But I was in a bar full of people, colleagues from work and friends, hundreds of people, I could have shouted, I could have screamed that he was attacking me and surely people would have taken my side. Michael would have been arrested, maybe even charged. But in those few seconds I had to weigh up the options and make a decision. His hand had never left hold of my body. His words and his eyes chilled me to the bone and somewhere inside, in the intrinsic, biological ancient part of you that keeps you alive I knew I couldn't scream. I might get away with it then, but sooner or later he'd make me pay. If I went with him I had a chance to live. We went home.

※

I might have known Michael wouldn't like Christmas. I loved it. I loved buying presents for everyone, choosing just the right thing and wrapping them all carefully. My house was always full of decorations, mostly tasteful, but there were the Santa Claus and reindeer collections that had to be accommodated. I loved the terrible programmes on TV and playing board games and eating too many sweets. The longer we stayed together the more dismal Christmas became. Michael's watchful eye on the accounts took the pleasure out of buying presents because I had to account for every penny even though we had plenty of money. And of course Michael couldn't abide family get togethers but civility meant he couldn't get out of them, or at least not all of them. We even had to endure his family at Christmas as well as mine and that was never a cheerful affair. Over the years I came to dread Christmas because it put Michael in a bad mood, and Michael in a bad mood was never a good thing for me. Still I have fond memories of the first Christmas in our new house.

'I got you an advent calendar.'

'Oh, what for?'

'Because it's nearly Christmas and it's fun and…don't you get advent calendars in your family?'

'No.'

'Oh. Oh well, I thought it would be nice.' I said, a bit deflated.

'It is,' he said, putting his arms round me. 'You're one of those people who loves Christmas aren't you?'

I nodded. 'Don't tell me, you don't?'

'Not really. Christmas is never that festive growing up when you're the only child and it reminds your parents that there's a child missing.'

'Of course. You poor boy. Well we'll have to make our first Christmas extra special then.' Michael didn't look enthusiastic at the prospect.

'What do you want for Christmas?'

'For there to be no Christmas.'

'Apart from that, Scrooge!'

'Hmm, I dunno. To go away and miss the whole thing?'

'That seems a bit anti-social. Maybe we could go away just after Christmas.'

Michael looked much happier at that suggestion. 'I know, you can dress up as Santa and ravage me!'

'Oh, now that does sound promising,' he said, wrestling me to the sofa, 'ho, ho, ho!'

I wonder what Michael's first Christmas without me was like. If he missed me? If he wished then that he'd let me enjoy Christmas more while we were together.

My mind seems to have blocked out most of that weekend. I was shocked, relieved, scared, and highly aware of the need for self-preservation and being totally on my guard all the time. That first night Michael clung to me like I was his comfort blanket, murmuring how much he'd missed me, how glad he was he'd found me, how he'd never let me go again, how he'd never hurt me again. It was so creepy I wanted to vomit.

I thought he was going to keep by my side constantly, that he wouldn't let me out of his sight, but Michael had another plan. Maybe he thought that if he did that it would drive a wedge between us, that I'd just struggle even harder to break free. He didn't seem to realise that he was the reason I'd left. He thought somehow we could go back to the way things had been. He didn't want to know where I'd been, or why.

'All water under the bridge Iz. I'm just glad you're back. It doesn't matter where you went. We need to work at things, make things great again.'

'Great'? Had things ever been great?

But at the same time he was able to instil fear with a single word or look. He didn't need to watch me day and night because now I had the fear more than ever. I knew what lengths he would go to, that he would camp outside my office building if he had to, or follow me, or even pay someone else to follow me, if that's what it took to make sure I never left again. If he'd hurt me before it was nothing to what I thought he'd do now. It's hard to describe, but I just believed he was capable of killing me. That he would kill me if I tried to leave again. And even living with Michael was better than being dead. I would find a way to make it work. I would promise to never leave if that's what it took. I would say we needed to make it look like we had no problems, like nothing was wrong, a united front against the world. That would appeal to him. In time I would say I needed to work and see Anna and my family so that no one would know anything was wrong, so that we could rebuild what we'd had. It was all about playing the game. If Michael could play, I had to find a way to play it better, to be smarter than he was. It was a challenge, but I did it. I played the game for months, with Anna as my reluctant counsellor and co-conspirator. If Anna had abandoned me, I think I would have just shrivelled and given up. Michael oscillated constantly between repentant, conciliatory lover and prison guard. Ironically, he hit me much less, though every now and then he couldn't help himself, but mainly he concentrated on control, on mind games, on keeping the fear alive.

I got so tired. Tired of Michael always needing to know where I was and who I was with. My attempt to leave had unnerved him and made him vulnerable and Michael did not like being vulnerable. He hated it. And as his hate grew, his control of me grew. He did everything he could to keep tabs on me and make sure I didn't slip away again. He barely tolerated Anna any more. He was convinced she was behind my wish to leave him, that left to make up my own mind I wouldn't even consider running away. He tried to prevent me seeing her, but we always managed somehow. I still met her for lunch from work sometimes, and we talked on the phone every Saturday while Michael was at squash, and any chance we got when he was out she would sneak round.

Michael bought me a mobile phone and insisted that I kept it on all the time when we were apart, but not when we were together, obviously. He didn't want *my* friends interrupting our perfect marriage. Not that I had many friends left by then. On the rare occasions when he let me go out, other than to work, he'd call, always at the most inopportune moment, to ask when I'd be coming home. No wonder I had so few friends – they had to be very long suffering to spend time with me, especially as I'd still told no one the truth except Anna and Louise. I'm sure people could tell I was lying when I said I was all right, and that things with Michael were fine. It was clear something was wrong – what normal husband calls you five times when you're out for a quick drink after work? I began to hate mobile phones for the constant communication they provided. I swore when I got away, if I ever got away again, that I'd never have a mobile. It didn't do any good to ignore it and not answer, he'd just keep calling until I did answer, too embarrassed by the beeping flashing security tag by my hand. I tried once or twice turning the thing off, but you can guess what happened then, it provided the perfect excuse for his behaviour – 'what have I told you about keeping your phone on?' Usually answering it didn't help much either, I'd still be home too late, or gone too long, or spent too much money. It served no purpose except to sour my evening, make me feel uncomfortable, like I shouldn't have friends, or a life, as if I was being disloyal by not being at home with him. But if he felt in the mood he'd go out and leave me at home alone. He always told me about his plans at the last minute, so that it would be too late to arrange anything with my friends, so I'd be at home, waiting for him to get back, so I'd know what it felt like, he said; the selfish bastard.

But I was too scared to go out, scared he'd come home early to find me not there and then there'd really be hell to pay. Sometimes I would call Anna since she's a workaholic and has no life, and she was often on call so she could be expectant just as well at my house as anywhere else. It was safer if she came to me, because if Michael did come home unexpectedly she could dive out the back. We made all sorts of preparations. We were always plotting. I positioned the garden bench in such a way that she could climb on it and then over the low wall. She always used to leave her coat and bicycle pannier (Anna didn't do handbags) next to the unlocked back door so she could grab them on the way out (Michael is a creature of habit and always came in the front.) She very reluctantly left Molly the Moulton out in the street with her helmet locked to it, for a quicker get away. We even used to drink out of one wine glass so that if she had to leave in a hurry I wouldn't be caught out by him discovering two glasses.

Later on I got braver, after I realised that he was going to hit me whatever I did or didn't do, dependent only on his whims. That was quite liberating, the realisation that it didn't matter what I did, I could do whatever I wanted. It took away his power. Well up to a point it did, I paid for my freedom of course, because it gave him excuses, but still it gave me a certain edge. That's probably what saved me, what made me start planning how I could get away again. What a fool! Clearly a little bravery is as dangerous as a little wisdom. But survival is a mental thing and the thought that maybe he didn't always have the upper hand, that I could get around his minefield of restrictions and curfews and punishments kept me going.

I still had my job. No matter how much Michael begged and bullied me to give it up, I stood resolute. I knew if I lost my financial independence I'd never have a hope of getting away from him. Leaving Michael every day to interact with normal (I use the term loosely – we are talking about insurance brokers!) people was one of the few things that kept me sane. I know he would have preferred me to stay at home and play the model housewife – that had been one of the topics on our list of standard arguments from the day we got married – why I couldn't just stay at home? Can you imagine, being dependent on him for everything? Not having any money of my own? But I'm getting off the point. I still had to put my salary in the joint account. There was no way Michael would let me get away with doing anything else, but for years I'd been putting my bonuses in my own account that he didn't know about. He was also reasonably generous with the housekeeping and I usually managed to save a little each month from that. After a while I started to think of it as my escape fund. I kept the pass book in my desk drawer at the office and I used to look at the balance every day, watching it accrue, calculating how far I might get with it.

Sometimes he'd say, 'They don't appreciate you much at that place. Why do you stay when they never give you a raise? When they never promote you? All that time you've been with the company. What good does it do you?'

He liked to put me down; it was one of his favourite occupations. I'd just say, 'I like it there,' and he'd shrug and change the subject. I think he was afraid if he went on too much I might leave and get an even better job, and he wouldn't like that because then he'd have to start all over again finding out where my new office was and building a rapport with the receptionist so he could keep tabs on my whereabouts without it seeming too weird. And he wouldn't have liked it if I got a job that was too impressive, it would show him up. He had to be top dog, top wage earner. My salary was good, but nothing compared to his – that was the way he liked it. I didn't tell Michael much about my work, I liked to let him think I was just a glorified secretary. He knew I left the office sometimes, it was one of the things that most rattled him, because he couldn't be sure exactly what I was doing then, but he thought it was just to deliver papers or something. He didn't know that I often went to visit clients. If he'd seen me out and about in London, meeting mostly male clients he'd have had a fit. I wonder what those brokers would have thought if they'd known I was perfectly comfortable in their presence and scared shitless of my own husband.

It was one of those nights when Michael was out with his work colleagues. He'd come in as I was cooking dinner and said he was going out again. I felt like throwing the pan at him, not because I wanted him to stay in, by then I was thankful for any respite I got from him, but just because it was so frustrating. Some of the girls from work were going out to celebrate Jackie's engagement and I'd had to turn them down to avoid causing a scene at home. I looked at my watch and wondered whether I could still go and meet them, but I knew I wouldn't relax if I went. Michael would be bound to call the house a couple of times during the evening and it wasn't worth the effort. I had to save my strength and my battles for things I really cared about.

I called Anna at work.

'Hi, you just caught me.'

'Doing what?'

'Going home.'

'So early. You feeling all right?'

'Very funny. There's an article on the pathophysiology of haemostasis I want to read.'

'Ooh, fascinating. Well, I've got some chicken in white wine and rice simmering, if you're remotely interested.'

'I'll be right over! I take it Michael's not around.'

'No, last minute plans with his work chums. If I had a dog his dinner would be in it, but since I don't...'

'Thanks very much!'

We'd finished dinner and were sitting in the lounge with the telly on in the background.

'I'm surprised Michael hasn't called yet. He usually "checks in" when he's out.'

'I don't know how you stand it Iz.'

'Neither do I. It's only by constantly thinking about how I can get away next time.

And you,' I said, 'I don't think I could keep going without you.'

Anna sidestepped the emotion implied by that confession. 'So, what's your next cunning plan?'

'I don't know. I've been thinking about what you said ages ago, about moving away, getting a transfer. My friend Sarah lives in Edinburgh, that's a good long way away, maybe I could go and stay with her. Unless you've had any bodies tip up at the hospital that look just like me!'

'Maybe we could just kill somebody who looks like you.'

'Oh Anna, don't even think about it. You know we couldn't.'

'Do you?' she said, with a peculiar look on her face. She rubbed her hands together, 'You know how I like cutting up bodies!'

'Oh shut up.'

'Or let's just bump off Michael. Think how satisfying that would be.'

'Yes, wouldn't it?' said a voice from the door. Michael. We hadn't even heard him come in. 'I might have known you and this bitch would be plotting against me, but I never thought you'd stoop to murder.'

'Michael, I...'

'What, didn't think I'd be back so soon? No, obviously you didn't.'

'I mean, we were just...'

'Shut up,' he said, slapping me across the face.

'Oi,' said Anna, standing up.

'And what are you going to do, you interfering bitch?' He grabbed hold of her jumper. 'Get out of my house.'

'Not if you're going to hurt Izzy.'

'And how are you going to stop me, you midget?' He half pushed, half pulled her towards the door. Anna's knee came up sharply into his groin. Michael groaned and let go of her. He straightened up. His face was red and sweating. I hadn't seen him this angry in a long time.

'You'd better go,' I said.

'I'm not leaving you with this monster.'

'You're making it worse.'

'Get the hell out of my house, before I kill you.' Michael lunged at her, but Anna sidestepped back out of the door into the hall. Michael threw his right hand at her, but caught the door frame and yelped in pain.

'Go Anna. I'll be all right.'

Michael held his hand in his left armpit, desperately trying not to show the pain he was in. Anna said, 'OK, I'm going, but if Isabel doesn't call my mobile in half an hour to say she's OK, I'm calling the police and they will come round, and they will arrest you.'

She made for the door. Michael glared at her. Before she left, she said, 'and call me at work first thing tomorrow. If I don't hear that Izzy is all right, I'll be sending the police to look for you Michael.'

The front door banged and Michael slumped into the arm chair.

'Let me look at your hand.'

'Get away from me, you murderer.'

'Oh Michael, don't be like that, we were just fooling around. Come on.'

Eventually he relented and withdrew his hand. It was already swollen and turning blue. I went to the kitchen and came back with a bag of frozen peas and pressed it against his knuckles.

'Ah shit that hurts.' I wondered if he'd realise then how much he hurt me when he punched me or twisted my wrists. He began to calm down. 'Maybe you should put this on your cheek.'

'Huh?' I touched my face. It felt hot where he'd slapped me. 'It's OK, it's not bad.'

'I'm sorry Iz.' He looked down at his lap. When he raised his eyes they were moist with tears. 'Why don't you love me any more?'

Because you do shit like this, I wanted to say, but I knew it wouldn't do any good.

'I do, but you always spoil things. What's wrong with me having Anna round? You'd gone out and left me on my own, why shouldn't I see my friends too?'

'Because you plot to kill your husband with your friends! When I see my friends we just have a few drinks and talk about banking.'

'Oh and you never complain about your wives?'

He looked bashful. 'I love you Isabel. I'm so scared of you leaving me.'

I let him hug me. I wished he didn't love me so much, then maybe he'd let me out of his sight now and then. 'I'd better call Anna, unless you want the police round here.'

I still hadn't saved that much money by then, but after Michael's outburst with Anna, I thought the sooner I could get away the better. If I could just get away somewhere far enough, stay with a friend, they'd help me get settled, I wouldn't need a fortune to do that. My thoughts came back to Sarah. She lived about as far away as I could get. We'd been at university together. We hadn't seen much of each other since she'd moved back to Edinburgh, just Christmas cards and the occasional email, but we'd been very close at uni. Real hang out pals, mostly getting pissed, but we were there through the crappy boyfriends (her), the bad grades (me), and all the usual 'just left home, I wanna be an adult, but I'm not' angst. I was sure she'd welcome a visit and once I explained my situation, I knew she'd help me. I'd help her out in the same sort of situation, wouldn't I? Edinburgh was a vibrant place; I could get a job up there. I knew I'd get a good reference. Our company maybe even had a branch there. I could look into it. So I booked three weeks off work and emailed Sarah asking if I could come and visit her for a weekend. I didn't tell her what was going on, I thought I'd tell her once I got there, then it would be harder for her to refuse me staying a bit longer. I had this burning mania to run away, to stop my life the way it was and start a new one.

I thought I'd covered everything. I emailed Sarah from work and deleted the message and all subsequent ones, and wiped out my 'trash' box. The only person I told where I was going was Anna and in paranoid overdrive I only told her in person and made her promise not to try and contact me. She wasn't hard to convince. I didn't give her the address or any contact details, just in case Michael tried to bully them out of her. I booked time off work, but didn't mention my plans to anyone.

I packed a few things, just enough for a weekend, to tie in with my story to Michael and to not alert him to the possibility that I'd left for good. He was bound to go out of his mind as soon as he realised I'd gone even if he thought it was just for a weekend. By then I hardly ever went out on my own apart from going to work. I had to see friends at lunchtime, but even then unless he had a working lunch, he always called. But at least he'd cut back on spying on me leaving the office. When I first came back from the hotel he met me outside work every night, but gradually even he had started to relax and I think he'd started to believe I wouldn't leave him again. He turned up every now and then, just to remind me who was in charge and stop me getting 'any ideas.' He was going to go spare when he got home and realised I'd gone away for a whole weekend (so he'd think) without telling him beforehand. That gave me pause for a minute, imagining how he'd react, but not for long, I'd be miles away. I'd be safe! I left him a note on the fridge, 'gone to a friend's, an unexpected crisis (hers) – back Sunday.' I thought if I didn't leave a note with a viable explanation he might call the police and say I was missing or he would start hassling Anna. I didn't want to be found by the police or anyone else. I didn't intend to go back on Sunday, or any other day. I'd lie low at Sarah's for a while and decide what I was going to do.

I went straight from work, left early, caught the train. I felt so free. I couldn't remember when I'd last felt like that. There was always that shadow hanging over me. At work, every time the phone rang I wondered if it was Michael checking up on me. Every time we were apart and the phone rang I *knew* it was Michael. When I was at home, I felt like a prisoner in my own house, while he came and went as he pleased, never lifting a finger to help with the housework but always criticising the way I did things. I was a double prisoner – I acted as a warden too, self-censoring myself: don't stay out too late. What mood will he be in tonight? When will he phone? So that not even my thoughts were my own.

Just then my mobile rang. I looked at it – Michael. I ignored it. He'd be home by now, he'd have seen the note, he would start, 'What the hell do you think you're doing?' or some such. It kept ringing. I shoved it further into my bag and did up the zip. What I really should have done was ditch the phone, but I thought I might need it myself for something, and I wanted to be able to keep in touch with Anna. The train was packed, people going home for the weekend, or to visit relatives. Fellow passengers were looking at me. I smiled and tried to ignore them. As soon as my mobile stopped ringing I retrieved it from my bag and turned it off. I sat for a long time just looking out of the window, thinking how angry he'd be. I felt smug and pleased with myself for getting this far – why hadn't I done this before? It was so easy – just get on a train and go somewhere, he didn't know where I was. Unless I gave in and answered the phone and told him he couldn't know where I'd gone. And I wasn't going back to work this time, so he couldn't track me down there. I'd been careful not to order my train ticket online or over the phone, I'd just bought it at the station. I probably paid more that way, but the extra security was worth it. I'd even paid cash. I wouldn't put it past Michael to be able to look at the computer history, or call the phone company and see who I had called recently. See, I had his number up to a point. I just didn't realise quite how devious and desperate he'd be.

Mixed with the happy smug feeling was the tightness of fear in my stomach. What would happen if he did catch up with me? But I convinced myself he wouldn't. Scotland was hours and miles away. Scotland was safe. Eventually I took out my book and started to read, tried to keep up the pretence of someone ordinary. It was some sort of trashy Cinderella story where the unhappy single woman met the man of her dreams and they live happily ever after. I'd bought it at the station, just for something to occupy me. I thought how happy I'd be if I were single. All the things I would do. Would I ever be free of Michael? I couldn't divorce him – that would mean some sort of contact, if only through solicitors, he'd find where I was then and he'd never let me go again. It was hard to concentrate on such a banal book, well it was just hard to concentrate on anything with me taking such a monumental step, and the train so crowded, and being all jumbled up with feelings, the fear and the joy fighting it out in my innards. I took to people-watching, the young couple with a toddler in a push chair, the business man dozing over his *Financial Times*, the group of women chattering about shopping and clubbing. They were from Edinburgh by the sound of it, and they ran off names of places they would go to, restaurants and clubs. I tried to take in some of the names for future reference, but I couldn't concentrate on that either, I was too wound up, but Sarah would show me round and tell me everything I needed to know.

The journey went remarkably quickly. I threw the trashy novel in the first bin I saw – real life wasn't like that and the handsome man carrying me off into the sunset wasn't my kind of escapism. Sarah was there waiting for me. We hugged for a long time, maybe too long. I needed someone to hang on to. She pulled away first. 'Well this is a blast from the past,' she said in that soft Edinburgh accent of hers. She looked just the same as I remembered her from uni, funky blonde hair, tight jeans. 'Things must be bad for you to look me up,' she joked. 'Come on, we need to get you seriously drunk.'

We settled into a booth in a flashy bar on Queen Street. 'Wine or cocktails?'

'Cocktails.' She ordered two Long Island Teas. 'That'll get us started. So, should you not call the man, let him know you arrived safely?'

'No, let him seethe,' I said in a moment of bravado.

'Ooh, he's really pissed you off, eh! Is that why you're here? Let's have the whole gory story then.'

'No, I need to warm up to it. Tell me what you've been up to.'

'All boring stuff.'

'I doubt that. How's your love life? You haven't sent me any tantalising titbits lately!'

'I don't exist purely for your entertainment you know,' she said, taking a long gulp and doing that thing she used to do with her eyes – extreme eye rolling we used to call it – EER. I hadn't realised how much I'd missed her. 'Well, I had a very on off thing with a bloke who worked on the oilrigs. More off than on, obviously. Great shag, terrible conversationalist, so you know he had to go.'

'Mmm, and now?'

'I'm going through a celibate phase,' she held her hand up to her forehead like someone in a period drama, I laughed out loud. 'I don't believe that for a minute!'

'No, it's absolutely true. Two weeks, three days, six hours and thirty-two minutes.'

We laughed and finished our drinks. Sarah raised a hand to the man behind the bar and almost immediately two fresh drinks arrived. 'Do you know him?'

'Ex-shag.'

'Oh honestly!'

'So tell me,' she said, 'what's up with you?'

I sat staring at my drink. I didn't know where to start, how to start. I wasn't used to telling people about Michael. There was Katherine at work, who sensed my moods, who covered for me when I was off sick, who wondered why my husband called so much and intuitively knew it wasn't 'young love.' But I fobbed her off with 'we're going through a bad patch,' or 'over did it a bit last night.' She never asked for more details and I never gave her any. It was a natural collusion between women – all men are bastards sometimes, we have to stick together. There was Louise, who I now told very little, after she'd spilled the beans to mum. I'd let her believe things were better. I had told her about staying at the hotel and Michael making me go back, but I made out things were different since then, that he'd learnt his lesson, though I'm not sure how much she believed me. And there was Anna, who knew the whole story. That was it, one person in the world who knew what a monster Michael really was.

Sarah reached over and touched my hand. 'Come on, it can't be that bad, is it?'

I nodded. 'Yes, it is. He...He hits me.' There I'd finally said it.

Sarah looked shocked. 'Michael? But...Well, I never did like him that much, but I wouldn't have taken him for…'

'How could you tell you didn't like him? You only met him once at our wedding.'

'I dunno, sometimes you just have a feeling about someone.'

'Strange. You're not the only one. I wish I'd had a feeling about him.' I joked, trying to lift my mood.

'So how long has this been going on?'

I took a long gulp of my drink. 'A long time. Since not that long after we were married.'

'What? Jesus, but that's years ago! Oh Iz. Why are you still with him? You've told the police, right? Have you been to a women's shelter?' She was talking nine to the dozen like she does when she's flustered. I couldn't believe she'd come up with two options in thirty seconds, but it's always easier to solve other people's problems than look at your own. I started remembering Sarah's propensity for trying to fix everyone other than herself. Well, that could be a good thing; I needed fixing.

Anyway, where was I? I think I held up my hand, or maybe I just looked at her, but something stopped her in her tracks. 'I tried the police, it just made things worse.'

'But didn't you ask for him to be arrested? There must have been bruises and stuff. Surely they could see…'

I sighed. 'You don't know what he's like. He's so believable. He just said it was nothing, and then when they'd gone he went ballistic, said he'd kill me if I ever called them again.'

I could see her trying to fathom such an evil mind, clearly none of her undesirable and useless boyfriends had ever come anywhere close to a raised voice, let alone a raised hand, judging by her expression anyway, but maybe I'm being unkind. It's true what they say; you can never truly know what someone else is feeling, even if you've had a similar experience.

'What about a women's refuge? There must be loads in London, aren't there? I mean, I reckon there'd be places like that.'

I shook my head. 'I couldn't bring myself too. Then eventually I called and they were full, so I went and stayed at a hotel. I thought he wouldn't be able to find me, but he did. Long story.' I downed the rest of my drink. 'I haven't come just for the weekend Sarah.

I've come to stay. I've run as far as I could run. I'm going to stay up here, find a job...' my voice trailed off. It suddenly seemed like a farcical idea. A stunt I'd never pull off, and I had no reason to believe Sarah would help me.

'Bloody hell, Iz! I wouldn't have taken you for the kind to make an entrance. It's the quiet ones you have to watch! Don't see a girl for years, then she shows up on your doorstep having left her woman-hating husband and wants to move in!'

'No, I, it's just for a week or two 'til I get myself sorted out.'

She took my hand again. 'I'm kidding you tube! I know my comic timing is shite. You can stay as long as you want.'

We got well and truly hammered. It was just like being students again. Two more cocktails, while I told her 'all the gory details', well not all of them, but enough, and I was well gone. Sarah never had any problem holding her drink. Neither did I, back in the day, but I was somewhat out of practice. I never got the opportunity to go out drinking with friends and though I drank at home, I didn't overdo it. I never wanted to be so inebriated that Michael could take more advantage of me than he already did. I didn't want to turn into some old sad sack with a drink problem; I had to keep myself strong. Sure Anna and I had the occasional glass of wine, sometimes even a bottle, but that's not the same as really going for it.

Sarah led me out onto the street. It was still daylight, the sun just setting. The street full of people. I felt happy. I thought I'd really cracked it. Everything was going to be OK. We went to that curry house, the one we used to go to for special occasions, a step up from our usual student fare. I never did understand why people went for a curry when they were pissed, I'd always preferred chips, but it was perfect. We crunched our way through poppadoms and pickles to stave off our cocktail induced hunger, then found we'd ordered way too much and though we stuffed ourselves with rice, balti, chicken korma and that spinach thing we always ordered and then didn't really want, it didn't look like we'd made a dent in the dishes. Of course it was all washed down with the ubiquitous Kingfisher. I'm not much of a lager drinker, but it had to be done. It was like being twenty again. No worries. No Michael. Just me and Sarah, and a good time. The inevitable giggle at the waiter's accent, the bickering over who would pay the bill, the cold wait for a taxi.

I didn't take much notice of where we were, or what Sarah's flat was like. She did that fumbling with the key thing, while we both leaned against the door in hysterics, me crossing my legs trying not to wet myself, she going 'ssshh, neighbours'. She finally got the door open and we fell into the flat. Sarah pointed down a corridor to the bathroom and I made a dash for it. When I reappeared she was in the living room with a blanket and pillow. 'Sofa bed I'm afraid, I've only got one bedroom'

'Yeah fine. It's great. Thank you so much for letting me stay.'

'Don't wake me up early,' she said, pointing a finger at my chest. She knew from past experience that I tended to wake up early if I'd drunk too much, especially when we used to smoke, over stimulated and cranky, desperately wanting sleep but having to wait until a civilised hour to get up and make noise.

'Promise,' I slurred, and hugged her.

It was a big sofa, and I couldn't be bothered to open it out. I stripped down to Tshirt and pants, lay down under the blanket and passed out before my head hit the pillow. When I woke, the sun was streaming through the vertical blinds. I gingerly eased myself up. Bit of a headache, but not bad, not bad at all considering. I looked at my watch, ten o'clock. Another first. I swung my feet to the floor, still testing my hangover, but it was OK. No sign of Sarah, but I couldn't be accused of waking her early.

In the kitchen I downed a pint of water and put the kettle on, looking around for tea bags and opening cupboards to look for mugs. Back on the sofa, under blanket, I fished in my bag for my phone. I hadn't looked at it since I'd turned it off on the train. I put it under the blanket so the powering on noise wouldn't ring out. A blissful pause and then it started beeping. It took a few minutes before it fell silent and I could look at the display. Ten texts and sixteen missed calls. I knew they were all from Michael, and I knew what they would say, but part of me wanted to look at them, just in case they were from someone else, just in case there was something important, like that email that comes just as you're shutting down your computer and you can't leave it until tomorrow, you have to read it.

'Morning.'

I pressed the off button and flipped the phone shut.

'Hi. I didn't wake you did I?'

'No, no worries.' She looked half asleep still, and the epitome of tousled. 'You been up hours?'

'No, about quarter of an hour actually.'

'Wow, impressive. You've clearly improved with age. Unlike me. I need coffee.'

'Shall I?'

'No hen, you won't make it anywhere near strong enough. I remember that dreck you used to call coffee at uni.'

'Yeah but we were poor then and could only afford instant.'

Sarah grunted and headed for the kitchen.

'Nice place you've got.'

'Thanks, I'll give you the grand tour later,' she smirked, lifting her blonde hair up and over the back of her head where it promptly flopped back over her face again. 'So this is the way Saturday goes: coffee, papers, more coffee, brunch, and then we'll make a plan.'

'OK.'

'You want some?' She said, raising the cafétiere.

'No thanks, I'll stick with tea.'

Later I called Anna.

'You OK?'

'Yeah.'

'It's been crazy here. Michael's been calling me constantly. And he's been round already.'

'What did you tell him?'

'I said you'd gone, that you'd left him for good this time.'

'And?'

'He threw some stuff around. Said I'd better fucking tell him where you were. I said I didn't know where you are, but I don't think he believes me. He was a bit scary.'

'Shit. He won't be able to work out where I am though, will he?'

'I don't know, but he'll try something. Whatever you do, don't answer your phone. Don't talk to him.'

I fell silent. Part of me thought he'd never be able to find out where I was, part of me was scared shitless that he would.

'Isabel? You still there?'

'Yeah, I'm here.'

'OK, well take care. Watch yourself. Call me tomorrow, yeah?'

I flopped back on the sofa. Suddenly the future didn't seem so bright.

'What's up hen?'

'I just spoke to Anna.'

'Your big lezzer chum?'

'Leave her alone, she's pretty much the only thing that's kept me going all these years.'

'I'm sorry. And?'

'Michael's already been round to her place giving her hell. He's in a real rage.'

'Well you knew he would be.'

'I know. But... I dunno, everything was so great yesterday. I thought I'd got away for good, and...'

'You have. You will. He won't find you up here. I know what you need. Put your glad rags on, we're going shopping and drinking.'

It was nearly a week before Michael found me. A week of normality, of doing things normal women do, shopping, drinking, chatting, looking at job advertisements, looking in the paper for cheap flats. I was working on a job application when the knock on the door came. I didn't think anything of it. In only a week I'd got used to ordinary life, to not looking constantly over my shoulder. I really thought I'd got away. It was so different to when I'd stayed at the hotel. Being in a completely different city so far away made me less nervous, less fearful. Sarah put down her book and went to the door.

'Oh Michael, what...what are you doing here?'

Michael? My heart missed a beat, my stomach rose to my throat. It couldn't be. The door pushed inwards. 'Is she here?'

'Who?'

'My wife.' He marched in. I thought he was going to physically lift me out of the chair and carry me away. He came in like a whirlwind, or so it felt to me. But his anger dissipated almost immediately. He sank into the sofa next to me and took my hand. 'Why didn't you call me? Why didn't you let me know where you were? It's been a nightmare trying to find you. I'm so sorry Izzy.'

He had a strange, plaintive, almost tearful face. This wasn't his ordinary sorry.

'Sorry about what?'

'It's Louise.'

'What about Louise?'

'She's been in an accident. They don't know if she's going to make it. Your mum's been calling, didn't know where you were. I said you'd gone on some spa holiday with the girls. Said I'd bring you back.'

'But mum hasn't called me.'

'Well you haven't had your phone on, have you?' he said pointedly.

It was true. I'd got tired of the myriad of texts and messages there'd be from Michael even if I put it on just once a day. I hadn't had it on for days. I'd been calling Anna from the landline.

'Oh God. Where is she?'

'Bart's. Come on, get your stuff. I'll drive you back. We'll drive straight there.'

It never crossed my mind that he wasn't telling the truth. Not even Michael would lie about my sister being at death's door. Except he did.

He was very convincing, I'll give him that. All the way back in the car he fed me snippets of the story – knocked over crossing the road – a big lorry, in his blind spot, head injuries, they didn't know what the prognosis would be even if she woke from the coma. He did a bit of needling – why had I left, why hadn't I called him, how worried my parents were, how he didn't understand me, but he kept it all understated and concentrated on how lucky it was he'd found me, how I'd be able to be at Louise's side now, how I wouldn't have forgiven myself if I wasn't there, when she, you know, if she didn't make it.

'How did you find me, Michael?'

'I figured you were probably staying with a friend, that you just needed some space from me, though I couldn't think what I'd done wrong. I looked for your address book, but of course you had it with you. Then I remembered your Christmas card list, how you keep a list of people you're going to send cards to. Took me ages to find, had to go up in the loft and fish out all the Christmas decorations, but I found it. I worked through that, called a few people. Narrowed it down to Sarah. It wasn't that hard to find an address once I had a surname.'

His lack of recognition of his part in my leaving was amazing – thought I needed some space, but he couldn't think what he'd done wrong! I wondered about that a lot later, I couldn't get over it, how strangely his mind worked, that nothing was ever his fault. But then, on that long car journey all I thought about was Louise, my baby sister and how we might not get there in time.

We were quite near the house before I realised we were in Stoke Newington and not going to Bart's. 'Why aren't we going to the hospital?'

'We're going home.'

'But I want to go and see Louise. You said we'd go straight there.'

'There's nothing wrong with your sister.'

'What?'

He looked at me then, a look of pure evil and I knew I'd been duped. I collapsed against the side of the car. My eyes filled with tears. He'd fooled me again.

☙❧

Michael stayed with me every minute after we got back. And I mean every minute. I got to go to the loo on my own, but that was it. When I had a bath, he either came in and sat on the toilet seat, or he sat right outside the door. I could hear him sighing and flipping the pages of a magazine. That was when he started insisting I never lock the bathroom door (before it had just been a preference) and sometimes while I sat there I saw the handle move down – him testing to see if I had locked it or not. It was like some Hitchcock movie, one of the old black and white ones, where they would do a close up of something like that, like a door handle moving, just before the psychopath bursts in with a dagger, hand raised, and the piercing violins start.

And I was scared, I won't deny I wasn't, but I had even more resolve to get away again. All I had to do was bide my time and wait for another opportunity. He wouldn't be able to use the sick or dying relative ploy any more. I pretended to be sorry I'd left, and faked that I understood how upset he'd been. I went along when he almost cried and said didn't I know how much he loved me, didn't I know how much I'd hurt him? How much I'd hurt him?! I hope that irony isn't lost on anyone; it certainly wasn't lost on me. But I played his game for self-preservation, while I planned how to get away again, and how to do it better.

He must have called in sick or something. He never let me out of his sight. When we needed food, we went together to the shops. At least it got him to the supermarket! If I said I was going to bed, he went too. What did he think I was going to do, throw an overnight bag out of the window and make a rope out of sheets? Actually I might have tried that if I thought it would work. I'd love to see his face now that I'm free of him. I wonder what he's thinking? I wonder what he's doing? Is he grieving? Is he missing me because he loved me, or because he has nothing to control? Who am I kidding? He'll have found someone else; some other poor sap.

At one point I said, 'How long are you going to keep this up?'

'Until I'm convinced you won't leave me again.'

I am going to leave you again, I thought, and again and again until I succeed but I didn't say anything.

'We have to go back to work some time, you know.'

'Correction, I do.'

'But it wouldn't look very good, would it, if I don't go back to work? What are people going to say?'

He just shrugged.

Michael seesawed constantly between wronged lover, trying to win back my affections, and control freak. Some sort of modern day Jekyll and Hyde. It was sheer hell. It was worse than being in prison because the guard never left my side. I never got a minute's peace. If I was reading, I could feel his eyes on me. If we were watching television, I could feel the heat of his skin emanating to mine, making the fine hairs on my arm rise up. We barely spoke. What was there to say? There were hundreds of things we could have said, but both of us were too afraid. Yes, I think he was afraid too in his way, frightened of losing me. He knew how close I'd got to getting away.

He wanted me to forgive him for bringing me back, for the scene he'd created. The quiet, restrained, seething scene. He was like a party popper on the verge of popping, so desperate to beat the crap out of me for daring to leave him, but knowing that would only make me run harder. If he'd hit me then I swear I would have called the police. I would have taken the risk and tried it again. I would have taunted him into hitting me in the face, into creating evidence against him and I would have had him arrested. I would have gone to a women's refuge, given up work, whatever it took. But he didn't hit me, instead he silently forced me to stay.

Once or twice I tried to taunt him, but it was a lost cause, I couldn't break him.

'Come on hit me,' I said, 'you know you want to. Go on, do it. Here Michael,' I stroked my cheek, 'show me what a man you are.'

'You don't really think I'm that stupid, do you? I tracked you down. I found you, all the way in your little hideaway at the other end of the country. I'm cleverer than you are.'

He was. I knew he was. That was a scarier weapon than his fists. I had to work out a way to deceive him, a way he'd never find me. Our life was a battleground from then on; both of us fighting, both of us scared, neither of us able to leave, though I at least kept trying. We never made love again. If we had sex it was violent, rough, lashing out at each other as a way of breaking the tension. He got my body back, but he didn't get me back and that gave me hope that somehow I would endure and have a life after Michael.

Following the hell of that first week back, the next week was blissful. I'd told Michael I'd only taken two weeks' holiday. He assumed I had to be back at work on the Monday. And he let me go, since he'd realised he'd either have to go back to 'normal' life and take the chance that I might leave again, or have the cracks in his marriage start becoming apparent. Michael was messed up, but he wasn't a psycho and I believe he seriously thought he could make me love him again, make me want to stay with him. Inside Michael was a timid, pathetic boy who desperately needed love, and he thought I was the woman who would give it to him.

I dressed in my work clothes, walked to the Tube station, got the train to my usual stop, walked to the office, hid in the downstairs loos for half an hour just in case he'd followed me, and then I was free. Free for the entire day until 5.30 p.m. when I had to reappear from my office building, in case Michael was waiting for me and then make it home to prepare dinner and fabricate work chitchat. Free for five whole days. Of course it wouldn't be real freedom; I'd have to be constantly looking over my shoulder and being careful, but it gave me a little breathing space from my prison cell.

I called Katherine from my mobile and said I'd suddenly remembered that one of my bigger clients might be calling me so could she divert my work phone to my mobile.

'Not like you to forget a thing like that.'

'I know,' I said, 'but you know I've been a bit stressed out lately, and taking three weeks off was a bit spur of the moment. I'd rather just speak to him, if he calls, than have a problem to deal with when I get back.'

'OK.'

It wasn't that unusual for us to get the switchboard to divert calls to our mobiles or home numbers, especially among the more conscientious types.

'Oh, and can you take my email vacation message off?' It would be just like Michael to send me an email and then want to know why my vacation message was on.

'But you are on vacation.'

'I know, but Michael's off playing golf all the time. He's always wanted to play St Andrew's, and sitting around waiting for him is not my idea of a good time, so he left me here in Edinburgh. I'm hanging out with an old university pal, shopping, getting manicures, drinking cocktails, you know the whole girly thing he can't stand! But if I get bored I might check my email a bit, save me wading through hundreds when I get back.'

'Whatever,' said Katherine. I could see her rolling her eyes and thinking what a saddo I was. 'You'll have to give me your password. So you're having a fantastic time then?' She added sarcastically.

'Oh yeah,' I laughed 'It's great now I've got rid of Michael! I'm in a gorgeous hotel. It's even got a spa.'

'I thought you were staying in a cottage?'

'That was last week. We decided to spoil ourselves a bit this week. Anyway, look I've got to go. You'll sort that stuff out for me, yeah?'

'Sure. Just think of me while you're lying back getting a mani and pedi!'

I stepped out from the doorway of the building and breathed. I inhaled the dirty fumes of London like it was cool mountain air, like it was the first time I'd ever taken a breath. It felt good to be free of Michael, if only for a few hours. What would it be like to always feel like this? I'd had a taste of it in Scotland and I liked it. I wanted it again; I wanted it all the time. I just stood there, probably for ages. I'm hopeless with time. I never know if a few moments have passed or hours, especially now. Now I let hours and hours pass literally doing nothing. I realised then I didn't know what to do. I hadn't had real free time for so long, I honestly didn't know what to do with myself, so I walked. I thought about the time in Edinburgh, how short-lived it had been. I needed to email Sarah when I got back to work, and let her know I was OK, let her know that Michael's sob story had been a bunch of lies and Louise wasn't in a coma. What a bastard, playing a trick like that. I couldn't get over it. I never have got over that one. Just like my fall down the stairs, it stayed with me always as a totally despicable thing to do. I could have gone home, emailed her from there, but I was out of the habit. I never emailed anyone from the home computer. I was scared that Michael would find a way to read the messages, even if I deleted them all. Anyway, I didn't want to go home, I'd been a prisoner in that house for a week. I didn't ever want to go back, and certainly not before 6 p.m. So I walked.

I can't say I didn't contemplate finding a women's shelter right there and then and staying there. I could have easily collected some stuff and done it. But various things stopped me. The incident of Michael bringing me back was too new; I didn't want to go through something like that again. I couldn't go through it. And at that point, I was a hundred percent sure he'd find me again. He'd done it before. I know those places are supposed to be secure, they have all these measures in place so the men can't find you, but I was too fragile, if Michael had tracked me down hundreds of miles away, I was sure he could find me in London even in a supposedly safe place.

I was tired. I needed to re-coup my mental energy before I could take on Michael again and win. I had to plan. If I was going to get away successfully, I needed military-style precision. Just then I felt we were about equal. It may have been hell on earth, but I'd scored points during our week of confinement. I had him worried, and that put him a little off his game. He had to balance controlling me with not pushing me over the edge so I'd try and leave again, because he knew that the tiniest push would make me try it and bugger the consequences. And maybe all the fighting, and manipulating and calculating, took its toll on him too.

But above all, I had a week to enjoy myself. As long as I was careful, I could do want I wanted during office hours and fool Michael into thinking I was at work. I needed that time. I had to have it. I couldn't give it up to be in some shelter with no time to myself, desperately looking for another job and always looking over my shoulder to see if Michael was there. OK, so I did that anyway, that had become my norm, but I had play time and I intended to play.

I stopped at a café and ordered their largest latte and looked at the papers. It is surprising how long you can make a latte, and newspapers, and people watching last when you've nothing else to do. Then I called Anna to see if she was free for lunch. I hadn't been able to call her at all the previous week, obviously. So it hadn't dawned on me that she'd be thinking the Edinburgh plan had gone off smoothly.

'Hello.'

'Hi Anna, it's me.'

'You sound chirpy. I take it Edinburgh agrees with you then?'

'What? Oh, um I'm not in Edinburgh. I'm at home…'
'You're what?'
'It's a very long story. Are you free for lunch?'
'Um, no, oh…yeah, maybe I can get away.'

Anna looked worried when I greeted her. We kissed, sat, ordered water.

'What happened?'

'He came up to Edinburgh and brought me back.'

Anna looked appalled. 'But, I don't understand…'

'He told me Louise had been in an accident, serious head injuries, in a coma, and that if I didn't go back I might not get to see her again. Don't look at me like that. I know you're thinking how could I fall for that one, but what if it had been true? I couldn't take a chance like that. What would I have felt like if she had died?'

'But you know what he's like. Weren't you suspicious?'

'Not then. He was so convincing. And it was completely plausible. It's not like he said she had terminal cancer or something, she could have been knocked over, it happens all the time. Anyway it's not like it was a phone call where I could think about it before I acted. He was there, at Sarah's flat, for goodness' sake, causing a right scene. He's never been that devious before.'

Anna snorted into her water. 'Yeah right.'

'Sarcasm doesn't become you.'

'I'm sorry, but come on – not devious? Like finding ways to hurt you so he doesn't leave any marks isn't devious. How many wife beaters do you know who do that?'

'Fortunately I only know the one wife beater.'

'Well I'd rather have the drunken kind who just hits you and doesn't care if there's bruises.'

'Yeah well you don't get to choose what kind of wife beater you end up with.'

'Oh shit, Isabel, I'm sorry. I'm really sorry. I'm not being very sympathetic, am I? I'm just shocked that's all. I thought you'd really cracked it this time. I never thought he'd find you in Scotland.'

'Looks like we both underestimated him.'

'Are you ready to order, ladies?'

We hadn't even glanced at the menu yet. After a look at me for approval Anna ordered the special for both of us and a bottle of Pinot Grigio. 'I take it you don't have to cut up any dead people this afternoon, or were you planning to watch me drink a whole bottle of wine?'

'No, I don't have to cut anyone up, as you so tastefully put it.'

'Good, because we need to hatch a foolproof plan. I'm not underestimating him again, and I'm never going back next time I get away.'

'Don't you have to go to work? I'm assuming you do still have a job after the Scotland debacle?'

I gestured in a disparaging way having just put a large chunk of bread in my mouth. 'They never knew anything about it. They all think I'm still on holiday with Michael.'

'How ironic.'

'Mmm, it gets better. I took three weeks as you know, but I told Michael I'd only taken a fortnight, so he thinks I'm at work. I have a whole week of freedom!'

'Isn't that a bit risky? He calls the office all the time.'

'Got it covered. I told Katherine a story about a big client chomping at the bit, and she's diverting my calls to my mobile, and she's taken off my email vacation message.'

'Hmm, inspired.'

'I'm learning. The hard way, but I'm learning.'

'And he really hasn't rumbled you yet?'

'Well, it's only been one morning, though he has already called twice. I said I was swamped with having been off for a week. And he's penitent.'

'Now that I don't believe.'

'Well, as penitent as he ever gets. I swear he's so scared I'll leave again, and he knows he can't pull the dying relative stunt again.'

It seems, in retrospect, that I spent much of that free week walking aimlessly around London thinking about ways to get away, and having numerous late lunches with Anna at which we schemed and plotted a future escape, though of course I had to loiter around the office first in case Michael came to meet me for lunch.

I remember reading an article about how around 60,000 people disappear every year in the UK. Most of them never found. Sixty thousand – who effectively just disappear off the face of the earth – never found. After a while people stop looking. Why couldn't I be one of them? I didn't think Michael would ever stop looking. He wouldn't believe I was just a missing person, he would know I'd deliberately set out to disappear.

I mentioned it to Anna.

'Yeah, I know,' she said, shovelling a forkful of spaghetti into her mouth. God, that woman could eat.

'You know?' I didn't think *Red*, or whatever glossy I'd seen this snippet in was Anna's kind of reading material.

'Hmm, get a lot of those kind of statistics in my line of work.' She prised a piece of prawn out of a tooth with her fingernail.

'You eat like a pig. Why don't you savour it?'

'Sometimes I do, but right now I'm hungry and I have a liver to extract at 2.30 p.m., so get to the point. I presume you have one?'

'Yuck, thanks for that.'

She smiled her 'I love my job' smile and kept eating.

I moved my penne around on my plate, there was a thought in my head but I couldn't quite get to it. 'Well, how do they do it?'

'Well, some end up on my table, but otherwise easy, you just up and leave, no forwarding address, no mobile, change of name maybe.'

'Easy? What do you mean, easy? I tried that. Michael always finds me.'

'But you want to be found,' she said.

'What the hell are you talking about? No, I don't. I definitely don't want to be found. What about Edinburgh? What a spineless stunt to pull.' I gulped my wine too fast and coughed.

'But if you really didn't want to be found you wouldn't have fallen for that.'

'My own sister?' I was incredulous. 'But he was there on the doorstep, he'd already found me by then. You're cold. You're really cold, you are.'

'Yeah, can get chilly in the path lab. It's called tough love Iz. If you're going to get away and not have him find you, you have to get tough, and smart, way smarter than you've been up to now. Enough of this namby pamby sympathetic friend stuff, I need to tell you how it is, and you need to listen.'

'That's why you have no friends,' I mumbled.

'Except you.'

'Except me, but I'm desperate.'

'Glad you admit it. Anyway, I do have friends. There's George in the lab and Freddie, and OK, so they're mostly lab boys. Oh, and Jasmine.'

'Jasmine's your cat, she doesn't count, and she's not that friendly.'

'She is to me,' muttered Anna, scraping her plate.

'And what about girlfriends? When did you last get laid, huh?'

'I thought we were talking about you?'

'Your evasion tactics won't work that easily.'

'I think they will. I really have to get back to work, Iz,' looking at her watch. 'But seriously, are you that desperate?' I nodded, eyes wanting to fill as our light conversation slipped away. 'Cos there are ways to disappear, if that's what you want.' I must have looked puzzled. 'Google deed poll and call me.' She left a tenner on the table and airblew me a kiss as she grabbed her pannier and dashed out of the restaurant. Smug little know it all!

I did Google deed poll and discovered it really wasn't that hard to change your name, and once changed to get a new passport and other documents, open bank accounts in your new name and everything. I'd had no idea it would be so easy. I wanted to change my name right away, but I knew I had to do it later when I was ready to leave. I couldn't keep two identities. If I changed my name that would be final. I filed that nugget of information in my mental escape plan file and that helped me through quite a few horrible evenings cooped up with Michael.

I started to ponder what my new name might be if I ever changed my identity. If I could be a whole new person, who would I be? What would I do? I realised that it had never occurred to me to do anything different. Had I really only ever aspired to being married, having children, getting some kind of reasonable job? I'd somehow stumbled into my current job through a friend of a friend, but it wasn't exactly a career. Surely I'd intended more than this when I'd gone to university? But had I? It was a foregone conclusion in our house that both Louise and I would go to university and it didn't seem to matter much what we studied. I chose art history because it had been my favourite subject at school. The trips to art galleries with our laid-back art teacher were always the most fun. And I liked Italian. It was a bit out of the ordinary, not like French or German which everyone took. But hadn't I thought that I might put my degree to use in some way, working in a museum or gallery, teaching? Anna had always known what she wanted to do, or so it seemed to me, maybe not the pathology, but she was always fascinated by biology and had only ever considered being a doctor, nothing else.

On long evenings stuck at home with Michael, both of us reading or pretending to, I used to daydream about what my new life might bring. Maybe I could work in a gallery. Maybe I could live in Italy or Switzerland. I could try painting or photography, not that I harboured any particular artistic talents, but it would be fun to try. I almost cried when I thought of all the things I could do if I wasn't married to Michael. There was no way to branch out with him as my mill stone. I could just imagine what he'd say if I proposed going to an evening class, or joining some group or society. How had he come to dominate my life so completely?

Time marched on and I spent my life on a treadmill of work and home, trying to plan my escape and just surviving day to day – sidestepping Michael's rules and regulations, devising ways to get out of the house for a bit without him panicking, avoiding getting beaten, trying to have some kind of life beyond mere existence. My social satellite dropped to Anna and Louise. My parents I hardly saw, and Michael had given up any pretence of playing happy families and always cried off family visits. Louise I saw rarely. I never told her about her impending death and how Michael had used her to get me back. What would be the point? My conscious, rational brain knew she'd had nothing to do with it, but my emotional side couldn't help slightly holding her responsible for my being tricked into coming back. Things were never quite the same between us, at least from my side. I tried to hide from her how terrible and hopeless my life with Michael was, always steering her away from the topic if she brought it up, and tried to just enjoy her *joie de vivre* as a woman at the start of her life.

I had been ten when Louise was born and I'd been surprised and nonchalant, pretending I really wasn't interested in this new arrival, but secretly I found her incredibly cute and adored her. She was a happy baby, didn't cry too much, but there wasn't really much I could do with her except cuddle a bit. I certainly didn't want to change her nappies, and anyway mum seemed to be revelling in having a baby again, lapping up every precious moment of motherhood. No doubt my friendship with Anna was cemented as a result of my parents' sudden reduced interest in me. I wasn't jealous, at least I don't remember being jealous, I just couldn't understand why my parents would want a baby, why they acted so ecstatic. I didn't feel left out. I had Anna and her new tree house, and plenty of other school friends too. I did everything there was on offer – ballet, football, choir, Anna's spy club. Anna on the other hand was pretty much a loner. Her parents gave the impression of not being children people. Anna did everything for her own gratification, while I somehow still wanted my parents' approval. As Louise grew older I was able to incorporate her as a pliable plaything and depository for all my older sister wisdom. It seems she bypassed that and found her own wisdom for a carefree life, while I was stuck with Michael and no way out.

I tried to keep strong, but it was hard. I started drinking regularly. Michael either didn't notice or didn't care. A few glasses of wine per evening helped take the edge off reality, though I never got drunk. I needed to be in control and not give Michael any extra opportunities to take advantage of me.

I let myself go. I didn't bother painting my nails or putting on makeup. I got my hair cut less often and lost interest in fashion. All my energy was concentrated on staying one step ahead of Michael and it was exhausting. Anna was a rock, my absolute saviour. Despite her saying she needed to toughen me up, she still provided sympathy in large doses, along with food and wine in vast quantities. And she was always hatching plans, trying to come up with new ideas of how I could get away without Michael tracking me down.

More and more Anna kept coming back to the idea of passing off some unknown body as me and faking my death. I'll be the first to admit that I know nothing about pathology, or registering deaths, or what happens when someone dies, and I had no idea how many people died without anyone claiming them or knowing who they were, but I figured if 60,000 people a year went missing and weren't found, quite a few of those must wind up dead and unidentified in London. It still seemed like a long shot. I imagined drunks and homeless and missing people, not reasonably fit women in their forties, but the more we talked about it, the more Anna convinced me, and the less I thought about what might happen to Anna. She was a big girl, if she wanted to take that kind of risk, she knew what she was doing. I just didn't have the energy to worry about Anna and about me. It soon became a fantasy that I played over and over in my head. To get to sleep at night I imagined Anna calling me and saying she'd found the perfect candidate. I dreamt of sailing away into the sunset with my new name. I even pictured Michael at my funeral. I soon gave up thinking about any practical difficulties, I let Anna worry about the practicalities, while I daydreamed my way to survival.

One evening while Michael was at some work's do, Anna came round very excited. She sat on the floor, knees up to her chin, fluorescent cycle clips still on – she always forgot to take them off when she was excited or engrossed in something, glugging red wine and talking rapidly with lots of gesticulation.

'They've changed our jurisdiction.'

'Hmm.' I couldn't see why this was anything to get excited about. Anna didn't usually bother me with pathology or NHS-speak as she soon grew frustrated of my glazed over, non-interested response.

'So, we get more bodies.'

I was tempted to say, 'that's nice dear'. Keeping up with Michael sapped so much of my mental energy that I often had trouble remembering things and keeping up with complicated conversations. Anna was looking at me pointedly as though what she was saying was blatantly obvious. 'And...?'

'More potential for DOAs. You know unidentifiable people. Younger people... Oh do keep up, Isabel. People that might look a bit like you.'

'Oh right. Oh! And have you had any yet?'

'Well no, it's only just taken effect, but I'm sure we will.' She topped up her glass, and thought for a moment. 'And then there's people who die in hospital.'

'But surely you'd know who they are? They'd have to be admitted and everything.'

'Not necessarily, not if they come in as an emergency.'

'But wouldn't they be old? Young people would have relatives, wouldn't they?'

'Hmm, yeah maybe. Maybe you're right. Safer to stick to a DOA.'

'But how, I mean, OK, just hypothetically, let's say you get a woman's body, who looks vaguely like me, and who doesn't have any ID, which frankly I think is a long shot, but let's go along with it. How do you make people believe it's me? How do you make Michael believe it's me?'

'Firstly, Michael won't have to identify you. That's a TV myth. If the coroner's office is convinced it's you, job done.'

'But he'll want to see me. I know he will.'

'No problem. We say your face is too messed up as a result of the accident.'

'But...'

She held up a hand. 'Any distinguishing marks?'

'Eh?'

'Do you have any unique marks? Tattoos, birth marks, scars?'

'Yeah, I have a scar on my inner thigh.'

'Inner thigh?' She lifted an eyebrow mischievously. 'And how did you get that?'

'You know very well how I got it you idiot, you were there. In fact it was your fault, as usual.' She looked perplexed. 'Blackberrying, circa 1976, climbing over barbed wire...ring any bells?'

'Oh yes. Your mum wasn't very impressed, was she? Let's have a look.'

'What?'

'Trousers down, I need to see if I'd be able to re-create it. We need to give the impression that it's your body. Any distinguishing marks help. Would Michael recognise this scar?'

'Oh yes,' I said dropping my jeans and proffering my thigh. 'He used to like stroking it back in the old days when he fancied me.'

'OK, enough of your sordid love life! That's good. Should be able to match that. I'll take a photo next time I'm here.'

'Pervert!'

'The things I do in the service of science.'

'It's hardly science, is it, faking a body to be me.'

'Look, do you want to escape or not?'

'Yes, but…well, it's just not going to happen is it? I mean, how many bodies tip up that can't be identified?'

'Hardly any, that's the point.'

'Now I'm confused.'

'They may not have ID on them, they may not be claimed by anyone, but you can identify them by jewellery, possessions, scars, blood group, fingerprints. We just have to provide the Coroner's office with *your* ID.'

'You make it sound so easy.'

'I have to make it sound easy otherwise I can't imagine myself doing it. I have to plan every possible permutation. Do I do the post-mortem or not? How do I get the samples swapped? Oh yes, I'll need samples – cheek swab, blood, fingerprints. Come to the hospital tomorrow and I'll take them.'

'You're serious?'

'Yes, aren't you?' She gave me a strange look as though she couldn't comprehend what my problem was. I couldn't believe she was really contemplating it, but like I say it gave me a fantastic daydream to pin my hopes on that made getting through each day a little easier. It was kind of like being children again, me playing willing assistant to Anna's science lab.

'OK, whatever. I can come over tomorrow.'

I don't know why I never considered killing Michael instead of plotting to kill myself, but the thought never really crossed my mind. Even at his most violent, it didn't occur to me to fight back.

Maybe that would have been easier, if in a moment of passion, I hit him on the head with a heavy frying pan in self-defence, or grabbed a knife and fatally stabbed him. A good lawyer, I might have got off with a very short term, maybe even a suspended sentence, but that's not the way things worked out.

Once I'd bought into Anna's plan, we plotted incessantly. We made list upon list of what we both would need to do. Anna kept these in a tatty, scuffed A4 notebook that seemed to travel everywhere with her in her cycle pannier, which was itself a dirty, misshapen thing with loads of straps hanging off it. Every time we met, the notebook would emerge and Anna would earnestly run through the points, and any new updates. My escape plan was her new, all-consuming project. She was still a workaholic with no social life, but now she'd cut back on computer games and planning my escape took up all her free time. I don't know how many hours she spent surfing the Internet for information, or looking things up in books, and constantly revising the plan as she thought of more possible hitches that she needed to work round. I wondered if she wasn't becoming a bit obsessive about it, but to be honest most of the time it felt like a harmless game because I never truly believed that a suitable, female body with no accompanying ID would turn up at any London hospital never mind Anna's, so if it kept us both happy and helped distract me from the misery of my life, where was the harm?

'OK, let's run through it one more time.'

'Do we have to?'

'I sometimes don't think you're taking this seriously.'

'I am, and I appreciate all you're doing for me, really, but it seems to be all we talk about any more. And it's never going to actually happen, is it?'

'Think positive. It might. You do want to leave Michael, don't you?'

'Of course I do.'

'And you know what's happened every time you've tried before.'

'Yes.'

'So we have to have everything covered.' She patted my arm, in a slightly patronising way. 'Just one more run through and then we'll stop, OK?'

'OK.'

'So you're going to close your savings account soon and give most of the cash to me, and keep a bit to use when it happens.' I nodded. 'And you need to find all your documents, passport, birth certificate, everything, and keep them with you at all times. Then, when I call you to say that I've got a body, you need to go and check into a nondescript hotel, register under your new name and pay cash. You need to get a new mobile, or SIM card at least, and you only call me using the new SIM, and once you're out of the country you ditch both SIM cards and the phone.'

'Right.'

'As soon as I give you the all clear that it's viable, you get the deed poll and new passport as soon as possible.'

'Yeah, I checked, I can get both done the same day if I go to their offices.'

'Good, just be careful that you're not recognised anywhere.'

'It sounds like some kind of 1950's spy film!'

Anna smiled and drank more wine. 'It wouldn't hurt to think of it like that. Just keep thinking all the time that we have to ensure Michael doesn't suspect anything, that he can't trip you up on anything. Let's see, what else? Oh yeah, I come and meet you and give you the money and take your jewellery.'

'What about clothes?'

'Well you can't take any, because you're supposed to have just dropped down dead in the street. You can't take anything with you.'

'Good point. But if you're going to meet me with the cash, you could bring a bag with you, some undies and toiletries and a few clothes. I might need to change clothes so I won't be recognised. And what about my hair? In those films they're always hacking their hair off and dying it over a tiny sink in some nasty hotel.'

'Let's not get carried away! You could wear a headscarf and big sunglasses. I hear big sunglasses are in this season.'

'Ooh get you, with your fashion tips!'

'Seriously though, I could bring you a bag with a few things, and maybe you could get a new hairdo while you're waiting for your passport or something. Good thinking Robin, I'm glad you're finally getting the hang of things.' (We had gone through a brief stage in our youth of saying, 'to the Batmobile, Robin' every time we went off on an expedition, in case you were wondering who Robin was.)

'And what about you?'

'I think the less you know about what I'm up to the better.'

'But I need to know, Anna, at least some of it, otherwise how am I going to know it will work? It's all very well saying "trust me" but I'll be the one who pays if this all goes tits up.'

'Well, I think I'll probably lose my job, if it goes tits up, so I'm aiming for that not to happen. OK, what I'm thinking now is, that when said body arrives, I pretend straight away that I recognise you, i.e. I identify you immediately, and say I can't do the PM, and I'll get Gus or someone to do it. They don't usually get done immediately. The coroner informs us he's sending a corpse over, then we do the PM in the next few days. So meanwhile I pull your hospital records, put your jewellery on the body, make sure your samples get taken for analysis and fake the scar on the thigh.'

'That's kind of a lot to get done isn't it?'

'Yeah, but everyone knows I'm there all the time, it's not exactly unusual for me to stay late at night after the others have gone. And since I'm not doing the PM, I could say I took some samples to get ahead of the game, because since I know you I want it to all go quickly. I won't do the analysis, so it will all look above board.'

'Hmm. But what if the post mortem finds something that doesn't match with my records?'

'Like what?'

'I dunno, like this person is a smoker, or an alcoholic or has some congenital heart problem?'

'Don't start getting technical with me missy! You're almost an alcoholic, so that's covered!'

'Now who's not being serious?'

'OK, OK. I'll have to think about that one, but the cause of death is likely to be something traumatic not an illness, so underlying diseases will be less important. And between you and me, Gus is a bit slapdash, he'll probably leave the file lying around somewhere and I'll be able to read it. The main point is, if I, a respected doctor and pathologist and your closest friend identify this body as you, the coroner is not going to question it, especially if the hospital records and jewellery, and scar and everything matches up.'

I shrugged. 'If you say so. You're the expert!'

I had to keep a lid on my excitement about the plan, because I was still living with Michael, still having to deal with him every day and never knowing when he might become violent or kick off about me going somewhere I shouldn't. He still liked to keep tabs on me constantly, but he had relaxed a bit. I had worked hard at convincing him I wasn't going to leave him, and so he allowed me a certain leeway. He let me go to work so that his nice respectable friends and colleagues from the bank didn't wonder why I'd suddenly given up work. He also let me see Anna, but far less than I would have liked to. He had taken to brown nosing the higher ups at the bank, and often went to the wine bar after work, or to some dreary drinks party on a Saturday night so Anna could pop round, though we were very careful to listen out for his return so that he didn't catch us unawares again. Initially Michael insisted on dragging me along to these parties, but while I dressed nicely and tried my best from a purely self-preservation point of view, it must have been clear from my face that I was bored rigid and didn't want to be there, so he soon decided he was better off without me. He still used to call several times though to check I was at home. I kept the TV on while Anna and I plotted, so that when he called I could just hold up the phone for him to hear it. See, he wasn't all that bright, because the TV could have been on anywhere.

One night he again came home earlier than expected, but this time Anna just had time to scramble out the back door before he came in.

'What are you looking so pleased about?' he asked out of nowhere.

'Nothing. Just looking forward to *Casualty*,' I said guiltily, feeling that he must be able to see the joy in me at the thought of finally getting away from him.

'I don't know what you see in that rubbish.' He dropped into the armchair.

'Drinking alone, again I see?'

'Well you're weren't here, so I didn't have much choice, did I?' Anna and I had almost finished a bottle of merlot and his natural assumption would have been that I'd drunk the lot.

'You're bloody well letting yourself go.'

'Well, can you blame me? It's not as if I get to see anyone but you.'

'You should keep looking good for me, I am your husband. I don't want to be seen with some old lush. Look at the state of you.'

And look at the state of you, I thought, but didn't say anything. He was uncharacteristically squiffy and looking dishevelled.

'Anything to eat round here? I'm starving.'

I got up, there was no point saying there wasn't, or telling him to cook something himself. I knew exactly where that would lead. 'Frozen pizza, I expect, or oven chips.'

'Good. Egg and chips.'

'Please,' I muttered to myself as I went into the kitchen.

I made myself some too, and it was almost a scene of domestic normalcy with the two of us sat in front of the telly, bottle of ketchup between us.

It took Anna and me ages to come up with a reasonably workable plan. We speculated for months about whether the likelihood, or not, of a suitable body turning up made the plan impossible, but at some point we crossed a line. It didn't matter then whether we found a body or not, we just enjoyed the planning, and once I started on the practical things, it at least felt like I was doing something and that was all that counted.

One of the first things I did was close my savings account. By then I had a few thousand pounds. Not a lot, but enough to be able to travel to the continent and pay the rent on a place for a few months while I got settled. It felt like a satisfying wodge of money, and I was a bit loathe to hand it over to Anna, but we'd decided it was safer, because if Michael found it, I'd probably lose it all. I kept £500 for 'on the day' emergencies. I sewed a secret pocket inside the lining of my handbag to keep it in. That was another whole evening of entertainment, sewing that, and I was rather proud of my efforts.

My only window of opportunity to carry out any of the practical aspects of our plan was Saturday morning when Michael went to squash religiously. But it didn't give me much time. He'd given up having long lunches with Rob afterwards, and he always expected the house to have been cleaned when he got back. I perfected a technique of making the house look and smell clean with very little effort. If I was lucky they went for one pint and he was back in plenty of time for brunch with his wife, which was his new craze. He liked to spend the entire weekend in my company, partly to pretend that we were a happily married couple who actually enjoyed each other's company, and partly to make sure I didn't go anywhere else. No Saturday shopping trips with the girls for me! Very occasionally he gave me special dispensation to go shopping with Louise or my mum, but he wanted me back by late-afternoon for pre-dinner drinks and a blow by blow account of my day. One day I made it back with only minutes to spare and shoved my purchases behind a suitcase in the top of the wardrobe.

'Hi, I'm home,' he called from the hallway. He bounded up the stairs. 'Here you are. You look a bit flushed, you all right?'

'Yes, fine. I just finished hoovering,' I said guiltily.

'Well, get the coffee on. I picked up croissants,' he said disappearing downstairs again.

I let out my breath and smoothed the bed covers as I tried to compose myself. Get a grip Isabel. All I'd done was buy a few toiletries that I could say I needed anyway if he asked. It was horrendous the way I held myself in check and didn't do the simplest of things for fear that it would upset Michael. My life was in no way normal anymore. I felt I had to lie and deceive him about everything that most people do without even thinking about it – seeing friends, buying toiletries, buying the odd item of clothing. It was ridiculous.

'Iz, what are you doing?' He shouted and I went down and made coffee and pretended to enjoy listening to his comments on newspaper articles, and highlights from his squash game.

Another Saturday morning I went out and bought a small, nondescript back pack, and took great care selecting a five-pack of fresh, clean, cotton knickers from M&S to go in it, along with an old pair of jeans and a T-shirt, just in case. You can't imagine the pleasure I derived from such simple acts, thinking that one day Anna might deliver that bag to me in some dingy hotel and it would be my passport to a whole new life somewhere else.

I hadn't seen Louise for ages and I knew I wanted to see her again if I was going to suddenly disappear one day. I wondered how she'd take it – her only sister suddenly being gone? If I knew Louise, she'd manage. She'd be upset, possibly distraught, but in the long-term I knew she'd be OK, she was one of those people for whom everything turned out all right in the end. I caught Michael in a good mood and managed to get him to condescend to let me spend time with her one Saturday.

We met in Convent Garden and browsed round the shops, though I didn't buy anything. I was trying to save as much as I could, and I didn't want to incur Michael's wrath. We went to an Italian place that Louise liked for lunch.

'So, what's new? How are things with Michael?'

'Oh you know, the same old thing.'

'But you're still married, how come you haven't left him yet?'

I couldn't begin to explain to Louise how impossible it was to leave Michael, how getting a divorce wasn't really an option. It all took too much energy. 'He's not so bad, we plod along OK.'

'If you say so, but it seems to me life should be about more than just plodding along putting up with a crappy situation.'

It should indeed, I thought. 'So what about you? Got any gossip?'

We whiled away a couple of pleasant hours and then it was time to return to my prison cell. As we parted at the station, I gave Louise a hug. We're not in general a touchy feely family and Louise looked a little shocked. 'You all right?' she said.

'Yeah, fine. See you around sis.' I didn't though. I never saw Louise again.

'Drunk again?' Michael said by way of greeting.

'No.'

'Don't lie, I can smell it on you.'

'I'm not lying. I'm not drunk; I just had one glass of wine with lunch.'

'Hmm. Well what did you get up to all day?'

'Oh you know, just girl stuff – window shopping, lunch, chatting. Louise is teaching some yoga classes now.'

'Yoga? She's such a loser. Why can't she get a proper job?'

'I think it pays quite well actually,' I lied, not knowing anything about it.

※

Then one day, just like any other, my life changed. Anna called me at work. I almost didn't answer the phone because Michael had just called to say he was going to the wine bar and spelling out when he would be home for dinner. It made a pleasant change that he hadn't specified what he wanted for dinner. And I thought it was him calling again.

'It's me. It's all systems go.'

'Eh?'

'The coroner just called. There's a body coming over here later that might be suitable,' she whispered.

It took me a few seconds to work out what she was on about. 'Oh.' It was late afternoon, not that long before I would have left anyway, a miserable dark winter afternoon, made darker by heavy rain. Goodness knows what would have happened if she'd called later. I never would have been able to get out of the house with Michael around.

'Right, so go to a hotel and call me and I'll swing by later. I'm going to need your jewellery and stuff. And don't forget about fixing the phone.'

'What if Michael calls?' I said lamely.

'I think you're beyond that, aren't you? Anyway, change the SIM cards over and he won't be able to get you on your mobile.'

'But...?'

'I've got to go. Call me once you're safely at a hotel.'

I'd wanted to ask what would happen if this body turned out to not be any good. If I wasn't at home when he got back, Michael would go ballistic. I wouldn't be able to go home, whatever happened. I'd have to come up with a plan B fast.

I realised I was shaking. I wanted to throw up. It should have been one of the greatest moments of my life, but I was stunned, and scared out of my mind. I'd never really expected this would happen. I ran to the loos and locked myself in a cubicle. I sat there a long time, thinking, sweating. This was it, finally, the way out. But could I take it? Could I really do it? What if Michael found out? He'd kill me for sure. But would that be so bad? I couldn't go on anymore. And if I committed some crime and went to jail, at least I'd be safe. He couldn't get me there. But what if this body wasn't any good? Then what? I wouldn't be able to go back. I'd have to run again. I'd just have to get my new name and ID and go to Europe anyway. Then my decision was made for me.

'Isabel, are you in there?'

'Hmm.'

'You all right? You've been in there ages.'

'No, actually I don't feel too good. I'm going to go home.'

I went to my desk and got my bag. Katherine said, 'You do look pale, can you make it home all right?'

'Yes, no problem,' I said, feeling less than confident.

On my way to the Tube I kept looking around me, convinced Michael would see me, even though he said he'd be out drinking. Paranoia was driving me crazy. More and more I'd been having feelings that he was everywhere, that I was never alone. I hurried down the steps, feeling slightly safer underground, out of sight.

The Underground was busy, the start of rush hour. I got a seat, but only just. I felt like a fish in a glass bowl, swimming back and forth madly with my thoughts, while everyone else watched me mindlessly blowing bubbles. Excitement vied with fear in my stomach – that first day at a new job kind of feeling, or a first date. But what did I know about first dates? I couldn't remember my first date with Michael. I could barely remember what I did yesterday. If it involved Michael I blotted it out immediately. I fiddled with the strap of my handbag. Good job I'm not a Middle Eastern male or my nervousness would surely have been taken as an expression of guilt. But I was guilty. Guilty of wanting to get away from my husband; escaping from my life; guilty of taking someone else's life. I watched the Tube map assiduously, trying not to catch anyone's eye. Two more stops then a short walk to freedom. Maybe. Maybe it wouldn't work out. Maybe she wouldn't look like me. Maybe someone would claim her. Don't think like that, don't.

I got out at King's Cross. Walked away from the station into the smaller streets and found a seedy looking B&B, the kind of place that wouldn't ask too many questions. I'd let the rain wash over me so my hair was dripping and my mascara run. I knew I looked a mess, but I didn't want to be recognisable, even by a stranger. I know that makes no sense but I wanted to go in looking one way and go out looking another. I didn't want to be memorable.

I checked in under my new name. The name I'd chosen for just this moment. As I'd hoped, they didn't ask for any ID. I scribbled a signature and paid cash for one night. The room was crummy. A small double bed, a tiny en-suite, the ubiquitous TV, but it looked clean enough. I switched on the kettle for tea and sat on the bed. I still felt sick. I couldn't believe I was doing this. I could not begin to think about the things Anna might be going to do on my behalf. It felt too soon to call Anna, but I couldn't just sit around doing nothing. I had to keep myself busy.

I took off my soggy coat and hung it up and dried my hair with the thin towel. I washed my face and removed my makeup with the hotel's hand towel. I figured they weren't the kind of establishment that might chase me up for damage of one of their towels. Tea brewed, I took out my mobile, prized off the back and removed the SIM. Ages ago I'd got a new SIM card, which I inserted. I put the old one in my handbag, I might still need it for something. I put the phone on. Anna was the only person who knew that number, so if it rang I knew it would be safe to answer.

Then I tried to remove my wedding ring. It wouldn't budge. I'd put on a bit of weight, drinking and generally not caring. But with cold water and soap it loosened easily enough. I took off my earrings and put them all in the pocket of my coat. I wasn't wearing any other jewellery. I always thought tea in a crisis was overrated, but even the insipid tea of a low-rate hotel was soothing and I began to calm down. I was going to do this. I had to believe it would work. I emptied the contents of my bag onto the bed and checked that I had everything – passport, birth certificate, E1-11. I'd left my marriage certificate at home. I wouldn't be needing that in my new life. I took out my emergency £500 and counted it slowly and carefully. Address book – I'd better destroy that. I didn't want to think about it, but I knew if this was going to work I wouldn't be able to contact anyone in that book ever again. I'd never be able to contact Anna again.

We'd discussed it time and time again. I didn't know if I could manage without her, she insisted that we couldn't have any contact, at least not for years or until something changed like Michael died or got re-married. Part of me felt it was insane to think that if I was in another country he'd be able to find me just because I sent Anna a letter or email, but I knew too well what lengths he'd gone to in the past to track me down. We couldn't assume that just because I was dead and buried he might not get suspicious. So I knew that the times I would see Anna now were limited. They would be weird, brief times all about practicalities and not getting caught. No more evenings drinking wine, no more lunches, no more fighting over her lack of fashion sense and her ridiculous bike. I felt tears fill the back of my throat. I swallowed them back. I couldn't afford the luxury of crying. Once I was safely away, then I could cry.

I looked at my watch. Time was dragging. I tried calling Anna.

'Hi. How's it going?'

'I'm at the hotel. It's...'

'Don't tell me. I don't need to know.'

'Right. How about your end?'

'It's not here yet. Oh wait. There's someone coming up now. I'll call you later.'

Her abrupt hang up stunned me a bit, but I knew she had to be there to receive the body otherwise the whole plan fell through.

I turned on the telly. Early evening news. I don't remember what any of the stories were. There was no news that night other than my possible demise. I felt tired, already wiped out from the strain and I'd got nowhere yet. I re-checked my bag, recounted my money, let the TV wash over me, made more tea, went to the loo endlessly, and eventually the phone rang again.

'You OK?'

'Just about.'

'OK. It looks good. I mean, we're on. I've done it.'

'Done it?'

'Yes. I've said it's you,' she whispered. 'I can't say more. I'll come and see you.'

'OK. I passed a Burger King on the way, opposite King's Cross. Will that do?'

'Yes. Meet you there in half an hour.'

I didn't know whether to be excited or paralysed with fear. I retched pointlessly over the sink. As I raised my eyes to the mirror, I didn't recognise myself. I know those hotel bathroom lights are never flattering, but I looked terrible. Even if I bumped into Michael in the street I don't think he would have recognised me.

I ordered a burger and fries just to blend in, I didn't think I'd be able to eat a thing, but as I sat waiting for Anna my hand kept wandering to the fries and somehow I ate them.

When Anna turned up she was just the same as ever, not changed at all by what she'd done. 'I'm starving,' she proclaimed, dumping her pannier on the plastic chair before ordering a Whopper with extra fries.

'I can't believe you!'

'What. I'm hardly going to lose my appetite, am I?'

'Apparently not. I've certainly lost mine.' I pushed away my cold burger.

'Remarkable likeness. Really amazing. Hair's longer than yours, but no one need know that,' she said between bites and gulps from a monster coke.

'And how... do you know how?'

'Did she die? At this stage, from a quick look, I'd say she got hit by a car, though if she did, she came off relatively lightly. And whoever hit her must have been off his head, she had on a bright red jacket you could see a mile off.'

'How can you be so matter of fact about it?'

'It's what I do, isn't it? How do you think I'd survive if I got all sentimental about them?'

'And she didn't have a bag or anything?'

'No. A house key and a fiver.'

'They reckon she just popped out for a pint of milk or something. A man walking his dog found her.'

'But won't they check that street to see if anyone's missing?'

'They might. If she lived alone we'll be all right. But I've already said it's you, so they won't be looking to ID her, so much as looking for what happened to her. Who drove the car and didn't stop. But I've put a spanner in the works there, too.'

'What do you mean?'

'Well, when I said I knew who the body was. I also mentioned your husband and what a nasty piece of work he is, and how's he's beaten you up in the past. Gave quite a good performance, though I say so myself. I even remembered to mention that report you filed after he kicked you down the stairs, so there'll be some written evidence to back me up. I expect some officers of the Met will be speaking to your Michael fairly soon to ascertain his whereabouts.'

'And they'll tell him…'

'Yes, they'll break the news too. It really couldn't have been more perfect. Unbelievable.'

I sat in a sort of daze. I really couldn't believe this was happening. For all our planning and talking about this day I always thought it was just our fantasy, that it wouldn't ever happen. I dragged myself back to reality. 'Now what?'

'You've got your ring and stuff?'

I reached into my pocket and pulled out my ring and earrings.

'Good.' She took a plastic bag from her pocket. 'Drop them in here. So, the PM's on for tomorrow. Gus, which is good for us, 'cos he's not the most observant or conscientious of people.'

'So that's it?'

'As far as you're concerned, yes. You're dead.'

'Not officially.'

'A mere technicality. Look it's going to be OK. There is absolutely no reason for the coroner to doubt my word, and when a few tests corroborate it, we'll be clear.'

'But what about Michael? He's not going to buy it, is he? He'll kick up a fuss. He'll want to identify me. He'll want to see me.'

'Keep calm. Let me worry about all that. That's my field. He's not required to identify you. And it's not a given that he gets to see you either. And I reckon, for a while at least, Michael will be too occupied with the police to say much about anything.'

Anna screwed up her burger wrappings and belched.

'God, I won't miss your table manners!'

'That's more like it. Cheer up. You're finally free of the bastard. Now go back and try and get some rest. You need to get out of the country as soon as you can. If you can't go tomorrow, then change hotels. If I have any news, I'll call you on the mobile. Oh nearly forgot, here's your little going away bag.' She pulled out the backpack I'd prepared months earlier and which had been in her cupboard at work ever since. We hugged and went out into the damp night. It had stopped raining. My last sight of Anna was of her unlocking Molly, cycle clips gleaming, the smell of her burger breath in my nostrils.

❦

The next couple of days were something of a blur. I didn't sleep much that first night, so I felt less than prepared for the manic day of preparations that followed. I had a quick mug of tea and ate the little packet of hotel ginger biscuits. I put on the jeans from the backpack and put everything from my handbag into it. On my way from the hotel to the station I dumped my empty handbag and work trousers in separate bins. In my months of preparations I had pinpointed the nearest deed poll offices and had marked them on a map along with the location of the passport office. I was lucky, I didn't have to travel too far.

Changing my name couldn't have been easier. I filled out the form and was told to return in two hours to collect the certificate. Nearby was a hairdresser's. It didn't look great, not the sort of place I would ever have considered going to normally, but beauty was not the issue. It looked empty, so I tried my luck. They sat me right down, a girl who looked about fifteen and had very blonde dyed hair asked me what I had in mind.

'Something completely different,' I said, 'I'm tired of it. How about short and funky? And do you have time to colour it?'

She did have time. I almost relaxed drinking coffee and flicking through magazines while I waited for the colour to take. I was pleasantly surprised with the result, but I didn't have time to really think about it.

I picked up my certificate, no one commented on my new look, I'm sure they'd seen it all before, and dashed off to the passport office, making stops to get passport photos with my new 'do' and buying some trainers. My office pumps were not ideal for running round London or travelling.

By late afternoon I was at Waterloo booking a seat on the evening Eurostar to Paris. I sat with a sandwich and coffee, feeling reasonably calm and confident. I couldn't believe everything had gone so easily. I wondered how Anna was getting on. I rang her. No answer.

About half an hour later my mobile ran. It was Anna.

'How's it going?'

'Great. Got everything. I'm waiting for a train. How about you?'

'Not bad. Gus did the PM this morning. Injuries consistent with an impact with a car. Nothing unusual. I won't spell it out on the phone, but I did all the stuff we talked about. There shouldn't be any problems.'

'And Michael? Have you heard anything?'

'The coroner's officer who came for the report just said they had the husband in custody. He reckons the police will give him a hard time, what with the report from when you were in hospital and the couple of times the police went to the house it won't look good for him, but I reckon they'll have to let him go eventually. I don't think even the Met could find any evidence he was involved, unless he's got no alibi at all for the time frame, but the longer they hold him the better.'

'Won't he be suspicious that you're involved?'

'I've pretty much kept out of it. I know I identified you, but after that I haven't been officially involved. Everyone in the lab will say so. I know he's not rational when it comes to you, but I don't think Michael would be able to come up with a scenario as bizarre as the truth is. He might want to kick off about me saying he was violent towards you, but there's paperwork that will show he was even if you never pressed charges. He'll be better off keeping quiet.'

'Hmm. I wish you could come and see me before I go.'

'Me too, but I think I'd better not. It's too risky.' She paused, and it almost sounded as if she was crying. But Anna didn't cry. 'I love you, Iz,' she said.

'I love you too.'

She cleared her throat, all practical again. 'So, you've got rid of everything?'

'Yes.'

'OK. So lose the mobile phone. And...send me a postcard when you get there and that's it, right?'

I didn't say anything.

'Isabel? Promise me, no contact.'

'OK. Thank you for everything Anna. How can I ever repay you?'

'By having a good life.' She hung up.

I turned off the mobile and put it in my pocket. I knew I should get rid of it, but I couldn't quite bring myself to. Not yet. Only Anna had the number. It should be safe enough, and I might still need it for some emergency. I'd get rid of it when the money on it ran out.

I went out and wandered around a bit, killing time before the train. I dropped my old SIM card down a grate and ate something somewhere. I don't remember what. I wasn't hungry, it was only to pass the time and to keep me going. I felt a sadness I couldn't begin to express at the thought of never seeing Anna again, of never speaking to her. I had resigned myself to not seeing my family, though it hadn't really dawned on me that they would actually think I was dead, that they might have to go to an inquest, and my funeral, and...well I couldn't think about that yet.

I sat on the train looking out of the window. It was raining again and the raindrops streaking across the window as the train picked up speed mixed with my own tears. Relief mingled with excitement and sadness. I would never see London's grime again. Exhaustion took me and I slept.

※

I took my time travelling across Europe. It was a strange time – wonderful in many ways – it was the first holiday I'd had in years. The feeling of freedom was immense. I no longer had to look over my shoulder all the time. I was confident that Michael wouldn't be able to find me now, even if somehow everything went wrong and he realised I wasn't dead, I'd just run away, I didn't see how he could find me, or not for a very long time. And yet the happiness vied with despair at all I'd left behind, and all I'd had to give up, just because I'd married the wrong man. At times I seemed to have some kind of post traumatic stress disorder, never quite knowing where I was, or who I was. I often forgot what my new name was and shocked myself when I looked in mirrors. I had strange dreams and daydreams about bodies and accidents, and my family talking to policemen. I spent half my time in a daze, not speaking the language and barely being able to get around. At other times I surprised myself with how easily I got from place to place, how I took just the right train, and found perfect cafés and places to stay. I had a new confidence and a whole new outlook, and a very small new wardrobe. It seemed that being dead was marvellous.

I was tempted to just blow all my money on having a fabulous time, but I owed it to myself and I certainly owed it to Anna to stop travelling and start a new life that was worth all we'd gone through. I stayed in small B&Bs and ate simply. At one place I stayed, someone had left *The Talented Mr Ripley*. I read it eagerly, glad of anything in English and it seemed so appropriate. Not that I would ever kill anyone, but the captivation with another place, and another person's life. That's just what I was doing, living someone else's life.

I had no real plan. We'd planned my escape with elaborate precision, but I hadn't really thought about what I would do once

I got away, because I never really believed I would. I had a vague idea I'd like to live in Italy. I'd always loved it, and since I spoke at least some Italian I thought maybe I could get some sort of job.

It was only when I got here that I had what you might call an epiphany. As I sat, looking out over the lake, sunglasses on, glass of chilled wine at hand, I thought, nobody in the world knows where I am right now, and it was a wonderful feeling. The most amazing feeling ever. Nobody knew me here, and I knew no one. I knew that would change, all too soon I would have to start interacting with people. Soon I would count waiters at cafés among my friends, and chat in the market with local women, but for now I glorified in my total anonymity. Everything I owned was in the rucksack at my feet, and it was all I wanted. Time seemed to stand still as I sat there, sipping wine, watching the sun glint on the water. I thought about very little that afternoon. My mind could have been full with so many things, racing with all the things I needed to do to set my new life in motion. But the fact that I was alive, sitting there, unknown and unwatched was enough. I bathed myself clean in the sun and took on my new persona.

Eventually the café began to fill up with the pre-dinner crowd. The 'pretty' people in their smart suits and dresses out to be seen, drinking prosecco and saluting their friends and paying me no attention, and I realised I had sat there all afternoon. I began to re-enter the real world. I pulled out the postcard I had bought at a station on the way and performed my last act as Isabel Atkins.

'Ciao bella,

Arrived safely. Weather fantastic. Wish you were here. Will miss you, always. XX'

The next day I bought a stamp, addressed the card and sent it to Anna, before I crossed my final border and ended my former life.

In the mornings I teach English for a couple of hours. It isn't what I'd choose to do, but it pays the bills for now. In the afternoon and early evening I'm a waitress. I enjoy this more than I thought I would, interacting with people who I never see again, though of course there are a few regulars. When it's quiet Giovanni and I talk, and smoke (it's a new habit of mine, just socially, just because I can), and sometimes play cards, and he likes that I can speak to the tourists in English. I've also picked up a bit of French and German, so I manage to understand most people. It's surprisingly pleasant being a 'nobody'. I know everyone needs waitresses and I shouldn't run the profession down, but in a lot of ways people don't really see you, they only see what you can provide for them. The late mornings and after 8 p.m. are my own.

Every morning I stop at a café in Piazza Volta for a cappuccino. I love to sit there in the sun, watching the world go by. That's where I see her, most days. She walks through the square with a toddler. I don't know if she's the mother or the nanny. After a few weeks of seeing me there every day she's started to say hello. Now we've progressed to a few sentences of conversation. She's ascertained that I'm English and seems quite impressed with my Italian. I've ascertained that she is indeed the nanny.

Yesterday I invited her to join me for a coffee and though she said she really shouldn't, she didn't need much persuading to sit down and let little Francesco run around the square just in front of us. He seems to be a good boy and always does what she says, though she said he only behaves in public and is very naughty at home. Her eyes sparkled when she said this.

She is young, I'd guess twenties, but she may be older. She is fashionable in the Italian way, with tight jeans and knee-length boots. She has gorgeous big brown eyes which are accentuated by her very short hair. It's like a number two all over! The whole time she was sitting next to me I wanted to run my fingers over it and see what it felt like.

I think about Anna a lot. I wonder what happened in the end. I wonder if things did run smoothly, if my 'death' was accepted and where I'd been buried. Had Anna been found out? Had she lost her job? It drove me nuts sometimes not knowing. Sometimes it felt like all our precautions were ridiculous, that if it had worked then Michael thought I was dead. He wouldn't be looking for me anymore so how would he ever find out if Anna and I spoke or exchanged emails. I'd eventually destroyed my address book after I'd been here a couple of weeks. I knew I could never contact anyone in it ever again and it was just a liability, but I knew Anna's phone number and email off by heart. I knew her address too. I could write to her, but something always stopped me. I would send her birthday and Christmas cards religiously, never signed, never with a return address. I owed her that much – to let her know I was alive and doing well. Sometimes I thought about our last conversation and how she said she'd loved me. Maybe she had meant something more than friendship. You'd certainly have to love someone very much to do the things Anna had done for me. Maybe she'd always been in love with me and I'd just never seen it.

I never could bring myself to get rid of the mobile phone I'd brought from England. I know it was irrational and pointless, but it felt like my last link with Anna and if I got rid of it I'd never find her again. I took to putting it on for a few hours every few days. I don't know why. I don't know what I expected. I never expected it to ring, and then one day it did.

'Hello.'

'Hello.'

'Anna?'

'Well who else would it be you idiot. I thought I told you to get rid of this phone.'

'If you thought I'd get rid of it, why are you calling it?'

'Because I know you too well, I knew you wouldn't do it.' She laughed. Her throaty, mortuary laugh, and I laughed too, though it hurt so much trying not to cry.

'So why are you calling? Is everything all right? Are you all right?'

'Yes. I've just been to your funeral. Well, cremation to be precise.'

'What?'

'Yep, inquest was last week. Accidental death. They never did find out who killed you. They questioned Michael a fair bit, but there were plenty of witnesses who said he was still in the office at the time they think she was knocked over. There was no CCTV on that street. No one ever reported a woman missing. I'm afraid we'll never know who she was, or what drunk hit her. She just popped to the corner shop and that was it.'

'That's terrible.'

'Yeah. My guess is she was from another country, maybe hadn't been here that long. Anyway, good for us.'

I was silent. I didn't really know what to say. I didn't like to think of how I'd benefitted from someone else's suffering. She must have had family somewhere this woman, people who missed her.

'They made me say something, at the service.'

'Who did?'

'Your parents. It was torturous, worse part of the whole bloody thing. I had to say what a great person you were, all that crap.'

'Thanks!'

'At least I'll never have to do that again.'

'So it's all over?'

'Yep, burnt to a crisp, not anything anyone can do about it now.'

'How did they take it, my parents? And Louise and Michael.'

'No one copes well with their daughter dying, but they seem to be doing OK considering. They seem glad it's all over now. I think the inquest was the worst. Louise, what can I say, she's an odd ball. Turned up with some weird guy with dreadlocks. She's got her nose pierced now too!'

'Some things never change!'

'She'll be OK. Isn't she always? And Michael is still a slimeball. He did seem genuinely devastated. He actually cried at the funeral. He'd been pretty stoic up 'til then. I suppose the police suspecting him didn't do him any favours, he tried to play it down, but I think quite a few people finally woke up to what a piece of work he was, including your parents.'

'So we're free?'

'Yes. Well, you are, I still work for the NHS!'

'Very funny. So you could come and see me?'

'I don't think so Iz.'

'But why not. Obviously I can't come back to England. But you could come here. You'd just be on holiday. Who would know anything?'

'It's not that simple. It's... I don't know, it sounds ridiculous, but I've had to get used to the fact that you're dead. I don't think I could cope with seeing you just yet, and I dunno, after all that planning, all those precautions, I'd hate to screw it up. I could still lose my job if anyone found out.'

'But...'

'Please Isabel. I did so much for you. Please don't contact me. Maybe in a year or two,' her voice trailed off.

The phone beeped and the battery died. So that was that. I was officially dead. Nightmare over. And I felt dead, because I'd lost everyone. I'd won my life, but I'd lost everything else I'd ever known.

Before I went to work that day, I went to the medieval church beyond the station and I lit a candle for the woman who'd given me my new life and for the family who would never know what had happened to her. I can only say that somebody was looking out for me. That's the only way I can describe it. That woman getting knocked over and dying, with barely a scratch on her and no one claiming her was nothing short of a miracle. I haven't gone all religious or anything, it just seemed like the right thing to do. If I could repay that gift somehow I would. There's nothing wrong with a little gratitude and respect for the dead. In fact, I sometimes think there's nowhere near enough gratitude in this world. I wish I could thank Anna properly too. Maybe some day I will.

I got incredibly drunk that night. I stayed at the bar and at first it was fun. I told everyone I was celebrating, but I didn't say why. But then I couldn't stop. It was a celebration, and a wake. A wake for my old life and friends and family, all dead to me.

I would have liked to have gone to my funeral, just to see the look on Michael's face. Just to see how many people turned up and how sad, or not, they were that I'd gone. And to say goodbye too, in my own way, to my old life, my old friends. I imagined it like a film – it would be raining, everyone huddled together under umbrellas round the grave, my family tearful, Michael stoic but clearly upset. I would be standing at the back, the hood of my raincoat hiding my face, a mysterious stranger or distant relative no one would notice. The earth would be sodden and the sound of the heavy clods hitting the coffin would reverberate in a melodramatic way. Somehow I couldn't quite picture the sight of smoke pluming from the crematorium or Anna saying nice things about me. I wonder what she wore. I laughed out loud to myself as I stumbled home, tripping over cobblestones and falling down curb stones. I pictured Anna in black shirt and trousers with her fluorescent cycle clips still on. God, I hope she didn't go to the crematorium on Molly! I laughed until I began to cry.

Today Alessandra, that's the nanny's name, took me on a tour round the lake on her moped. I was petrified. I'm sure she drove cautiously, but we went higher and higher into the mountains, round sharp bends. I don't have a great head for heights and I gripped her tightly. Though scared, I felt strangely euphoric as well. This was the kind of thing I would have done when I was young. I felt like I'd re-captured something of who I'd been before Michael started breaking me apart.

After what felt like ages we stopped. It was glorious taking the helmet off and letting the breeze run over my damp hair.

'You look frightened,' she said, 'but I rode very carefully.'

'Yes you did, but I've never been on a motorbike before.' She shook her head as though she found that unbelievable. 'It's amazing up here.' We had a view right over the lake. We went and sat at the little café with the panoramic view. We were the only people there.

'Where is everyone?'

'It's siesta time.'

She ordered beer and cold meats and bread.

It was one of the best meals I've had.

Later we walked along the hill path and sat on the grass. I didn't need anything more than that amazing view and the sunshine. I closed my eyes and for moments at a time forgot that Alessandra was there. It was like time stood still, and the past was gone and there never had been Michael, or London, or the years of suffering, there was only that moment; not even the expectation of what would come next.

'You look sad sometimes,' she said.

'Do I? I'm not. Not any more.'

Then she lent over and kissed me on the lips. It was so soft and gentle. The last person who had kissed me had been Michael and he never kissed me like that. He never kissed me gently, only roughly in the heat of passion. He never kissed me as a wife, or in public. And here was this young woman kissing me right here in the open air. OK, there was no one around, but still it felt so daring, so shocking. I didn't know what to say. I had a dim recollection of another soft kiss, a long time ago in a time I couldn't recapture. It wasn't until I got home that night that I remembered it had been Anna, in the woods, when we were young. My heart ached for Anna then and I wanted so much to be able to call her, or write to her and tell her about the kiss — tease her a little and let her think it was going to go somewhere, but it wasn't. I know Italians can be incredibly flirty and demonstrative, maybe it was nothing more than friendship. Maybe that's just the way Italian women act with each other.

Would it really hurt to contact Anna? I'd been cremated; surely Michael wouldn't be looking for me anymore. Probably he'd already moved on, found some other poor woman to take care of him and for him to beat up. Michael didn't do well alone, poor pathetic creature that he was. God, I hadn't thought of Michael for so long. I pushed the image out of my mind. I didn't want Alessandra's kiss to make me think of Michael. No, it was best to stick to the plan, to not contact Anna. Not yet, it was too soon. Maybe in another year or so.

I looked at her, this young woman with the short hair who'd kissed me and I didn't know anything about her and that scared me a bit. I hadn't known anything about Michael either. I'd spent years married to him and had still never known him. I wanted to get to know Alessandra but not like that. 'How old are you?'

She laughed. 'What does it matter?' My face must have been serious. She dropped her head slightly to one side and said, 'twenty-nine.'

'And you're not married?'

'No, guys don't really do it for me,' she said with a knowing smile.

They don't really do it for me either, I thought, but as much as I was flattered by her attention, as much as rationally I would have loved to have fallen in love with her, I couldn't. Michael might have put me off men forever, or at least for a very long time, but unfortunately I couldn't bring myself to love women instead, or at least not physically.

Maybe Alessandra could be the new Anna in my life – my new best friend.

Mostly I tried to forget about England. I didn't want reminders of my old life. I didn't want to know what was going on in a country I could never return too, but sometimes I just couldn't help myself. Occasionally I would flick through an English paper left by a tourist or spoil myself and buy a new one, as much to read English as anything else. One day a small column a few pages in caught my eye:

Top City Banker Accused of Fraud

```
A senior banker at top bank Citibank, Michael
Atkins, has been suspended pending investigation
of a suspected fraud of up to £20 million. Mr
Atkins was questioned two years ago in the
mysterious death of his wife at the hands of a hit
and run driver, but no charges were brought and
the inquest returned a verdict of accidental
death. Mr Atkins denies any involvement in fraud,
but colleagues state he has not been the same
since the death of his wife and speculate that the
recent loss of many big contracts may have
unsettled him enough to commit illegal dealing.
```

I laughed out loud when I read that. You can't believe how pleased I was. It wasn't so much, I knew it would cause him to suffer even if the suspicions proven unfounded. It didn't begin to make up for all he'd done, but it made me smile. In fact, a smile kept coming to my lips for the next few days. Then I threw the paper away. That life was gone.